A NEW BEGINNING

Standing huddled together, Virginia and Rob watched the lightning flash in the charcoal gray sky. The wind wrapped her shirt around her body, revealing her shapely legs. It stung their faces and tried to dislodge Rob's hat. Virginia shivered at the sudden change of temperature, and pulled her cardigan closer. Rob wrapped his arms around her to keep both of them warm. The day had changed from scorching to freezing in a matter of minutes.

As they protected each other from the elements, Rob found himself responding to the closeness of Virginia's body and the vanilla sweetness of her hair. As if involuntarily, his hands began to caress her shoulders and back. He lifted her chin and planted a hungry kiss on her willing lips. His tongue possessed her as her arms glided around his neck, and she pressed herself against him. The wetness and the wind were forgotten.

"Let's go home," Virginia whispered, as she clung to him and his lips burned against her neck.

BOOK YOUR PLACE ON OUR WEBSITE AND MAKE THE ARABESQUE ROMANCE CONNECTION!

We've created a customized website just for our very special Arabesque readers, where you can get the inside scoop on everything that's going on with Arabesque romance novels.

When you come online, you'll have the exciting opportunity to:

- View covers of upcoming books

- Learn about our future publishing schedule (listed by publication month and author)

- Find out when your favorite authors will be visiting a city near you

- Search for and order backlist books

- Check out author bios and background information

- Send e-mail to your favorite authors

- Join us in weekly chats with authors, readers and other guests

- Get writing guidelines

- AND MUCH MORE!

Visit our website at
http://www.arabesquebooks.com

A NEW BEGINNING

Courtni Wright

ARABESQUE

★BET BOOKS

BET Publications, LLC

www.msbet.com

www.arabesquebooks.com

ARABESQUE BOOKS are published by

BET Publications, LLC
c/o BET BOOKS
One BET Plaza
1900 W Place NE
Washington, D.C. 20018-1211

First Printing: October, 2000
10 9 8 7 6 5 4 3 2

Printed in the United States of America

One

At barely eight o'clock in the evening, the ballroom was already filled with pretty women in elegant gowns and handsome men in tuxedos sipping mixed drinks from the bar, chatting in animated groups, and waiting for the dancing to begin again. They all wanted to be the first on the floor, and could hardly keep their toes from tapping as the deejay played Motown, soulful tunes, and the obligatory waltz for the more sedate set. They had shown an uncanny expertise in handling the swing and jitterbug music of their parents' generation. With the band on break, everyone had to resort to conversation to fill the fifteen-minute void. They could all use the respite, since the band had set the sparkling chandeliers to rocking wildly with its lively renditions. The deejay was calm by comparison.

Office parties, especially fancy ones, often promised much and delivered little. This one, however, looked as if it would live up to everyone's expectations. The big bosses of Phillips Corporation had decided that the sales force had performed so well the last quarter that it deserved a night of celebration. Timing the celebration to coincide with the holiday season, they gave it a 1940's Big Band New

Year's Eve theme. The firm's president had ordered his director of marketing to spare no expense in arranging an evening to remember. Always happy to obey, Jason Franks had lined up the best hotel in town, selected the most palate-pleasing menu, and hired the most talked about band and deejay.

Virginia gave her face another quick look in the gilt-framed mirror to make sure that she had properly applied the scarlet lipstick to her full luscious lips. She checked her shoulder-length light brown hair and adjusted the strand of lustrous cream pearls that lay at her throat and reflected the warm glow of her coffee and cream complexion. Her midthigh, red, satin dress with long sleeves ending in black cuffs highlighted the healthy glow in her cheeks. Her hazel eyes sparkled with confidence. Content, she closed the bathroom door and walked toward the dance floor. At twenty-eight, she possessed a strong sense of herself.

"Did you see the shrimp and paté, Virginia?" queried her friend Edwina Henderson as she adjusted the belt of her only slightly longer blue sequin dress with pearl and rhinestone spaghetti straps and deep plunging neckline. She and Virginia shared an apartment in a residential section of Washington, DC, near the National Zoo, and were successful marketing managers in the prestigious downtown DC communications firm.

"Indeed I did. What about that champagne fountain? I knew we'd trampled quota, but I didn't realize that we'd done this well. We must have set new sales records. The company is generous, but never like this." Virginia looked down at her slightly snug, black, satin evening shoes with sparkling rhinestone toes. She had purchased them one lunch hour on sale at a leading department store. This was her first time wearing the pumps. She hoped that none of her dance partners would step on her feet and ruin them. They looked so lovely on her feet, and accentuated the muscles of her calves to perfection.

"The music sounds wonderful," Edwina said as she gazed at the rhinestone rose glittering on her ankle. "I hope you're wearing dancing shoes."

"Even from here, it sounds great. I know that I'll dance until my toes go numb." Virginia breathed deeply of the white gardenia Edwina handed her before pinning it to the front of her dress. She was ready for whatever the evening would bring . . . or so she thought. The committee had thought of every detail, including corsages for the women and boutonnieres for the men.

As was usual at these mandatory company gatherings, the music was thumping. It always seemed to Virginia that the deejays played louder for these affairs than for any of the others she attended. She wondered if someone had decided that loud music would inspire those attending under duress to have a good time. However, tonight the melodious sounds of sweet soul music and swing did mingle with that of the Motown favorites and vibrate through the ballroom. Dancers did swing as well as the stomp, the slide and more. The sparkling chandelier illuminated the dance floor, and sent twinkling stars scurrying along the ceiling. Men wearing crisp tuxedos and highly polished shoes gyrated and laughed with women attired in pretty dresses and evening suits. From what Virginia had witnessed before the break, everyone was having a genuinely good time.

Virginia and Edwina took their seats at the table in the center of the room, one they had picked for its view. They wanted to be able to watch people's faces as they twirled around the floor, talked business, negotiated promotions, and gossiped about each other behind careful smiles. Company politics was never far away when groups assembled. An evening of glitter and fun provided the perfect opportunity for politicking. With the announcement of promotions scheduled for immediately following the holiday, Virginia knew that many in the room would make one last effort to win the favor of upper management.

As Virginia watched the faces of the late arrivals and nibbled daintily on a succulent shrimp, she looked up and caught a glimpse of a tall handsome man entering the ballroom. With a slightly raised eyebrow, she surveyed his broad shoulders, curly black hair, reddish-brown skin, narrow hips, and long muscular legs. His quick smile held the attention of many of the women, who flocked around him hoping that he would join them at their table, or at the very least invite them to dance. The determined set of the bare shoulders of many said that they would do the asking if he did not. Something in his carriage shouted self-confidence tinged with arrogance. She had heard all about him through the company grapevine, and knew that his position as senior vice president would make him a source of interest for many. Virginia was determined not to add her name to his list of admirers.

"Virginia," a gentle voice said, tearing her attention away from the newcomer, "I believe this is my dance."

Looking into the face of William Edwards, one of her favorite buddies, Virginia smiled and immediately forgot about the new arrival standing at the door. With a happy laugh, she placed her hand lightly on William's arm, she allowed herself to be propelled onto the floor and into a lively dance. Whenever the company held one of these social functions, William always claimed her as his partner, and Virginia enjoyed spending the evening with him. He danced beautifully, and had an entertaining sense of humor. Between dances, he told her funny stories about the sales representatives in his unit.

She had known him for two years, and would miss his bright smile and laughing gray eyes when he left on Monday. William's boyish face made him look much younger than thirty. Yet, since receiving his promotion, Virginia had seen little worry lines begin to pull at the side of his eyes. Like all the managers who desired upward mobility, he was a bit concerned about relocating to a new city, making friends, and rising to the challenge of the new job.

Tonight, however, he was his usual happy-go-lucky self, and would not allow her to mention the promotion as he twirled her around the floor, maneuvered intricate steps, and guided her movements with just the tip of his finger. Virginia and William enjoyed dancing together, and that made it easy for her to follow his lead. Their execution was always so perfect that they drew the attention of the other dancers. Tonight was no exception. She could feel people watching them from the tables that lined the dance floor. Ignoring the staring eyes, she continued to high step in time with William.

Standing together between dances and sipping a cup of punch, Virginia studied William's face, knowing that she would not see him again for a long long time. She had made him promise to visit her when he returned to DC, and to e-mail her often.

Reading her thoughts, William smiled at her, and with that simple gesture erased all concern from her mind. He had become like a brother, almost from the moment that they first met. He was one of the first people in her office that she had met after moving to the exciting area of Washington, DC, from her sleepy hometown of Towson, Maryland, when she had accepted her job at Phillips Corporation. They had become fast friends immediately, maybe because they danced so well together, maybe because they were both lonely living away from home. They often sat and talked about their lives back home and their experiences in college. When she was new and trying to develop her market plans, he was always at her side with ready suggestions. She would miss him terribly now that he had received a highly prized and deserved promotion to England, where he would head a new division offering cellular phone service.

Taking her hand as the music began again, William said, "Well, Virginia, this is it . . . our last dance. I've got to leave in a few minutes and get my stuff together. The movers arrive first thing in the morning."

Swallowing hard to keep back tears, Virginia responded, "It's your call. I can dance your feet off no matter what you do, or where you go."

"Oh, yeah! We'll see about that," he replied, pulling her onto the floor and twirling her into his arms for an energetic swing that sent Virginia spinning around his shoulders, down his body, between his legs, and onto the floor before pulling her back up into his strong arms. Breathless but happy, they laughed into each other's eyes one last time as the music slowed into a comfortable two-step amidst loud approving applause.

Before they knew it, the minutes had passed, and it was time for William to leave. Walking him to the ballroom door, Virginia quickly brushed aside the tears that trickled down her cheeks from the loneliness she could already feel. Holding her hands in his, William bowed low over them and planted a gentle kiss on each palm. Slowly, he pulled her into his arms for a tight squeeze. In a very short time, he had become the best friend she had ever had. They had shared so many thoughts, dreams, and silences.

Virginia had often wondered why her relationship with William had not blossomed into more than deep friendship. She had often sensed that he would have liked more, also, until he became resolved to the reality of their association. Now, looking into his eyes for what might be the last time, she saw the answer. Although William was incredibly handsome, he just was not her type. His boyish good looks made her feel protective, not amorous.

"I'll be seeing you. Take good care of yourself, kid," William said lightly through the hoarseness in his voice, looking into her brimming hazel eyes.

"E-mail and phone me when you can. I know you'll be busy. Let me know if any of those English girls can keep up with you on the dance floor. I hear they're pretty light on their feet." Virginia smiled, pretending to be jealous.

"Not to worry. I'll save all my dancing for when I come back to DC. See you then," he responded with a happy chuckle.

With that, William walked into the ornate gold-and-red lobby and through the revolving doors.

Watching him disappear into the darkness of the frosty December night, Virginia felt a chill run down her spine. She hoped it was just the result of the cold of the evening and the icicles clinging to the bare trees that lined the banks of the Potomac River.

"Your man will return for company functions, don't worry. The company likes to get us together on a regular basis, you know," said a deep voice filling the emptiness beside her.

"Not that it's any of your business, but he's not my 'man' as you called him. He's my friend, probably the best male friend I've ever had." Startled and angered by the intrusion into her thoughts, Virginia had spun around, furiously, and answered hotly. She came face-to-face with the newcomer whose entry had caused such a stir earlier.

Pushing past the arrogant intruder so he would not see the tears that ran down her cheeks, Virginia sought comfort in the music and gaiety inside the ballroom. The sound of other people's laughter only made her feel worse. She already missed William terribly, and suddenly felt very much alone in the big impersonal city of Washington, DC. Even the warmth of the laughing voices that filled the room could not penetrate the loneliness and darkness. Standing on the edge of the dance floor watching the others enjoying the music, Virginia felt utterly miserable and out of place.

She did not hear him approach her again until it was too late to escape. "I'm sorry. I shouldn't have intruded. I was only trying to make you feel a little better about sending your friend off to the British office. Separation is tough. I should know, since I'm leaving next week for England for a few weeks of training, and then off to France to manage that office. I won't bother you any more. I can see that you'd rather be alone," he added in a deep voice that Virginia would have found difficult to resist any other time.

"You're right, I would," she snapped without looking at him.

Raising his eyebrow and nodding his head slightly, the stranger walked away without another word.

"Virginia, what's the matter with you?" Edwina whispered as she pulled Virginia toward the ladies' room. "He's the catch of the evening. All the women want to dance with him, and the men can't wait to get him on the racquetball court. He's the new senior vice president for the European market. Have you lost your mind?"

"I don't care who he is. He shouldn't have butted into my life. I didn't invite him, and I don't want him. He can charm someone else. I just want to be left alone." Virginia touched the cold water to her puffy eyes.

"Wash your face and fix your makeup. You look terrible. It's amazing he even took the time to talk to you the way you look with your faced all streaked with tears. Besides, William wouldn't want you to be rude to the man, now would he? That guy might be his boss or yours one day," she added, helping Virginia reapply her makeup.

Looking into her friend's tortured eyes, Edwina had to admit that even with her streaked makeup and red eyes, Virginia was the prettiest girl in the room and, as always, the most popular. Yet, for all her beauty—her perfect skin, features, and her slim trim figure—and her outstanding sales figures, Virginia never acted high on herself. She was always ready to help out a friend. That's what Edwina liked most about her. Virginia was regular people, not at all conceited about her looks or her talents. Edwina often thought that Virginia did not even realize that she made men's heads turn every time she entered a room.

"I'll try to be polite to him, but he's too pushy and sure of himself. Although he entered the company at sixth level, he's still new. Already he's acting as if he owns the place. I just don't like him, that's all," Virginia said, adjusting the belt of her dress and preparing to return to the ballroom.

"You should still try to be nice to him. First impressions are very important, remember. You don't want John Robinson to think that you're one of those arrogant types," Edwina subtly informed her buddy.

"You're right, as always. I don't know what I'll do without the other member of my support team to keep me in line. With William on his way to England, you'll have to do double duty. I'll go make nice."

"Maybe he's nervous among this group of old friends. He looks like the big, brave, take charge type, but maybe he's afraid of not returning from the conflict, too. Remember, he'll have the livelihood of many people in his hands. That's a heavy load to bear," Edwina suggested. Looking across the room, she spotted the handsome newcomer sitting all alone at a table in the corner of the room. Seeing him occupied by only his private thoughts, she gave Virginia a gentle nudge.

"Well, I don't know if that's it or not, but one thing's for sure, he's pushy. But you're right. I shouldn't be rude to him," Virginia straightened her shoulders for what she knew would be the longest walk of her life. She was not one to kiss up, and this felt like it to her.

Edwina watched as her friend almost marched across the dance floor to the table where the new vice president sat sipping his drink. The sparkle from the chandelier bounced off her red dress as she walked. Involuntarily, her heels clicked an angry tattoo.

He looked up from his drink as she approached. Virginia could not tell if his penetrating gaze meant that he was glad to have her company. She did not stop to wonder. She was on a mission to make amends for her behavior, and could feel Edwina's eyes burning into her back.

"May I join you?" Virginia asked when she reached his table.

"Are you sure you want to?" John Robinson replied, rising to pull out the other chair for her. "I thought you found my presence detestable."

Taking the offered seat, Virginia saw that the corners of his mouth curved up ever so slightly at her obvious discomfort. As she tried to keep her temper under control, she thought he was the most arrogant man that she had ever met. Once again, she could not stand him. She decided instantly that she would spend a few minutes with him and then leave. There was only so much that she would do to restore his opinion of her.

"I'd like to apologize for my behavior. I'm not usually rude to people. You caught me at the wrong time. I was feeling pretty terrible after my friend left. Why don't we start again? Good evening, I'm Virginia Summers, Marketing Manager, Data Services." She offered her hand for him to shake after taking a deep breath. She was determined to make amends with this man if it was the last thing she ever did.

"Glad to meet you, Virginia. John Robinson, Senior Vice President, International Affairs. My friends call me Rob. Now that we're off to a better start, would you care to dance?" he asked with a slight smile and a nod in the direction of the highly polished floor.

Virginia had to admit that he was certainly smooth, and undeniably handsome. Maybe she had misjudged him; first impressions were often hasty. His deep, milk-chocolate brown eyes never left hers as he waited for her response. Against her wishes, she found herself once again drawn to him as she had been when he first walked into the ballroom. Only now, William was not there to distract her from this arrogant self-assured man with his quick laughter, funny engaging stories, and skillful dance moves.

"I'd love to," she responded, and he placed his hand on her elbow and escorted her to the middle of the dance floor. Virginia was grateful for the dimmed lights that would hide the blush that spread over her cheeks at the touch of his hand.

"I'm not as good a dancer as your friend, but I'm pretty good," Rob purred into her ear as he pulled her close and began gliding around the floor.

Virginia could smell the fragrance of his cologne and the wool of his skillfully tailored tux as Rob pressed her expertly against him and propelled her along in a very respectable dance. He was not as energetic as William, but he was easy to follow as he skillfully executed the turns and moves. She could feel the ripple of his shoulder and back muscles under her hand, and the firmness of his well toned thighs against hers as his hand pressed more firmly into the small of her back. She hoped that he could not feel the rapid beating of her heart as the nearness of him made her light-headed and a little giddy.

When the dance came to an end, Virginia mentally gave herself a little shake as they returned to the table. Although she found Rob more pleasant than she had initially thought he was, she reminded herself that he was not the kind of man to whom she was ever attracted. He was too sophisticated and worldly, not at all like the boys at home who had pursued her during high school or her dear friend William. Yet, her body tingled from the memory of his warm breath on her ear and his muscular body pressed against hers.

As she sat opposite him sipping her wine cooler, Virginia waged a fierce battle with her emotions. She found herself having fantasies out of a romance novel as she was drawn to him against her wishes. In her imagination, she could envision herself running her fingers through his curly brown hair, leaning against his strong chest, and kissing the mischievous corners of his mouth. She could see him rising in the morning to join her in the shower, where the water would glisten on his reddish-brown skin. Her fingers would tighten in his wet hair and pull his face down to hers so that she could kiss his lips under the thin line of his mustache. Using a fluffy towel, she would dry his body before applying lotion to his muscular limbs and lingering to caress every inch of his six-foot, five-inch frame. Virginia had to use all of her willpower to keep from touching the hand that rested casually on the white linen tablecloth.

Virginia reminded herself that his overconfidence would never allow a relationship to develop between them, even if he were not leaving almost immediately for Europe. She had not allowed herself to fall in love with William, who obviously cared a great deal for her. She certainly would not let down her defenses regarding the arrogant Rob. Placing her empty glass on the table, Virginia decided that she had read too many romance novels and that her Prince Charming was a long way off.

Virginia did not guess that John Robinson fought the same battles against her charms. Ever since he'd entered the ballroom, he had been drawn to her physical beauty. After seeing her eyes brim with tears when her friend left, he could not help but be attracted to her gentleness. He wanted someone to care that he was leaving, but he knew that none of the beautiful women he usually escorted would give it a second thought. He had deliberately avoided emotional attachment and placed his job ahead of his personal life. His dedication to the company had paid off. At thirty-five, he had earned a fabulous promotion. He had searched for that special someone, but he had not been able to find her. Many of the professional women he had known had been cold and calculating. He did not blame them for assuming the personas of some of their male counterparts. However, they had made him understand the long-standing complaint of women that a balance sheet made a poor bedfellow. One in particular had all but destroyed his belief in love and kindness.

Just his luck—a special woman would appear on his last weekend in the States under the glittering lights in a ballroom.

Rob sat across the table from Virginia, wondering how it would feel to walk in a spring garden with her, to watch the tide come in with her at his side, and to share a heaping bowl of ice cream with her on a hot summer day. He thought of how it would feel to hold her in his arms, to caress her naked shoulders, to kiss her lips and eyelids, and to run his hands over her body. He imagined the sight of her first thing in the morning after awakening from a deep sleep. In his mind, he pushed the hair from her face and buried his lips in the honey sweet warmth of her neck and breasts. He envisioned her lithe body covered in bubble bath as he gently massaged her shoulders and back to remove the stress of the day. He could almost feel her long trim legs lying across his as they lay spent from lovemaking. If only there were more time, he would make this woman his. But, on Monday, he would board a plane for far places.

"I think I've danced just about all I care to for one evening. How about some dinner? I saw a little steak place in the next block. You never know when I'll have a good, thick, juicy, filet mignon smothered in grilled onions again. We can grab a bite and still get back in time to toast the New Year. I'm hungry after missing dinner. Care to join me?" Rob asked, looking deeply into her eyes and willing her to say yes.

"Well, I don't usually mix my professional and personal lives, but I guess I could break the rules just once. Besides, a good friend of mine was on the planning committee, and told me that we won't have breakfast until five. I'll get my coat and meet you at the door," Virginia answered. She had surprised herself by accepting his invitation. Despite the attraction of his fabulous good looks, she continued to find him too self-assured.

Walking across the room to where Edwina sat, Vir-

ginia could not believe that she would soon be going
for a light supper with this impossible man. She still
did not care for him, but she could not help feeling
the power of this sexual magnetism. Even if she
could get past his attitude to uncover warmth beneath the self-possessed surface, Virginia would not
have the time to get to know him.

While waiting for Virginia, Rob decided that the
impact of their meeting had been a pleasurable one.
He had liked her spunky personality when he first
met her. Dancing with Virginia and chatting with
her had only made him want to get to know her
better. Now, instead of looking forward to his new
job, he was actually wishing that he did not have to
go.

Taking her arm, Rob gently steered Virginia down
the street toward the steak house, a famous Washington establishment. The night was surprisingly
quiet for a Saturday and New Year's Eve. She decided that everyone must already be at parties, waiting for the countdown. Even the usual laughter of
passersby going from one bar, restaurant, or movie
to another did not pierce the silence. They had the
cold silent streets to themselves.

Glancing quickly at the beauty on his arm, Robinson could not believe his good fortune. Tonight
when he entered the ballroom, he had not expected
to meet anyone as charming and lovely as Virginia.
He had attended many corporate parties and usually
left disgusted because of the way in which low-level
managers fawned over him. Instead, he had met Virginia, a strong-willed but caring young woman from
whom he wanted more than only a few hours and
a fistful of good times. Reluctantly, he forced himself
to remember that his plane reservation called for

him to fly out early Monday morning. It would have been nice to have had the time to become better acquainted with her.

As the silence of the wintry Washington streets enveloped them, Virginia felt her heart surrender to the majesty of the frosty night. The magic of the evening whispered to her with promises of love and adventure. Even the subdued lights peeking from behind the lace curtains of the nearby apartments made her feel the mood of the city, and made her expect that something bewitching was about to happen. The occasional blasts of a horn or shout of "Happy New Year" made the sense of anticipation grow. Like everyone else, Virginia wondered what the new year held in store for her.

Shaking her head slightly, she reminded herself that Rob would soon be leaving. She knew she would probably never see him again. The company was massive, expanding by leaps and bounds as it reached into the European market. Days passed without her seeing Edwina, and their offices shared the same floor in the headquarters tower. She could not allow herself to care for him . . . she could not afford the pain of losing someone she loved. Still, the nearness of him was exciting and comforting at the same time, even though he carried himself with an abundance of confidence and assurance.

Virginia had made a New Year's resolution to cut back on her consumption of chocolate. Fortunately, she had not committed to reducing the number of men in her life. Her work schedule usually took care of that for her. Joining the only other couple on the sidewalk, Virginia decided that she would let the new year take care of itself.

Two

The warmth of the restaurant greeted them as they opened the door, releasing the aroma of wine, onions, cheese, fresh bread, and steaks sizzling in the kitchen. Statues filled the corners, and photographs of famous people lined the walls. Only one other couple sat among the white linen tablecloths and candles twinkling in hurricane lamps. They looked up as Virginia and Rob entered, but they did not stop their subdued conversation as they clasped hands together hungrily across the table. The candlelight cast a soft shimmer on her thin gold wedding band and tiny diamond, making Virginia wonder if they were newlyweds.

The menu offered reasonably priced steak and chicken dishes that had earned the restaurant many rave reviews in the *Washington Post* and a position as a focal point for political and social dinners. As Virginia and Rob waited for the water to bring their order, they chatted about their families. Virginia told Rob about her two brothers, who had attended service academies and were newly commissioned officers in the air force. They always had interesting stories to tell of their first assignments. She had not seen them in six months, but they phoned their mother almost every week. Her mother taught school in rural Maryland, not far from their farm in Towson. Her father worked the land on weekends and ran a prosperous law firm during the week. He called farming his hobby, claiming that the demanding work relieved him of the tensions of his practice.

Rob said that he was an only child whose family had moved to Washington from Richmond when he was a little boy. He had grown up in one of the stately old houses on the edge of Rock Creek Park in a fashionable section of Washington, DC. His father had practiced medicine, and his mother was a professor at a local college who loved to entertained the black intelligentsia at dinner parties. The list of his parents' friends included many famous names from the arts, politics, and literature. They had been especially proud of him when he entered Harvard Business School, from which he graduated with honors. They had glowed with pride with each step he took up the corporate ladder, although they had secretly longed for him to follow in his father's footsteps.

As Virginia watched Rob speak, she could not help but notice the way the dimples played at the corners of his mouth. The movement of his hands and long slender fingers as he gestured for emphasis intrigued her. She was held captive by the deep rumble of his voice, and the twinkle in his deep brown eyes. She found herself thinking how lovely it would be to get to know this man, to rest against his broad shoulders and chest, and to feel his strong arms protecting her from the world. There was something magnetic about Rob that Virginia could not deny.

Pushing away the thoughts that made her cheeks redden, Virginia realized that if she had not hungered for life in the center of political and social energy, she would not have moved to Washington or met Rob. She would have stayed in Maryland after college. She would have taken a marketing job in nearby Baltimore. From there, she would have followed one of two paths. She either would have met a nice man, married, and raised her family, just as many of her friends had, or she would have moved through the corporate ranks on a smaller scale. She might have journeyed to DC to see the theater, but this bustling city would never have become her home. If the lure of the big city and its adventures had not called her from Towson, she would not be sitting across the table from Senior Vice President John Robinson. She would have been at a friend's house, sipping a drink and waiting for the ball to drop in Times Square.

At least, that was the way Virginia had always thought her life would turn out. She had always dreamed that she would marry one of her childhood friends or someone she met while studying business at Johns Hopkins University. She had never imagined that she would leave home for the adventure of Washington. When her brothers left for the Air Force Academy and then active duty, she had changed her mind. She had grown dissatisfied with her quiet life and had longed for something more, so she had packed her things and headed for DC with a masters degree in business under her arm. Her parents had not been happy with her decision, but they understood the loneliness she felt without her brothers and their friends who had also left Towson for more exciting locales. They understood her need to spread her wings and try out the freedom that women had not enjoyed in her grandmother's day. They had let her go with the promise that she would phone home often, thinking that she would stay away for only a few months before requesting a transfer to the Baltimore suburbs. They accepted her decision to remain in DC with a sense of resignation. Her parents missed the happy laughter of her carefree brothers, too, and found home a bit gloomy without their children, but they faced the realities of their new lives and let them go.

Now, sitting across the table from Rob, Virginia knew that she would find it difficult to return to the quiet farm days she had loved so dearly as a child. There was something about the excitement of DC. The fabulous clubs and the theater, the paddleboats on the Tidal Basin, the lights on the monuments, and the smell of the fog on the Potomac would not let her return to the days of her childhood. The cold wind blowing past the front door of the National Cathedral would not let her return to her old life on the farm. Although Baltimore considered itself cosmopolitan, it could not hold a candle to DC.

Virginia felt that Rob had entered her life to distract her tonight from the loneliness of her brothers' and William's absence. She would accept the few hours with him as a gift, and enjoy them as she would a box of chocolates, savoring each for the surprise under the rich coating. She would try not to take their short time together too seriously. She would remember that he was a big city man and a corporate big shot, while she was a small town girl from Maryland and a successful manager. He was the opera and the theater; she was state fairs and carnivals. He was caviar and champagne; she was hot chocolate and homemade buttermilk biscuits. She had come to Washington for adventure, and to for-

get her loneliness. She had found all of that, and
more.

Yet, Virginia found it difficult to keep from being
interested in the handsome arrogant man in the
smartly tailored designer tux. She wanted to know
what made him happy, sad, amused and tearful. He
had entered her life from the frigid winter night.
Her curiosity made her want to uncover all there
was to know about him. She wondered about the
forces that drove him to fight against corporate
prejudices and rise to positions of power.

John Robinson sat thinking some of the same
thoughts as he munched on his perfectly cooked
medium rare steak. He had smothered his baked
potato in sour cream with chives, soaked his broccoli
in cheddar cheese sauce, and slathered his hot roll
in butter. As he chewed, he gave his full attention
to Virginia. He listened as she talked about the farm
and the city that had been her home until two years
ago, when she had come to Washington. Seeing her
in the glow of the candlelight, he wondered why he
had not noticed her at meetings during the course
of those years. They must have attended some of the
same sessions. Perhaps it was the dreamy glow of
candlelight that made her appearance so stunning
now. Maybe the fluorescent lighting in the office did
nothing to bring out her lovely complexion. He
would have enjoyed learning more about this beauty.

Rob could not believe his good fortune at meeting
Virginia at the company party that night. He had
only stopped by on his way home, since he had
needed to be packing his things, an arduous task he
hated and did not mind postponing. He had heard
that the music would be lively, and the food delicious. Besides, he did not want to start the new year

alone. He had not expected to find someone as stunning as Virginia there. His heart had almost leapt out of his chest when he first saw her. Her radiant complexion, slim figure, and quick laughter had made her stand out above all the other women. He could fully understand her popularity as he watched her mingle with the other members of the marketing staff.

Rob had been instantly drawn to her, though he suspected that her friend William planned to monopolize her evening. When William left, Rob could not believe his luck. He had hoped that if he worked fast enough, she would spend her evening with him, but he had not been prepared for the way she looked at him when he first approached her. The expression on her face and in her fiery hazel eyes quickly told him that his attentions were not desired.

Rob almost smiled at the memory of the way Virginia initially treated him. As a man with a prominent position, he was not accustomed to being ignored. Women always flocked to him, drawn by his free-spending style of living and his easy laughter. Their eyes said that they also found him very attractive, even handsome.

Growing up as an only child, Rob had become accustomed to being pampered. All the women in his life had always doted on him. Virginia had definitely been different, because she seemed to find him repulsive. It was only as she got to know him while they danced and chatted that her attitude toward him softened. Her conversation had gradually turned more relaxed, and the angry tension left her shoulders.

Looking at her now as she licked lemon meringue from her fork, Rob was happy to see that she had changed her mind. The sight of her tongue darting in and out of her mouth in search of the sweet stray tidbits made him long to pull her against his chest. Rob knew instinctively that he could not move quickly with Virginia. He could tell that she was the kind of woman who needed to feel secure before she would open up to a man. She needed time to learn to trust. Unfortunately, time was something of which he had very little. He would have to be content with holding her hand as they walked if she would let him, and imagining how she would feel in his arms. If only he had the rest of his life, Rob knew he could make Virginia fall in love with him. He was already being pulled magically to her.

After dinner, Virginia and Rob quickly walked back to the ballroom for one more dance. They arrived as the band struck up the first chords of "Auld Lang Syne." Taking her into his arms, he led them around the room to its leisurely tempo. Virginia rested her hand lightly on the back of his neck and her cheek against his. Despite her resolve to dislike him, Virginia found comfort in his arms. She felt warm and comfortable in his arms, yet, she couldn't forget that their time together was almost over and he would vanish into the frosty night forever. Instead of forever, they had only a few remaining hours. This new year was definitely off to an exciting beginning.

Rob read the hesitation in her body as he pressed Virginia closer to his chest. She fit perfectly against him, almost as if she had been made just for him. His mind and arms longed to hold her, to make love to her, and to wake up every morning of his life with her sleeping beside him. Breathing deeply of her clean soap and water fragrance, he wished again that she had entered his life sooner. He would have held her and drawn strength from her slight frame and soft voice. Now, it was too late.

"Happy New Year!" Rob whispered as the horns blared the new beginning.

"Happy New Year!" Virginia echoed as she smiled into his eyes.

Looking into her soft hazel eyes and feeling her gentle hand in his as they walked toward the door, Rob saw that Virginia shared his feelings although she tried hard to hide them. Daring to voice his thoughts, he cleared his throat and said, "I'm going to the Washington National Cathedral for service tomorrow morning at eight o'clock. Would you meet me there? We could have breakfast afterward and spend the day visiting the zoo, museums, art galleries. Then, if you think you can stand me even longer, a few friends are having a little going away party for me. I'd like you to accompany me. What do you say?"

"I'd love to, Rob. I'd really like to spend the day with you. I'll meet you there," Virginia replied quickly, surprised at her reaction. She had been determined to remain cool to this confident man, but, she had felt her resolve fade.

"I'll see you in the morning," Rob whispered as he returned Virginia to her table and the waiting Edwina. Turning, he waved, and then disappeared into the cold of the black starry night.

"Well?" Edwina demanded as soon as Rob was out of view.

"OK, so I was wrong. He's a nice guy. We're going to church together tomorrow, and then to a little party his friends are giving him," Virginia replied as she threw her black mink jacket over her shoulders.

"I'll say you changed your mind! You were all set to hate him, and now look. You're even going on a date with him," Edwina chirped as she followed Virginia for the walk to their apartment down the street from the hotel.

"Who said I can't change my mind if I want to?" Virginia rebutted as they almost sprinted in the cold air of the new year. "Besides, Rob spoke lovingly of his family, and sincerely of his plans for the future. When he did, I saw this incredible warmth and gentleness in his eyes."

"Don't tell me you find him attractive now. I thought you couldn't stand the guy," Edwina said as they waved at their doorman and boarded the elevator to the third floor.

"He's okay," Virginia said with a nonchalant shrug as she threw her purse onto her closet shelf and hung up her jacket. "Anyway, I'm certainly not going to allow candlelight, New Year's Eve, champagne, and music sway me too much. Besides, he's leaving on Monday for Europe. There's no point in becoming interested in someone who won't be here. Long-distance relationships don't work."

Calling from her room next-door, Edwina offered, "A occasional vacation trip to Europe wouldn't be a bad way of keeping in touch. The distance would keep the relationship fresh."

"I don't call that fresh. It's more like frigid. No, when I settle down and fall in love, it'll be with a man who lives in the same city that I do. No E-mail or long-distance romance for me. I want handholding and evening walks in the park together, not transcontinental messages passing in the night." Virginia slid under her crisp sheets and turned out her light.

Edwina continued to chatter in the darkness about the benefits of distance, the element of mystery, and the ability to date other people while being somewhat committed. After a while, Virginia did not hear her. Her mind was reeling with thoughts of tomorrow, when she would meet Rob at the cathedral. She would have to remember to keep her feelings for him on a strictly friendly basis. It would not be easy, since the sound of his voice made her heart skip a beat, the touch of his hands caused her knees to buckle, and the feel of his arms around her lifted her heart to new heights. She was forced to admit to herself that she could easily fall in love with a man like him. Even his arrogance now had an appeal. She knew it was too soon, but everything happened quickly in this fast moving town.

With a deep sigh, she turned over and adjusted the sheets. As she drifted off to sleep with a heavy heart, for the first time she regretted coming to Washington. If she had stayed at home in Baltimore, she would not be experiencing such conflicting thoughts and emotions. She would be happily sleeping in her own little bed in the same room in which she had spent most of her life, played with her dolls, and dreamed of one day marrying her Prince Charming. Her life had been so simple. Washington and its bright lights had seemed far away; the excitement DC offered was only a rumor. Now, in the darkness of the first day of the new year, the city was all too real, and life was much too complicated. Virginia was confused and unsure of her next move.

By eight o'clock the next morning, the cold night had turned into a bright, shining, Washington winter day in all its glory. Thousands crammed the early service at the Washington National Cathedral. Vir-

ginia had never seen so many people on the
sidewalk and steps. The crowd reminded her of the
Easter Sunday service she had attended her first year
in DC. She wondered if any of them were nursing
hangovers from partying the night before.

At first Virginia feared that she would not see Rob
in the crowd, although his six-foot, five-inch frame
made him difficult to miss. As she pushed and
shoved her way through the mass attired in heavy
suits and dresses, she saw him standing on the top
step, waving both of his arms over his head to attract
her attention. Smiling and waving back, Virginia
found herself once again impressed by Rob's stature
and his handsome face. Secretly, she had hoped that
her feelings for him would lessen in the sunlight,
that the candlelight and music had confused her and
made him appear more handsome than he really
was. Seeing him with the sunlight sparkling on his
reddish-brown skin and playing on his broad shoulders, Virginia knew that the night had not cast its
magic spell on her. Rob was everything she had ever
dreamed of, and more.

Rob squinted into the bright light, looking over
the sea of faces as he watched Virginia making her
way through the crush of people slowly walking into
the cathedral. When she saw him, her face lighted
up with joy that outshone the sun that played in her
light brown hair. His heart lurched painfully at the
sight of her, knowing that he had found the love of
his life only to have to leave her tomorrow. As the
ache swelled in his chest, he wondered if she would
still be in DC when he negotiated a transfer. Sadly,
he faced the reality of separation and the effect of
distance on a relationship. Virginia would probably
marry someone else and forget all about him if his

stay in Europe lasted too long. He would become a memory of her new life in Washington.

Taking his offered hand as they joined the masses seeking something greater than themselves inside the cathedral, Virginia once again wished that she could have more time to get to know Rob. She would have liked receiving flowers, sharing long telephone conversations, and going on picnics. If only they had met before he was promoted to the European branch. Virginia sighed in resignation. This was the only opportunity she would have to get to know the man who occupied the pew beside her.

Resting his shoulder lightly against hers as they sat together with the incense filling the high ceilings of the cathedral, Rob gazed at the fabulous stained glass windows and wondered when he would ever see them again. He had looked forward to this promotion and the opportunity to head an international work force until last night, until meeting Virginia had dulled his enthusiasm. He felt an inexplicable pull toward her. Although he had known many women, Rob had never met one who had such an immediate impact on him. After all, they were really strangers. When next they met, Rob wanted Virginia to come to him willingly, without the influence of the excitement of New Year's Eve or the sun shining through the stained glass windows and the incense in the Washington National Cathedral. He wanted her to give herself to him freely without the romanticism of last days, and sensual music and dances clouding her vision.

After the service, Virginia and Rob strolled briskly down Connecticut Avenue toward Rock Creek Park and the zoo. Holding hands and chatting, they stopped to browse at shop windows and to buy toasted bagels with thick slabs of cream cheese. Sitting together on an isolated bench on a quiet side street, they contentedly munched their snacks in silence. Virginia cast furtive glances at Rob as she fed the pigeons which gathered at her feet, cooing happily each time that she dropped a piece of bagel for them to share.

In Virginia's mind, Rob looked especially handsome as the sun glinted off his hair. Rob looked so different from the boys in her neighborhood and in college. He was graceful and patient. They'd had a swagger and a boldness that belied their youth, and an impatience to be involved and busy. They had always been in a hurry, whereas Rob acted as if he had all the time in the world.

Virginia still tried not to become attracted to this tall handsome executive, but she could not stop herself. She dreaded the passing of this day, knowing that she would probably never see him again. Even if he returned to an office in the States, she feared that he would not search for her. Why should he? They had known each other barely twelve hours. She had no reason to think the expression in his eyes was anything other than his concern about starting a new job and leaving home. She would not allow herself to believe that Rob might actually have the same kernel of attraction growing for her. Virginia kept her thoughts locked deep inside her. She could not afford to risk showing them. If Rob did not feel anything for her, she would appear foolish by making a premature announcement of interest.

Little did she know the Rob fought with the same emotions as he watched the sun play in the red highlights of her light brown hair, making it look like the horizon at sunset. He, too, was torn between feelings that swelled within him and his need to remain silent. He thought that if he did not mention his growing fondness for her, he would spare her the anguish of waiting for his letters, calls, E-mails, and eventual return. He wanted to take with him the memory of her smiling face, her happy easy laughter, and her light step. He could not bear the thought that his last picture of her would be one with sadness written on her face as she waved goodbye at the airport.

Taking her hand again, Rob led Virginia deeper into the park. They strolled slowly until they reached the zoo, stopping along the way to watch the birds and squirrels playing in the trees. The warm January sun on their backs made them feel relaxed and enfolded in the embrace of love and comfort.

Squinting into the sun, Virginia looked at Rob as they walked under the gate to the zoo. The sun brought out the red in his hair and skin. She could see the eyes of other women, who looked longingly in his direction as they passed. Several of them touched their hair, adjusted their hems, and moistened their lips as he approached. They wanted to look their best for this fine specimen of black manhood. Virginia struggled to conceal her feelings of triumph as they stared boldly into his face.

Rob did not notice them. He mind would only be on her until he had to fly away tomorrow. Oblivious to stares and whispers, he concentrated only on Virginia.

Pulling a small bag of peanuts from her shoulder bag, Virginia tossed one into the chimpanzee cage. The happy little animal grabbed it and scampered to the top branch of the perch. He almost smiled at the gift as he munched hungrily. Rob threw another to his companion. The cute little animal rubbed his head in a gesture similar to a salute. Continuing to the elephant house, Virginia and Rob tossed the rest of their nuts at the mother and her youngster. They raised their trunks and trumpeted clouds of dust in thanks. Grasping the offered treats, they contentedly munched their snacks before lying down in the dirt for a cleansing roll.

Virginia and Rob rounded the corner and meandered to the indoor seal pond, where they found a family of seals sitting on the mounded rocks. The animals clapped their flippers together and barked at the spectators. When their handlers threw fresh fish toward them, they lunged and jumped to catch them, then quickly devoured their meal. Virginia and Rob applauded the animals' behavior, and laughed with glee along with the others in the crowd at their antics.

Rob smiled down at the top of Virginia's head. The light brown curly hair showed off the curve of her graceful neck to perfection. She wore a kelly green suit with big black buttons and a wide, black, patent leather belt. The white collar of her blouse showed at the open throat and cuffs. Her shoes were fashionable wedge patent leather pumps with three-inch block heels. She looked like a fashion model waiting her turn to walk down the runway. He lightly patted the small hand he held in his own massive one. She was so tiny compared to him, yet so strong and proud. He could not help but feel the strings of love pull at his heart and his groin. Rob decided that he could not leave without at least one kiss from her red lips. He did not know when he would return. He only knew he needed the memory of Virginia in his arms to take to Europe with him.

Virginia, sensing his eyes on her body, could feel the blush rising to her cheeks. She quickly turned as if looking farther down the path that led to the bird house. She did not want Rob to see the affect his nearness and his gaze caused. She did not want to admit to herself that she felt an irresistible pull to him. Yet, as the warmth spread from her cheeks to the pit of her stomach, Virginia knew that she was fighting a losing battle against him and her feelings. She no longer thought him arrogant or unreachable. His anecdotal stories had illuminated his softer side.

Not since Virginia had been in college had she experienced such a flood of emotions. Then, she had fallen for an engineering major with gold-rimmed glasses. One day, when he bent over to pick up her fallen book, the glasses that always slid down his nose landed on the ground. In his nearsighted hurry to pick them up, he had stepped on them. After that, he had bought contact lenses. The transformation was phenomenal. The glasses had been hiding deep gray eyes and a penetrating gaze. He and Virginia had been inseparable for the rest of the year until he graduated and moved to MIT for his master's degree.

"I'm hungry," Rob said, breaking the silence that separated them from the laughing children playing along the walk. "How about a hot dog smothered with onions, mustard, ketchup, and relish?"

"Sounds good to me," Virginia replied, grateful for the opportunity to put some distance between them. Although she loved the feel of his hand on hers and the nearness of his arm as it lightly pressed against hers, she needed to move away from him to

sort out her feelings. Being close to him only added
to her confusion.

Munching on hot dogs and sipping hot chocolate,
Virginia and Rob strolled along the path leading to
the giraffe house in silence. Thoughts of the next
day crowded their minds, although neither spoke of
their parting. Both wondered if they would ever
meet again. They tried hard to keep the sadness
from their faces, not wanting to ruin the little time
that was left to them.

They arrived at the giraffe house to find that the
giraffe stood at the center of a large gathering of
onlookers and admirers. Virginia and Rob joined
the others, who marveled at her antics with the ball
the handlers tossed into the confinement area. The
little giraffe family appeared to be having a good
time playing with their toy.

Standing there with children running around her
legs, Virginia was suddenly sad that they had come to
the zoo. As she watched the happy families playing in
the sunshine, she fought hard against the love that
bloomed inside her for this man who would soon be
leaving her. Sneaking a quick peek at Rob, she knew
in her heart that she had found the man of her
dreams, but she could not allow herself to love
him . . . not now . . . not until after he returned from
Europe, and they knew each other better.

Rob was feeling the same way, and he wore a wistful expression on his face as he watched the children
running in and out of the trees and playing tag at
their parents' knees. Beyond them, he saw other
couples walking hand in hand in the sunshine. He
saw one man pull his woman into his arms as if they
sat all alone on a deserted beach despite the cold.
If he were not leaving for Europe tomorrow, he

would press Virginia against his chest with the same hunger.

Exchanging quick glances, Virginia and Rob read each other's minds as they stood apart from the reveling families and lovers. As they looked into each other's eyes, they could feel an electrical charge pass between them. They longed to reach out their arms to enfold each other, and they ached to feel their bodies lock in a passionate kiss. Their lips itched with the need to share the sweetness of their new emotion, their hands burned with the desire to explore the strange but exciting bodies, and their skin tingled in anticipation of an embrace that would not come. Sadly, the timing was not right for them.

Virginia was the first to speak as she looked away into the setting January sun. "I think we should be heading back. I'm getting a little chilly." She could no longer tolerate standing close to him and not being able to hold him in her arms, kiss his lips, or run her fingers through his hair. She wanted him with a consuming fire that was new to her. She had never felt this way about any of the boys back home who had held her too closely at parties, stolen kisses on the Ferris wheel at carnivals, or danced with her in the moonlight at the prom. She did not dare stand there with Rob any longer. She did not trust herself and her resolve not to fall for him.

Rob felt cold, too, but not from the waning of the day. The emptiness of his arms made his chest ache and his heart feel heavy. It was not his leaving for Europe that made him sad. It was parting company with Virginia that made him wish he had never heard of the branches in Europe that needed his special managerial touch. She had come to mean so much to him in only a few hours. He wanted to be with her more than anything else in the world. He knew his thoughts were selfish, but he made himself a promise for the future—their future—as the red light darkened her light brown hair to deep rust. It was a promise he intended to keep.

Three

On the way home, Rob and Virginia stopped briefly at his friends' home in a very fashionable section of Washington, DC, near the zoo. Tulips and azaleas bloomed in the well-tended flower beds that lined the walk and porch. Inviting cushions lay ready on the porch furniture. Inside, the house smelled of gingerbread, baked apples, and freshly brewed coffee mixed with a slight scent of roses and cold cream. The heavy furniture, with its colorful but tasteful tapestry fabrics was a testament to their financial success and position in the neighborhood.

Joe and Donna had planned a little dinner for Rob's going away, and were happy to invite Virginia to join them. They sensed that something special and unspoken united Rob with the new woman in his life. Seeing the play of emotions on their friend's face, they thought that maybe this time Rob had found the right woman, and was regretting a business decision. For the first time in the fifteen years that they had known him, Rob did not look completely confident about, and comfortable with, a decision.

Even in college and graduate school, when everyone was trying to make decisions for the future, Rob seemed to have his life mapped out. He'd never vacillated in his decision to major in business at Haverford College. Once in graduate school at Harvard, he'd never questioned his focus on international business. Rob made plans to become a corporate big wheel while Joe and Donna were still trying to figure out the directions in which they wanted to go.

Donna's eyes never left Rob's face as they chatted amiably over sumptuous filet mignon, baked potatoes, delicately seasoned green beans, and sweetly steaming rice. They all deliberately stayed away from discussing business and Europe, focusing instead on music and theater, which Virginia discovered were two of Rob's passions. When Donna served dessert, they sipped their coffee and ate delicate gingerbread topped with whipped cream and slices of fruitcake spread on dainty rose pattern china. The good friends laughed happily about past golfing exploits, their college days, and business deals, all in hopes of refreshing memories that would have to last a long time before they could make new ones.

Looking over the rim of her cup, Virginia watched as Joe chuckled at the jokes he and Rob shared. Often he placed his hand affectionately on Rob's shoulder. They had shared so much, and now had to part company until Rob could return. As a successful bank executive, Joe understood that opportunities like this one did not come along every day. Regardless of the personal hardship involved in relocating, Rob had to take the job. In his career, he needed the change.

They spent the evening looking through old photo albums and chuckling at college memories. Virginia saw the eighteen-year-old Rob play flag football on the green. She watched the twenty-year-old

Rob accept an award for scholarship in business. The handsome twenty-one year old smiled proudly standing beside his friends on his graduation day from Harvard. They stood together in front of the church on the day of Donna and Joe's wedding. One of the sweetest photos was of Rob, the new godfather, holding their firstborn at his christening.

Virginia hardly felt the hours pass as she sat enfolded in the comfort and love of Rob's friends' home. When they finally rose to leave, Donna and Joe kissed her warmly and asked her to visit them often while he was away. She knew that they genuinely meant the invitation.

Walking down the almost deserted streets and avenues, Virginia and Rob finally reached her apartment building in a little residential section across from the National Cathedral. The red brick glowed a deep russet as the setting sun shone on the front of the building. She and Edwina had consulted countless magazines and finally sought the assistance of a decorator as they made the large, two-bedroom-plus, den apartment feel like home. She had covered her double bed with an antique spread that she had found in a quaint shop on Connecticut Avenue. The window treatment picked up the dominant turquoise in the ring pattern, and coordinated well with the Oriental rugs on the floor. Edwina had gravitated toward a more modern look, and decorated her bedroom in a stunning teal and creamy white. They had painted the two bathrooms a subtle shade of teal. In the gourmet kitchen equipped with the latest in appliances, they grew flowers on the windowsill and the marble-top bistro table. The bright mauves of their violets showed from the sidewalk.

Standing on the pavement in front of the building, Virginia pretended to hunt in her shoulder bag for her key, trying to delay their inevitable good-bye. She knew the tactic would not work, but she wanted to relish the last moments with Rob. The nearness of him helped to block out the increasing coolness caused by the setting sun. She was very aware of his gaze as he tried to memorize every contour of her face.

Finally unable to stall any longer, Virginia looked into his eyes and said softly, "I've never enjoyed a walk through the zoo or any afternoon more than I have today with you. Donna and Joe were most gracious, inviting a total stranger into their home. I felt so comfortable with them, and with you. I kept hoping that it would never end."

Rob had been studying Virginia's face as she dug into her shoulder bag. He had memorized the way the moonlight flickered across her cheeks, the upturn of her nose, the thickness of her lashes, the slight downward tilt of her lips, and the playful light brown curls that topped her head. He would hold these images in his mind while toiling in Europe. The attraction that drew him to her grew stronger every minute.

"So was I," Rob replied from the depths of his heart. "If I didn't have to pack, it wouldn't end now. I don't want to say good-bye. I'm having difficulty believing this turn of events. I've been looking for the one woman who would make me feel like settling down, and now I've found her. Virginia, you're everything I've ever wanted. I don't even know when I'll be able to arrange a transfer to the States, though. These assignments don't usually last more than a few years. They move someone like me into a job to get it started, and then someone else comes along to keep it going. I'm a corporate opener, I guess. It sounds strange to say that we can keep in touch, but I'd really like to hear from you when you have the time. I always answer E-mail, although snail mail and telephone calls often go unanswered. I know it sounds strange and much too fast, but I think I'm falling for you. This has never happened to me before, and I'm at a total loss. Help me here, would you?"

"Strange thing is that I feel the same way," Virginia responded truthfully. "I'm always in control of my life. The truth is, I didn't like you too much at first last night, but it's amazing how fast you've grown on me. I'll e-mail you often. I've got accounts at school, and at home. I wish you didn't have to leave tomorrow. This might just be the beginning of something big." Now that Rob had spoken first, she did not need to worry about sounding foolish.

As the moon and stars provided the only light on the quiet street, Virginia and Rob found themselves in each other's arms. Holding on as if life itself depended on it, they clung to the last moments before he would have to leave her. The minutes ticked away as they breathed in the sweetness of each other. Their mouths hungrily tasted kisses and the tears that mingled on their faces. Her hands stroked the stubble of his five o'clock shadow and wisps of curls. She lovingly committed the little lines between his eyes and the quickness of his smile to memory. He recorded the sound of her voice and the feel of her warm trembling body against his in his mind. Those memories would have to last until they could be together again.

As the bells from the National Cathedral tolling

the lateness of the hour filled the darkness, Rob drew a handkerchief from his pocket and dabbed the tears from Virginia's streaked face. Never releasing his hold on her, he walked her up the stairs of the apartment building and to the front door. Opening it, he turned and eased her inside.

Pulling his school ring from his pinkie, Rob said, "I can't believe that I'm doing this, but think of this as a friendship ring. If the lines of communication remain open between us, and if our relationship continues to grow, we'll exchange it for something more permanent. If at any time the relationship becomes too heavy for you, return it to me. You'll always know where I am. The company directory is revised constantly. You won't even need to send a note. I'll understand."

"All right, but don't expect to get it back," Virginia replied as he pulled her tightly into his strong arms. For the moment, Europe was far away. Again the cathedral bells sounded sonorously, telling them that it was time for them to part.

Reluctantly, Rob pulled away and said, "I'll wait until I see the light come on in your apartment before I leave. I don't want to go until I know you're safely inside. Take good care of yourself, Virginia, until I see you again," he said with a heart that almost split in two at the thought of leaving her.

Releasing his hand for the last time, Virginia barely whispered, "I'll be looking for those E-mails."

Quickly she dashed inside as tears blurred her vision. The ride to the third floor seemed to last forever. Reaching her apartment door, Virginia could barely see the lock as she struggled with the key. Running to the kitchen window, she looked down as the moonlight cast a shadow on Rob's face. Virginia saw her happiness through a fog of tears. She raised her hand and slowly waved to him, then blew him a kiss. Rob raised his right hand to catch the kiss and then he transferred it to his lips. Darkness hid from her sight the tears that filled his eyes, making it difficult for him to see her face at the window.

Squaring his shoulders, Rob walked toward the subway stairs. As his hand touched the railing of the escalator for the ride to the underground entry, he cast one last look over his shoulder at the figure barely visible at the apartment window. Then, he descended toward the waiting train that would take him to his apartment and then onward to the beginning of his journey to Europe.

Virginia watched as Rob disappeared down the steps, into the crowd entering the Washington, DC, subway station. When she could see him no longer, she turned from the window, wiping tears from her stained cheeks. She had to compose herself before Edwina returned from her Sunday afternoon visit to her aunt and uncle's house. Virginia could not let her see that she had been crying. She did not want to explain that she had fallen for Rob even though she knew that he was leaving. She busied herself with dusting the already clean living room. Virginia would tell her friend about Rob when her emotions had settled a bit.

At that moment, Edwina burst into the apartment carrying a bag filled to overflowing with carefully wrapped food. Bubbling with the happiness of the day spent with her family, Edwina did not notice her friend's discomfort as she exclaimed, "My aunt really loaded me down this time. There's plenty of pot roast, baked chicken, biscuits, and cornbread."

Turning from the imaginary dust, Virginia forced

herself to smile at her friend's happiness and the promise of good home cooking. "She shouldn't spend all of her time cooking for us. What do they do for spare time, with her always in the kitchen?" she asked. As usual, her first concern was for other people.

"You know it makes them feel good to feed us. With my two cousins away in college, they don't have anyone to take care of except us. Besides, Aunt Evelyn doesn't know how to cook for two. All this food would go to waste. Hey, what's wrong with you? Your mother hasn't called, has she? You look as if you've been crying."

"No, I haven't heard anything from home. As far as I know, my brothers are safe. I was just feeling a little lonely, that's all," Virginia responded, trying to cover her sadness with a small crooked smile.

"I guess you're missing your friend William. He's a smart guy. He knows how to dodge the traps set by corporations. It's a wonderful opportunity for him," Edwina said as she loaded their refrigerator with the goodies her aunt had packed for them. The fragrance of the still hot food filled the apartment, reminding Virginia of her family home in Towson, Maryland. Suddenly, her heart filled with homesickness, and worry about her brothers mingled with her loneliness for Rob and William.

"I'd better hurry, or I'll be late. Don't forget that it's our night to work at the USO," Virginia called over her shoulder as she darted into their shared bedroom. She did not want Edwina to see the tears that welled in her eyes and threatened to overflow and run down her cheeks. She was not ready yet to tell her of her relationship with Rob, or of the plan that gnawed at her mind.

Their company encouraged its managers to do-
nate time to service organizations. Both of their
mothers had worked for the USO during WWII, and
Virginia and Edwina happily joined the staff of hostesses who now spent evenings talking and dancing
with servicemen and women stationed around the
world.

Quickly she brushed the dust of the zoo from her
curls. Rushing to her bathroom, Virginia washed her
face, neck, and hands. As she carefully removed all
traces of the mustard from the hot dog that stained
her fingers, the topaz in Rob's class ring sparkled
in the garish light of the bathroom. She changed
into a black sweater dress with a V-neck and long
sleeves and snapped a single strand of pearls around
her throat. She slid pearl earrings onto her ears.
Looking at herself in the mirror, Virginia saw a
poised young woman. Her face did not mirror the
turmoil in her heart and soul. She was ready for
whatever the evening would bring.

"I'll see you at the USO hall. I have a few things
to take care of before the dancing begins," Virginia
said, grabbing up her purse before Edwina could
ask to accompany her. She needed to be alone. She
did not want her unhappiness to transfer to the soldiers, who might be spending their last nights in
town before going off to places distant and unknown.

As she walked down the dark silent street, Virginia's thoughts traveled involuntarily with Rob on
what she knew would be his journey across the
ocean to England then possibly onward, to France.
She knew that their company was in the process of
negotiating a partnership with the French government that would allow them to team up with the

French telephone industry. Since Rob's specialty was opening offices and establishing business, Virginia imagined that, after his stay in London, he would move to a high-profile job in Paris.

Virginia could almost see the fog settling over Dover Castle, and the poppies growing in Flander's Field. She smelled the sea air blowing off the English Channel. In her mind, she watched the white chalk cliffs of Dover fade from view as the ferry moved farther and farther from shore. In her heart, Virginia knew the decision that lay ahead of her, and she was filled with a mixture of fear and excitement.

Opening the door to the USO hall, Virginia smelled the comforting aromas of coffee, tea, cakes, and cookies. The fragrances of chicken stew and biscuits wafted from the kitchen. She breathed deeply. Somehow, as the gentle breeze enveloped her, Virginia knew that her life would never be the same again. Her growing feelings for Rob had changed it forever. The decision she was about to make would add yet another dimension.

"I'm so happy to see you, Virginia," Mrs. Patterson said as she pinned a heady gardenia to Virginia's sweater dress. "So many of the girls have decided to stay out. I think some of them have fallen for reservists, and are planning to see them later tonight. Falling in love is such a difficult thing to control, isn't it?" She looked deeply into Virginia's eyes. Virginia quickly diverted her gaze, afraid Mrs. Patterson would read the anguish written there. She was thankful Mrs. Patterson had not noticed the class ring. She would tell her about Rob later, too.

Little had changed at the USO since Virginia's mother had attended dances during WWII. Celebrities still entertained the troops in far-off countries, and women still cooked and provided company for servicemen and women far from home. Virginia imagined that as long as there were wars, duty stations, and homesickness, the USO would be there to help out.

As the music started, Virginia drifted away from Mrs. Patterson toward the groups of men and women standing together and tapping their feet. Finding that their happiness did little to lighten her mood, she strolled over to the punch bowl for a glass of the sweet, pale pink, fruit drink. As the cooling freshness of the juice trickled down her throat, Virginia found herself thinking of her first dances with Rob at the party, and of her last minutes with him. Already his face, the sound of his laughter, and the touch of his hand were engraved on her memory. She lovingly touched the ring that served as a reminder of their wish to make the long-distance relationship work until they could be reunited.

Watching the laughing dancers as they gyrated around the floor, Virginia found it more and more difficult to keep up the pretense of happiness when her heart sat in her chest like a cold clump of iron. The room, which was usually such a relief from her hectic demanding job in the marketing department, looked dismal and used. The worn spots in the carpet showed thinly in the light from the revolving twinkling ball. The spots on the tablecloths shouted their ugliness against the dingy gray of the once white and sparkling fabric. The chips in the punch bowl and cups looked like jagged razors waiting to slice and rip into unsuspecting fingers and lips. She had not noticed any of these things before when she had volunteered her time. Virginia decided that meeting Rob in the glory of the hotel's ballroom had amplified the appearance of wear in the USO hall.

Virginia no longer found solace there from the world. She was not safe from her thoughts, or the headlines that shouted the involvement of the United States in wars and peacekeeping operations. Her protective bubble had been burst. Rob had entered her life and removed her confidence. Now she'd had to say good-bye to someone special, too.

Circling the dance floor in the arms of a handsome sailor in his crisp white uniform, Virginia forced a smile to brighten her face. She had to give him a good time tonight. She did not want to send a man to his duty station far from the States without one last exciting evening. The sailor did not appear to notice that her cheery attitude was a facade. He seemed happy to hold her in his arms and twirl her around the floor. He pulled her close and breathed deeply of the perfume that drifted around her neck and mingled with the clean smell of soap. His hands clung to her, and his arms held her close to his chest. He chattered contentedly into her ear as the music played all around them. He was very sure of himself and the contributions he would make to the protection of freedom.

Virginia heard nothing of his happy conversation. Her mind was miles away with Rob as he prepared for his early morning flight. At this moment, he was probably packing his clothes into huge trunks. Rob had already sublet his furnished condominium to a graduate student couple from Georgetown University. At least he had saved himself the chore of crating or covering the furniture, and the financial burden of paying the mortgage on an empty condo.

As the music stopped, Virginia scanned the room

for Edwina. Not finding her among the clusters of laughing men and women, she excused herself and walked toward the ladies' room. Inside she found the usual combination of laughter and clouds of perfume, but no Edwina. Beautiful women lined up in front of the mirror as they checked their hair and makeup. Peering at her own face over the tops of their heads, she was surprised to see that the worry and pain in her heart did not show in lines at the corners of her eyes or at the edges of her mouth. She was relieved that no one could read the concern that kept her heart from dancing as lightly as her feet. Yet, she could see a strange light and a new determination glowing from her brightly shining hazel eyes. Strange, that light had not been there yesterday or the day before. Virginia could not deny its existence now.

Leaving the ladies' room, she spotted Mrs. Patterson sitting at the welcoming table near the door. Virginia squared her shoulders and marched over to her. She would liked to have spoken with Edwina first, but what she had to say to her could wait until after her conversation with Mrs. Patterson. She knew her friend and roommate would understand. She was not as sure about Mrs. Patterson.

Virginia cleared her throat as she approached the formidable presence sitting at the table. Mrs. Patterson always wore her heavy black hair in a tightly coiled bun on the back of her neck. She dressed in black with only a single strand of pearls or a modest brooch at her throat as accessories. She discreetly tucked a linen lace-trimmed handkerchief into her sleeve. Her shoes were not the stylish high heels worn by the younger women. She preferred the sturdy, stack-heel oxford worn by women of much more advanced years. She could have been any age from thirty to sixty the way she dressed, but Virginia knew that she was a young widow of forty with two teenage sons who were almost old enough to join the army. The lines from suffering, loss, and worry worn by so many of the women in Washington marked Mrs. Patterson's face, too. Virginia knew that she only wanted the best for the young hostesses in her care, despite her sometimes gruff exterior.

"Mrs. Patterson, may I have a minute?" Virginia asked with newfound courage rushing through her veins.

"Certainly, Virginia. It's rather quiet tonight, isn't it? What can I do for you?" She put aside the night's tally and the entertainment schedule so that she could focus her full attention on the slim young woman standing resolutely before her. Something in the set of Virginia's shoulders told Estelle Patterson that this would not be a discussion of the latest fashions.

Pulling up one of the black, straight-back, wooden chairs with its worn, faded, red cushion, Virginia sat down at the table opposite Mrs. Patterson. She could feel the older woman's eyes on her every move. Taking a deep breath, Virginia began her story. Speaking clearly and with conviction, she said, "I followed your advice and kept my distance from servicemen. However, last night at a company function I met a senior vice president by the name of John Robinson. He's leaving tomorrow for Europe, to open a branch of the company. I didn't plan to fall for him. In fact, I didn't even like him when we first met. Rob seemed arrogant, and all too sure of himself. But, when I got to know him, I found out that he was really very gentle and quite sensitive.

"He took me to dinner . . . nothing fancy . . . and we talked about ourselves. He's from here, you see, and the son of a doctor. I told him all about my family in Towson, and my brothers in the service. Then today, we spent the day together. After services at the National Cathedral, we went to the zoo, fed the animals, and talked some more. We even stopped at the home of his best friends. "They're really nice, and seemed to like me. They asked me to visit them while he's away.

"Seeing him leave, I've decided not to wait for him to return to Washington. I really don't like long-distance relationships, and Europe is just about as far away as you can go. I'm going to England, to be with him as much as I can before he leaves to open another office. I'll ask my company to transfer me to the branch there.

"I'm not asking you to understand. This is simply something I have to do. My parents won't understand either, when I call to tell them. I'm only asking for your support, and the address of the USO headquarters in London, because I want to continue volunteering. After he leaves, probably for France, I'll stay in England. With all the time I'll have on my hands, I should be able to help out quite a bit. If my company won't cooperate, I'll get a job at one of the British communications firms. I'm always hearing from international headhunters, so it shouldn't be too difficult. Besides, I've saved quite a bit from my job, and can live on that for a while if I must. Sharing a life with him is just that important to me."

Folding her hands quietly in her lap, Virginia waited for Mrs. Patterson's reaction. To her surprise, she saw tears begin to fill her eyes and flow gently down her cheeks. Pulling the handkerchief from her sleeve, Mrs. Patterson dabbed at them before she spoke, gently saying, "I knew from your face this evening that something had happened. I'm sure that I don't have to tell you that you might be making a big mistake. However, sometimes we have to do things that appear foolish, to have the things that we cherish the most. There's no USO in London, but here's the name of the Red Cross hall. They give comfort and food to our brave servicemen and women, just as we do here. Always know, Virginia, that my prayers are with you. I hope your young man understands what a wonderful woman he has in you. Come back to visit me when you return. Take care of yourself, Virginia."

Taking Virginia's face between her trembling hands, Mrs. Patterson deposited a kiss on her cheek. Then she rose and walked toward the kitchen. She did not want Virginia to see the concern she felt. This was a bold decision. Virginia could be very hurt if she had misunderstood Rob's intentions, a ring and a promise of E-mails or not. Mrs. Patterson knew that many men talked of love when they would soon be out of reach in foreign lands. Virginia was such a sweet girl. Mrs. Patterson hated the thought that she might get hurt, yet she knew she could not stop her. The look of determination glowed on Virginia's face with such brilliance that Mrs. Patterson knew that effort would be wasted on her.

Later that night, as they closed the hall together, Virginia said her last good-byes to Mrs. Patterson. Then, squaring her thin shoulders, she walked bravely into the cold January evening and toward her future and Rob.

Four

As she sat opposite her dear friend, Virginia's heart ached from the worry she was causing Edwina, but she had to go regardless of the possibility of heartbreak. She had to be with Rob. Even if their love cooled, she had to experience all the joy she could. Life was too short to allow a moment's happiness go unfelt.

Thinking back on the events of the last two weeks, Virginia was amazed at the speed with which she had made the arrangements. She had facilitated her transfer to the London branch office without a hitch. It seemed that her bosses had been planning to ask for volunteers to move to Europe on a long-term temporary basis, and were thrilled when Virginia offered her name for the list. They were delighted that she wanted to join the new staff, which would provide the needs of their international customers in much the same manner as they had the domestic ones. As it turned out, her bosses had been searching for just the right promotion for Virginia. Her interest in the overseas position handed them the opportunity to offer her the recognition for a job well-done. The transfer would make Virginia the youngest female vice president of marketing in the organization.

Her desire to continue helping out with community service work related to servicemen was not as easy to accomplish. Without Mrs. Patterson's help and contacts, Virginia would not have been successful in her attempts to position herself with the Red Cross. Using Mrs. Patterson's friends in high places, Virginia did manage to get permission to join the ranks of the staff in England.

Finding accommodations proved easy with the assistance of her company's relocation manager, who connected her with a realtor in London. The gentleman had quickly found Virginia a very acceptable flat, located in central London overlooking Hyde Park. She would have a perfect jogging area across the street, the best stores a brisk walk away, and the theater only a few stops on the tube. She could not ask for anything more.

"But, Virginia, you can't go. I'll be so lonely without you," Edwina moaned as she sat on Virginia's bed watching her pack the last of her things into two large, overstuffed suitcases. "What if Rob's already moved to France? What will you do, then? Even if he is still in London, how will you react if he doesn't feel the same way? What if he isn't as handsome as you remember? What if you look at each other and the spark is dead? You don't know anyone in England. You just can't go. Stay here with me. We have such a good time together. If you're really meant to be with him, the relationship will survive the long-distance." Edwina could tell from the set of Virginia's shoulders that her pleas would have no effect on her friend. Balling up yet another soggy tissue, she began to cry again.

"Edwina, please stop crying. We've been through this a thousand times in the last two weeks. I told you I have to go. Rob called this morning, so I know he'll be in London for a while longer. I didn't mention my plans to join him, but I'm a big girl and I can make my own way. Besides, he's probably read the company bulletin and knows that I've transferred to London and been promoted, although he didn't mention it in our brief conversation. I don't care how short our time will be together. I'm going to spend whatever there is with him. If I wake up one morning and find that he's really a total stranger, at least I'll have wonderful memories. Besides, I want this promotion. I've earned it. Even if Rob weren't in England, I'd go for the job. Please dry your tears and wish me well. I've gone to considerable trouble booking this flight and renting an apartment sight unseen, and nothing you or my parents can say will stop me. I'll be just fine, don't worry. Anyway, I've made up my mind, and that's all there is to it. I've always wanted to tour Europe. This might just be my chance. If this relationship sours, sightseeing will make a delightful salve for my hurt feelings." Virginia gave her soft bag a determined squeeze and a firm tug on the straining zipper.

Edwina was not the only one who opposed the trip. Her parents had been horrified at the thought that she had volunteered for a position thousands of miles from her family. They were thrilled with the promotion, but they did not understand why the new position would have to take their youngest child so far away. They realized that their thoughts were old-fashioned, but they did not like the idea that their daughter would live alone in a distant country. They still believed that female children should live at home until they married.

Seeing how determined Virginia was to join Rob and to begin this new assignment, her parents finally relented, but not before many tears had been shed by both of them. Virginia could tell by their expressions as they hugged her that they had resigned themselves to her decision. After all, she was a grown woman, and the experience of working in international commerce would look great on her resumé.

Rob's friends, Donna and Joe, thought that Virginia was making a smart decision professionally and personally. The exposure to an international work force and environment would strengthen Virginia's marketing acumen and broaden her horizons. Living in the same city with Rob would give her the opportunity to see if their relationship would grow, and if she could live with his little quirks. If the relationship did not survive, Virginia would have still expanded her experience base and added to her net worth in the marketplace. From Donna and Joe's perspective, Virginia was undertaking a win-win experience.

Looking around the apartment that had been her home since moving to DC, Virginia could not believe that she was actually leaving for England. She was a girl from Towson, Maryland, whose biggest trip before coming to Washington was going to college in Baltimore. She had found the hustle and bustle of the harbor wonderfully exciting and a little frightening, too, though. She did not want to be like her parents, who waited all their lives to travel and took their first trip for their thirtieth anniversary. At twenty-eight, Virginia wanted to grab all the fun and opportunities she could now, while she was still young. Moving to DC and taking the job in telecommunications had given her that opportunity, and

Virginia's life had changed drastically. Not only had she met Rob, but she had worked her way up to the inner circle of management. She had earned the respect of men and women who now championed her decision to move to England with the same enthusiasm with which they had welcomed her thoughtful research on projects and her ability to manage personnel.

As she picked up her bags and walked toward the door, Virginia knew in her heart that this was the right decision. She could not bear the thought that she might have to wait years for the opportunity to hold Rob in her arms, to awaken in the morning with him by her side, or to watch him sleep beside her. She planned to marry him as soon as she arrived in London . . . although she had not told him!

With one last look around the cheery living room, Virginia kissed Edwina on her tearstained cheek. She did not stop or look back until she was on the sidewalk. She feared that her friend's sad face might change her mind.

National Airport was a busy place on that January morning. The bright sun from the skylights almost blinded Virginia as she stepped from the subway into the main terminal, where she would check her luggage, buy a magazine, and wait for the departure of BA 1202 to Gatwick Airport. Through the lounge window, Virginia could see planes of every size as they taxied down the runways and took off over the Potomac River. The one that would take Virginia to England had not yet arrived, although she knew that it would be a wide-body jet, probably a 767.

Finally, she was airborne. As the vista of Washington faded and the field of clouds thickened under the plane, Virginia already missed her homeland.

She thought of Towson with its lush, green farm-
lands. She could smell the fragrance of strawberry
fields on warm summer days, hear the songs of rob-
ins in the evergreens, and watch the stately flight of
the yellow and black oriole. She was leaving so much
behind. But she had so much to gain when she arrived in England . . . her whole future lay before
her, across the Atlantic Ocean. As she looked into
the distance, Virginia imagined herself safely in London, with Rob's head on her shoulder. She could
feel his strong arms enfolding her, protecting her
from the cold mist off the ocean. The stale air of
the plane magically changed into the smell of spices
and vanilla, of Rob's cologne. In her imagination,
she ran her fingers through his newly clipped curly
hair and felt his clean-shaven cheek.

The piercing sound of the voice of the woman
next to her shattered her peaceful reverie. Pulling
herself from her thoughts, Virginia turned and
looked into the woman's smiling face. Beaming, the
woman said, "Wasn't that thrilling! I love takeoffs
and landings. They're my favorite part of the flight.
My name's Sylvia. We'll be seatmates for this glorious
flight."

Virginia smiled with as much enthusiasm as she
could muster. She hated having to chat with people
on planes, and had hoped that she would be able
to nap. Now, as Sylvia chattered away, Virginia closed
her magazine and said good-bye to any opportunity
for rest or reflection.

Sylvia Everly was from Boston, Massachusetts, and
on her way to meet her husband in Paris. He had
left her behind to finish the details of selling their
house while he got settled in an apartment on the
Rive Gauche. They had been married for thirty years

and, according to Sylvia, were still on their honeymoon.

"My Edgar found the most wonderful apartment for us. It's within easy walking distance of the Eiffel Tower, fabulous restaurants, and all kinds of small museums. I'm thrilled with the idea of living in Paris and traveling all over Europe whenever he has vacation. My husband is an executive with an international finance concern. We're thinking of retiring to Paris after this assignment. What does yours do? I'm sure he'll be as happy to see you as Edgar will be when I arrive. He has missed me terribly."

"I'm not married," Virginia replied with a smile. "I work for a corporation, and I'm relocating to England."

"Oh! Well, do you have a significant other? Surely an attractive woman like you has someone at home. Or maybe someone is waiting for you? That's a mighty big college ring you're wearing." Sylvia nudged Virginia with her elbow, as if the prod would bring forth more information, perhaps a tasty personal tidbit.

Seeing no harm in giving Sylvia a little something to repeat to Edgar over dinner, Virginia smiled and said, "My friend is in England, which is my incentive for relocating. I'm looking forward to joining him and getting to know my new home. However, being with him isn't my only reason for moving. I'm looking forward to the challenge of a promotion, and a new position."

Satisfied with her detective ability, Sylvia cooed, "Oh, that's wonderful . . . the promotion, I mean. I'm always envious of you successful businesswomen. That wasn't an option for me when I was your age. Women have so many more opportunities now. And

I knew you had to have a boyfriend. No attractive single woman with your charm would be without one. Tell me about him."

Realizing that there was no possibility of peace until she had satisfied Sylvia's curiosity, Virginia launched into the story of her job and her association with Rob. The older woman's constant nodding and questioning for detail made the flight seem shorter than its six hours. By the time Virginia finished her story, the movie had begun. They had talked through dinner, and would have ignored their snack if the flight attendant had not taken it upon herself to make sure that all the first-class passengers were pampered. Before Virginia knew it, they had landed at Gatwick Airport.

The plane landed at seven o'clock in the morning, and by nine o'clock Virginia was ensconced in her new apartment. She had boarded the train at the airport, changed to the greenline at Victoria Station, and walked the two blocks to her apartment near Hyde Park. The view from the train window had been spectacular. Virginia had settled in for the ride to London, she watched as the horizon passed before her eyes. The train sped through fields of yellow and green, past barns and grazing pastures, and along rivers and streams. It slowed down at every little town, stopping at many on the line to pick up passengers who boarded and quickly unwrapped their sandwiches and opened soda cans. To her delight, Virginia found that winter in London was much softer than in Washington, DC.

To her delight, Virginia met a young woman on the plane returning from a business trip to Scotland. Rita Timberlake had flown from Edinburgh beside a talkative seatmate, too, and had been all too happy to be free of the woman in the baggage claim section of the airport. As they talked, Virginia discovered that Rita lived in her new neighborhood, actually in the building next door. To make the similarities even greater, Rita worked for the same telecommunications firm, Phillips Corporation, in a different division. Rita said she would be more than happy to show her around town, and promised to visit as soon as she unpacked and refreshed herself.

London was a city teeming with life and activity. Looking at the crowds in the station, Virginia tugged her bags from the overhead compartments. The larger cases would arrive separately the next day. Quietly, Virginia joined the single file procession as it moved from the warmth of the car onto the platform. Getting a tighter grip on her belongings, she walked into the busy station for the transfer to an Underground train and Hyde Park with Rita at her side.

All around her, people spoke in accents strange to her ear. Virginia had thought the Washingtonians' somewhat nasal clipped speech sounded odd, but at least she understood them. Listening carefully to snippets of conversation, she picked up terms like blimey, loo, and quid. All were foreign to her uninitiated ear. Virginia often had to ask Rita to repeat phrases so that she could be sure that she understood.

Boarding the crowded subway, Rita stood with her bag between her feet. Virginia quickly caught on to the trick, and soon adopted the balance of an experienced rider. She watched as the train whizzed through the dark tunnels, stopping at streets with names like Earls Court and Paddington, until it finally reached Hyde Park. She and Rita walked on

crowded streets past quaint stores, upscale bou-
tiques, and charming little shops. People smiled and
waved happily as they pulled their collars higher
against the nippy air.

Waving good-bye to Rita at her apartment building, Virginia looked past the stately iron gate at a
tall, old, Victorian house. Long ago, its four floors
and attic had been converted into flats when the
population of London had swelled with farmers dis-
enchanted with the hard life of farming after WWII.
Now, they were occupied by upwardly mobile young
business executives, physicians, and attorneys. Looking around the neighborhood before entering the
building, Virginia noticed that this was not the only
converted house on the block, In this elegant section of Mayfair, the long row of homes on the block
all sported multiple mailboxes and intercoms.

She had heard that London was a gray town in
winter, with only a few weak streaks of sunshine. As
tiny flecks of snow fell into the palm of her outstretched hand, Virginia realized that she would
have to adjust to the overall gray color of the city
and its often lifeless sky and buildings. Somehow she
knew in her heart that the warmth of the people
would soon make her forget the flashiness of Washington, DC.

The lobby of the building had much of the elegance of the original foyer. A massive chandelier
hung overhead and reflected its light off the highly
polished marble floor. The vibrant colors of thick
Oriental rugs echoed the hues in the landscapes
that graced the walls. Plush tapestry settees provided
seating space for those waiting for a resident to appear. An attendant in the mailbox area greeted Virginia with a smile and handed her the key to her

new home, along with maps of London and its underground transport system—the tube, as it was known to the locals.

As the elevator came to a stop on the fourth floor, Virginia smelled the fragrance of new and enticing dishes cooking on the stoves in the flats behind the closed doors. Passing wood-paneled walls with elaborate sconces and paintings that resembled old masters, Virginia finally found her door at the end of the hall, neatly tacked away from the noise of the elevator and laundry room.

As it swung open, Virginia was pleasantly surprised by the appearance of the two-bedroom flat. Although the realtor had faxed and e-mailed photos, she had not been sure they were not retouched. To her surprise, Virginia found that the living room and the spacious dining room were filled with light from the floor-to-ceiling windows. One wall was completely covered in bookshelves, broken only by an ornately carved mantle surrounding an apparently functional fireplace. The landlady had placed a bowl of cut flowers from her garden on the hearth as a welcoming gift.

The kitchen had been freshly refurbished, and housed all of the most modern appliances. Her boss had sent a fruit basket that she found on one of the wraparound marble counters. Overhead, cabinets that would have been the envy of any chef awaited her new china.

The bedroom was equally welcoming. To her surprise, Virginia discovered that she could see Speaker's Corner in Hyde Park, and a jogging trail from the window. Almost unable to contain herself, she began to unpack her things so that she might venture into her new city. All that the flat needed was furniture, and she would take care of that as soon as she showered.

She would call the office and Rob after her return from her outing. She knew that Rob would not be available until much later. He had told her in the previous day's phone call that he would be in meetings all day. London belonged to her.

Hearing the doorbell, Virginia opened it to find Rita's smiling face.

"Going somewhere?" Rita asked as she noticed that Virginia's purse still swung from the strap on her shoulder.

"As a matter of fact, I do have a list of things to do today. The office took care of having the phone and utilities turned on, but I need to buy some furniture. I don't even have a bed to sleep on. After I do that, I want to see Parliament, with Big Ben, Westminster, St. Paul's, and Number Ten Downing Street. Then, I'll visit the Victoria and Albert Museum, Hyde Park, Buckingham Palace, and St. James Park." Virginia recited all this without stopping her rapid unpacking of items that would fit on the shelves and hangers in her closet.

"You don't have to see everything in one day, you know. We'll be here for a tong time. This is your home for a while. These places survived the bombings of WWII and the IRA. I think they'll be here tomorrow, too." Rita chuckled at her new friend.

Realizing just how silly she must have seemed, Virginia stopped in her tracks and laughed at herself. She had been running around crazily, she knew, but she was so excited that she could hardly contain herself. She had never dreamed of being so far from home, of being in London. She wanted to see everything about which she had always read.

"You're right, I don't need to see everything to-day." Virginia admitted, sitting cross-legged on the hard window seat. "I'm just so excited I don't know what to do. I'll slow down. But I have to order the furniture, if I don't do anything else. After that, what do you think I should see first?"

"My schedule is clear for the rest of the day, so I'll show you around. You can sleep at my place for the next two weeks until your furniture arrives, or I can lend you a sleeping bag. There's a lovely furniture store two blocks to the north, and a grocery store on the corner. I suggest that we visit both, since you don't have anything to eat except that fruit." Rita picked up her coat and bag. She had already discovered that the pantry was indeed quite bare.

Strolling down the street with their coats securely buttoned against the sharp winter winds, they peeked into storefronts and spoke to vendors along the way. At the grocery store, Virginia purchased some basic staples—spices, rice, cereals, tea, and milk—with which to stock her kitchen. Rita threw two bags of frozen green peas into Virginia's cart, as a reminder that peas were a staple not to be over-looked in her new English diet. The butcher happily sold her choice cuts of lamb, with which she would make curry. Farther down the street, she discovered a baker selling flaky crust bread that would be good for sopping up leftover juices. From the liquor store, Virginia bought a merlot to accompany the meal.

After loading her refrigerator with groceries, Virginia and Rita returned to the street for a trip to the furniture shop, which proved to be a pure de-light. The manager was only too happy to assist Virginia in decorating her apartment in a heavy leather sofa and matching chairs. The end tables she se-

lected were made of the best mahogany. The bedroom furniture consisted of standard pieces, in
cherry. Fortunately, every item she selected was already in the warehouse. Promising to have the furniture in her flat by noon the next day, the manager
waved good-bye.

Although Virginia's energy was running on re-
serves, she could not stop. Jet lag had turned to
a strange speed that propelled her forward. With
Rita's skillful assistance, Virginia navigated the underground walkways until she stood for the first
time on Speaker's Corner in Hyde Park. From
there, they walked the few blocks to the Victoria
and Albert Museum, where she marveled at a col-
lection of ancient artifacts. Later, they shopped at
Harrod's, where Virginia purchased curtains and
bed and table linens.

On the way back to their flats, Rita looked at the
droopy Virginia and said, "I won't take 'no' for an
answer. You're spending the night in my flat. I've
an extra bedroom, and a perfectly wonderful video
that I've been dying to watch with someone. You can
take a nap while I cook dinner. You can tell me all
about yourself and your posting to London while we
eat."

"I'm too tired to fight you. I'd love to take a nap,"
Virginia agreed as they stopped at her flat long
enough to check her messages. Leaving one on
Rob's voice mail in which she told him to come to
Rita's flat, Virginia dragged herself next door for a
meal, bath, and a bed.

Over a sumptuous meal, Virginia and Rita shared
personal information and chatted about the trips
they would take on their days off. Sitting in front of
the fire with their teacups balanced on their chair

arms, Virginia realized that she would not miss Edwina as much as she thought, since Rita had quickly moved into the position of valued friend and confidante. The only thing that would make Virginia's first night in London more perfect would be Rob's head resting in her lap. She knew that he would be with her as soon as he could get away from the office. Until then, she could wait.

As Virginia rested in Rita's flat while the video played in the background, Rob locked the door to his office and began the trip from the business district to Mayfair. The tube was almost empty as he slipped into a seat and opened his paper. Finding that he could not keep his mind on the articles, Rob allowed himself to think about the last time he had seen Virginia. He remembered the touch of her soft hand, the smell of her freshly washed skin and hair, and the feel of her body against his as they danced away the night as if it were only yesterday, instead of two long weeks ago. The memory of her upturned face warmed his heart, and made his groin grow tight. He wanted her in his arms so much that he ached.

Although Virginia had not told Rob that she had arranged a transfer to England, the office bulletin, as she suspected, had informed him of her plans. At first he had planned to go along with her surprise, and not let on that he knew of her pending arrival, but the sound of barely suppressed excitement in her voice loosened his tongue. During their last phone conversation, he had admitted his knowledge, and had been happy that he had. He could hear the relief that spread through her as soon as Virginia realized that he longed to see her, that her presence would be a welcome addition to his life.

Almost sprinting up the fashionable street in May-fair, Rob entered the elevator and impatiently pressed the button for the third floor. The doors closed slowly, and the creaky cables of the old machine groaned as they inched their way upward. Rob tapped his foot and bit at the cuticle of his right hand anxiously. After two weeks away from Virginia, he could hardly bear the tedious ascent.

Rushing down the hall with the slip of paper bearing the address and flat number in his hand, Rob searched every door. Finding number 3A, he rang the bell and waited as the clock in the hall ticked away the seconds that felt more like hours. He had envisioned their reunion, and was now ready to have Virginia in his arms again.

"Yes?" an accented voice answered through the thick paneled door.

"It's Rob Robinson, Virginia's friend," he replied almost breathlessly.

Again Rob waited, and the person on the other side unlocked the three bolts that secured the door and protected the inhabitants from the outside world. Slowly, the door slid open to expose the interior of Rita's flat. The warm glow and aroma of dinner flowed out to embrace him.

As Rob crossed the threshold, he saw Virginia rising from the semidarkness of the living room. The light from the television shone behind her. Wanting to take her into his arms, Rob waited for a sign from her that distance had not changed her feelings toward him.

Virginia walked slowly toward him, into the light that played on her hair. Stretching out her arms, she mouthed his name as his lips pressed hungrily on hers. Taking her cue, Rita vanished into her bedroom to give the lovers privacy. She knew that her new friend would not sleep alone that night.

...

Five

Virginia had anticipated that on her first trip to England she would want to do tourist things before settling in to work. She had arranged to use some of her accrued vacation before reporting for work. For the next two weeks, she would have time to herself. Between waiting for furniture deliveries and visiting museums, she needed time to establish herself in her new home. Now that her relationship was off to a sound beginning, she would be free from worry to enjoy her outings.

Although Rob was tied up in meetings most of the day, he found time to spend extended lunch hours with Virginia. They whipped through the British Museum the first day, and the Tower of London the next. On the weekend, they traveled out to York and Stonehenge. The next weekend, they visited Leeds and Bath. In between, they stayed in London, where they toured Whitehall, visited a famous wax museum, and enjoyed the thrills of the London Dungeon.

Whenever Virginia was not with Rob, she visited little museums off the beaten tourist path, or worked to turn her flat into a home. She sponge-painted the living room and dining room walls a deep cranberry, and tiled the kitchen wall in a charming floral pattern. She painted the walls of her bedroom a deep cream, and the guest room a pale raspberry. From Harrod's she purchased gaily patterned bedspreads that picked up the colors perfectly. At a local flea market, Virginia found inexpensive prints that complemented the color scheme. Thankful that the English did not require carpets on condo floors, she left the hardwood floors bare with the exception of an area rug. Their luster added to the elegance of the Queen Anne furniture.

Virginia called Edwina almost nightly, telling her of the places she had visited with Rob and the increasing bond between them. Edwina promised to visit as soon as she could arrange her vacation plans. She wanted to visit England in the spring, so that she would be able to see the flower show at Kew Gardens. Virginia looked forward to a nice long visit, knowing that neither of them had used any personal or sick days in two years. Vacation was not something that either of them scheduled on their calendars.

The days passed quickly, and the evenings even more rapidly. Always on the surface was the fact that Rob would not remain in London for long. His departure had already been postponed once, much to Virginia's delight. She would have more time for nestling against his wide warm chest and sharing their thoughts and dreams.

"Rob, I hope you don't mind that I followed you here," she whispered into his neck one night as they snuggled on the sofa in front of the roaring fire. "I couldn't stay in Washington without you. I had to try to see you again. I promise not to be in the way, or make any demands on your time."

"Oh, Virginia, I've dreamed of seeing you again and holding you in my arms. I just wish we could have more time together. As it is, we've been very lucky that the office in Paris isn't ready. If it hadn't been for that labor strike, I'd be packing my bags right now. We'll have another month together before I have to leave. Beside, London and Paris are not that far apart now. The Chunnel train makes the trip in no time at all. We can spend our weekends together, in your place or mine." Rob smiled, looking into Virginia's upturned face.

Putting on a brave smile of her own that she hoped would mask her disappointment at losing him again so soon, Virginia said, "Let's make the most of the time we do have. I'll have to go to work on Monday. I tried to extend my vacation, but couldn't. I'll make dinner here tonight, so that we can spend all of our time together without being disturbed." The idea of doing something domestic made her feel that she had some control over her life and his.

"Great! I'd enjoy some of that famous Maryland cooking. I've a few pounds in my pocket. I'll buy the ingredients." Rob beamed at her without releasing the hold he had on her trim body.

The cold wind buffeted them as soon as they left the building. As they walked along looking for her favorite butcher shop, Rob and Virginia held hands. Neither wanted to let go as they eased their way around women with baby carriages, a few couples strolling leisurely down the street. After buying the chicken, rice, and peas that were to comprise the night's dinner, they returned to her flat.

Busying herself in the kitchen with Rob standing close by, Virginia fried the chicken, steamed the rice, and simmered the bright green peas until they were tender. For dessert they would eat a tasty berry cobbler made from fruit they'd purchased at the corner stand. Rob was so busy watching and memorizing her every move as she set the table in the dining alcove that he did not notice the delightful strawberry pattern dishes and the sparkling freshly polished silverware. He was too taken by the sight of her soft hair glowing in the candlelight and the aroma of the delicious meal.

Sitting opposite him at the table, Virginia could hardly eat for sharing stories of the people she had met on her independent outings. She wanted Rob to be a part of everything she did. She was already learning her way around London's great subway system, which efficiently covered all of the city and its suburbs on a system of tracks that connected to stations for travel to outlying areas. The efficient and inexpensive means of transportation made driving her new company car unnecessary, unless she wanted to travel into the countryside beyond the reach of trains. Since she was a bit nervous about negotiating the numerous roundabouts—traffic circles—she usually took the subway as far as she could, transferred to the train, and then either walked or hired a cab for the rest of her trip.

Sitting on the comfortable sofa after the dinner dishes had been stacked in the washer, Rob pulled Virginia against his chest and rested his face on the top of her head. He wrapped his arms around her small frame. *This is the way we should always be,* he thought, *just the two of us, holding each other and saying nothing, letting our silence speak for us as words never could.*

Virginia felt the same tranquillity and peace as she allowed herself to melt into his warmth. Her small hands closed over his massive ones as she snuggled into the fold of his arms and drank deeply of his masculine aroma of wool and soap. She loved the way Rob smelled, the way he walked, the gestures he made with his hands, the touch of his lips on hers, and the feel of his fingers in her hair. She sighed softly and listened to the beating of her heart as it joined with his, becoming one synchronized rhythm.

As the news on the BBC television changed to soft music, Virginia felt Rob's breathing deepen and his head become heavy as it rested on hers. A gentle rumbling sound told her that he had fallen asleep. Even though she, too, was tired, she did not want to go to bed. She did not want the evening to end. With half a startled snore, Rob awoke, as if he, too, realized that the evening was over.

"I guess we might as well turn in. I want to show you St. Paul's Cathedral and Windsor Castle tomorrow. Fortunately, there won't be too much of a crowd, but we still need to get an early start. Part of the fun of visiting Windsor is taking the special train," Rob said, pulling Virginia to her feet and holding her against his muscular body.

"Oh, do we have to go to sleep now? I was enjoying listening to you snore," Virginia teased as she hugged him close.

"I don't snore, and I wasn't asleep. I was simply resting my eyes. Besides, I said that we should go to bed. I didn't say that we would sleep," Rob rebutted as he playfully pulled Virginia toward her bedroom.

Since her furniture had arrived, Rob had spent most nights in her apartment. His lacked the charm and warmth of hers, and felt more like a hotel than a home. The company owned the condo, and used it for visiting executives who were in London for relatively short stays. The rooms were pleasantly but institutionally furnished. The kitchen was adequate for quick breakfasts, but not for preparing large meals or feeding guests. Before Virginia arrived, Rob had eaten all of his meals except breakfast in restaurants recommended by his colleagues. Now that she was in London with him, he relished their quiet dinners together.

Pressing kisses to her forehead, eyes, and lips, Rob tasted the sweetness of Virginia's love and pulled her even closer. Leading the way down the hall and into the bedroom on the right, Rob flipped the switch that illuminated the comfortable room in which he had stored a few of his belongings so that he would not have to return to his place in the morning. Helping Virginia remove her wool and silk slacks and silk sweater, he quickly tossed his clothing onto the floor beside hers. Slipping into bed beside her, Rob slipped on a condom and turned off the lamp on the night table before turning his full attention to the gorgeous woman lying beside him. As always, he marveled at his good fortune at having such an intelligent exciting woman in his arms.

The next morning dawned bright and warm for a late winter day. A sorely needed break from the rain invited them out to the streets. Birds sang cheerfully in the trees, boats floated leisurely down the Thames, and children played in the streets on the way to school. After a breakfast of bangers and eggs served with tea and toast, Virginia and Rob walked with Rita to her office before starting off to explore London together. Their first stop was St. Paul's Cathedral in the highly congested section of town in which lawyers, judges, and litigants spent their days oblivious to the cathedral's majesty. During the bombing of London during WWII the cathedral had miraculously been spared. Even now, it was never the target of the IRA's attacks. It stood in the center of a large square as its stained glass windows reflected the sun's rays. Even though winter was not one of the most popular tourist times in London, a throng of visitors stood on the steps waiting to enter.

Virginia and Rob mingled with the faithful who came to the cathedral's peaceful shadows to pray and to take in the majesty of its architecture. There were old women with prayer veils, young women with bare heads, children in strollers. Old men with wrinkled hands sat together on the highly polished wood of the pews, their lips moving in silent prayers. Sitting a little away from the others, Virginia and Rob joined in the quiet meditations as they studied the intricacy of the windows.

Feeling the majesty of the cathedral flowing over them, they linked arms and strolled the aisles and gazed into the alcoves. They strained their necks to study the vaulted ceilings, peered into the semidarkness at the statuary, and studied the ornate carvings that shouted man's tribute to the glory of God. They joined a guided tour group traveling to the heights of the cathedral for a better look at the splendid ceiling.

Outside once again, Virginia and Rob mingled with the crowd of workers and visitors. Walking down the street toward the river, they decided to take a detour away from the Thames and toward the banquet hall of the Henry VIII's Palace at Whitehall. Rob wanted to show Virginia the detailed frescos that decorated the ceiling and walls.

Taking her hand and guiding her through the

streets, Rob marveled at the small size of her fingers and the warmth that flowed from them into his cold body. He knew that for the rest of his days he would find comfort in this small angel who had entered his life one evening at a company dance. She had already enriched his life by loving him. He could not imagine how his life would be without her in it.

Sensing his mood, Virginia walked quietly at his side. She found comfort in the silences that passed between them. Her heart sang, knowing that they were not afraid of the long periods free from words yet filled with the emotions that joined them. None of the boys and young men she had ever met had made her feel this complete. Even dear William could not touch her soul with his laughter the way Rob did with his silence.

On the way to St. James Park, they stopped at a little bakery smelling of cookies and fresh bread. They bought two huge cookies and a loaf of marble rye to take home with them. The aroma of the bread made their mouths water, and they knew that the tasty treat would not make it back.

It was still early when they reached St. James Park. Along the way, Virginia and Rob had stopped at a shop and purchased slices of Swiss cheese and ham. Sitting on one of the benches facing the lake, they tore off sections of bread for sandwiches. They laughed as they squeezed the little packages of mustard into heart shapes and flowers. Sitting on a wooden bench, they enjoyed the simplicity of the meal together and laughed at the antics of the pigeons and sparrows that flocked around their feet, pecking at the tiny pieces they threw to them.

Lunch finished, Virginia and Rob gave their full attention to the swans and ducks swimming on the pond. The birds dove under the surface of the water for a few moments to reappear with tiny fish in their colorful beaks. The sight of their little feathered bottoms pointing upward to the sky while their heads furiously hunted for morsels to eat made them laugh.

They had not planned to linger in St. James Park—they had wanted to stroll through Hyde Park and see Speaker's Corner before Rob had to return to the office for a late afternoon meeting—but sitting with the warm sun on their faces, they had almost forgotten about his pending transfer.

When they reached the flat, Big Ben in the clock tower of the Houses of Parliament had just struck five o'clock. The cozy rooms were awash with the last rays of the late afternoon sunlight. The oranges and reds sparkled off the mirrors and mingled with the colors of the upholstery.

Picking up his briefcase, Rob turned to Virginia and said with a boyish grin, "I love you, Virginia. I love our days together. We'll have to find time to play hooky from work again before I leave for France. I'm going to my flat tonight, since I don't want to disturb you This meeting will last into the night. We have a very important deal to close before we adjourn. Why don't we drive into the countryside tomorrow afternoon? My calendar's free, and I should be able to get away."

"I love you, too, Rob. That sounds like a great idea. I'll get a map and plot a course for Stratford," Virginia replied, pressing her hand lovingly to his cheek.

It was the joy of hot dogs in Central Park, feeding the birds in St. James Park, and waving from windows that made her love Rob so much. For a man who had grown up with so much, he seemed to enjoy the little things in life the most, and Virginia loved sharing them with him. Their exploration of side streets and little cafés and museums would give them something to tell their children.

Virginia was not sure who moved first, but suddenly they were in each other's arms. As the warmth of their bodies mingled, she melted against his strong chest. Her lips responded, to every one of his hungry kisses, and her hands memorized the muscles in his back and shoulders. She breathed deeply of his smell and stored it in her memory until they would be together again tomorrow.

Holding her ever so slightly away from him so that he could gaze into her eyes, Rob traced her eyebrows, nose, lips, and cheeks with his finger and burned the memory of her dear face into his senses. Taking a deep breath and straightening his shoulders, he gently led Virginia to the window, kissed her one last long time, picked up his briefcase, and walked out of the flat. He closed the door behind him with a soft but final click.

The tinkling sound of her doorbell finally made Virginia turn from her sentry post. Rita smiled happily as Virginia welcomed her. "I'm surprised to find you here. I thought you and Rob would be out seeing the sights. I found this in a little shop near the office, and thought you might like it."

Taking the little wooden music box from Rita's outstretched hand, Virginia carefully opened the cover on which an artist had carefully painted a moth orchid in full bloom. Immediately, the music softly began to play—"The White Cliffs of Dover," an old favorite from the WWII era.

"It's lovely!" Virginia said happily. "Now, I have

even more reason for wanting to visit Dover Castle. I must see the white cliffs."

"They are a fabulous sight. Don't forget to take the tour of the WWII defenses. They're a real historical wonder. You should take Rob with you. I doubt he's seen them either."

"That's what we'll do this weekend. We'll take the train, so we can see the scenery along the way. I certainly don't want my knowledge of England to be limited to just London," Virginia placed the music box on the mantel.

"Well, we'll have to see. After all, this is only our first date. Gotta run. I'll call you later if I don't get home too late," Rita said with a wicked wink. She let herself out the door and headed toward her flat to prepare for her date.

As the oranges turned to gray on the living room wall and the shadows lengthened, Virginia flicked on the lights and turned up the heat. Suddenly, she felt a chill run down her spine that was more than the change in the room's temperature. An eerie sense of foreboding fluttered over her. She had a strange feeling that Rob's transfer would cause them considerable trouble. She wondered if the separation, although less distance than from England to the States, would be the downfall of their relationship. Scolding herself for such a silly thought, Virginia turned on the television for her solitary dinner . . . the first one since her arrival in London.

Six

The London winter morning bloomed unusually bright and sunny. The sky gleamed a glorious clear blue without a trace of clouds or fog. Children scampered about, seeming happy to feel the sun on their faces as they jockeyed for seats near the windows on buses.

The weekend with Rob had been glorious, but now it was time for Virginia to report to work. She had enjoyed her time off to learn the city, and felt wonderfully at home on the tube as she gripped the strap and swayed to the rhythm of the train with the other passengers in the crowded car. She smiled as she followed the crowd that moved through the exit gates and into the teaming London streets. Monday morning, and everyone was returning to work.

Virginia and Rita walked past smiling Londoners on their way to their corporate offices. The sunlight and warmth made everyone cheerful. Gentlemen nodded at women they recognized along the streets, lanes, and avenues. Women waved in recognition. For a short time, in the glow of the spring sun, all was right with the world.

Reaching the office, Virginia and Rita rode the elevator to the third floor, where Sylvia Morgan, the office manager, awaited Virginia's arrival. A small breakfast meeting over coffee and scones had been arranged in her honor. After the staff welcomed the new marketing vice president, they began their task of contacting customers and building accounts. The expanded force had a very cosmopolitan flare, and representation from almost every country. Everyone Virginia met smiled greetings of welcome, and looked genuinely grateful that the Yank had joined their group. Then, they went to their respective offices and work, including Rita, who winked good-bye and mouthed "Good luck" as she eased from the room.

As she settled down at her new desk, Virginia hungrily scanned the list of the accounts and salespeople in her charge. The company wanted to continue its penetration of the London communications market, especially the data side. With so many companies expanding their business to the Internet, the company·wanted its share. In Rita's unit, market managers like her had the responsibility for keeping the customers happy and servicing their accounts after the sales. In Virginia's division, her people had to develop the product and position it with the user.

Looking rapidly over the lists, Virginia found clients ranging from small mom-and-pop companies to huge insurance firms. From what she saw, her sales force would have more than enough opportunity to position the company and expand its base. Virginia looked forward to the chance to show what she could do. After all, her unit had been the highest producer in their division. Virginia saw no reason why she could not inspire this organization to the same level of success. She had certainly worked for the best. Now, it was time for her to show that she ranked up there with them as the vice president responsible for this group's success and development.

After a few hours of studying sales volumes and product plans, Sylvia interrupted the silence, saying, "I'd like to show you around, if you're available. I think you'll appreciate the efficiency and economy of the work units."

"I'm all yours," Virginia replied. She pushed the papers away and joined Sylvia in the hall.

Virginia could hardly believe her ears as she followed Sylvia to the next room, where the telemarketing group was busy on the phones. They focused most of their effort on contacting residential customers with the new offerings that promised to improve their lives. Lists of customers to contact, orders not yet processed, and call-back requests littered their cluttered desks.

"This is certainly a busy section," Virginia commented as she watched a representative hang up from one call only to have another ring through to her.

"They do a tremendous sales volume, and give wonderful customer support. Not only do they respond to the calls generated by the direct mail campaign, but they also make outgoing calls to targeted customers. They're an invaluable asset to the company," Sylvia explained proudly as she led Virginia around the office.

"It's amazing just how similar the function of this group is to the one in the States. I guess no matter where the company establishes an office, it sticks with a tried-and-true plan," Virginia commented as she continued to follow Sylvia.

As they rounded the corner that led to the adjoining division, Rita appeared. Happy to continue the tour, she guided Virginia into her unit. Except for meetings and company functions, the two groups worked together very little, although they shared the same corner of the floor.

"I don't think I told you, but I'm going to Ipswich tomorrow. Why don't you see if you can join me? You said that Rob will be tied up in meetings all day. The trip will give you a chance to see other areas of England that come under your department's jurisdiction," Rita suggested as they left yet another beehive of activity.

Nodding, Virginia replied, "That sounds like a great idea. I'll tell Sylvia that I'll be away for the day. I'm not expecting any calls, but you never know. I'm holding a meeting this afternoon with my division, so I'll tell them then. Maybe we'll be able to get passage on an early train going that way if we leave in the morning."

As Virginia returned to her office, she found her mind wandering to Rob and the trip to Ipswich, despite the folders of facts and figures on her desk. For a girl from Towson, Maryland, she sure was putting a lot of miles between herself and home. She would have to remember to phone her mother and Edwina to tell them all about her new position and the trip to Ipswich. Thus far, Virginia had discovered that being in charge meant having more time to understand interaction between divisions and the operation of hers, in particular.

The rest of the morning, Virginia's mind was busy making plans for the next day and arranging her notes for the meeting with her division. Over and over, she mapped out her journey into the countryside. Sylvia told her that regular service ran between Ipswich and London, and that with proper timing she would be able to get there, tour the facility, and return to London before darkness came. She thanked her lucky stars that night came late in London. She would still have time for an evening with Rob.

The time passed so quickly that Virginia completely forgot about breaking for lunch. She looked up to find Rita standing at her desk with her purse on her shoulder and her hand on her hip. She had been waiting for Virginia to pick her up for their planned lunchtime exploration of the areas of Soho and Westminster.

"I didn't think you'd ever look up. I've been standing here forever. You are hungry, aren't you?" Rita queried. Her face wore an amused smile. She knew that Virginia's mind was only partially on Ipswich. Her greatest concern was in making the round trip in time to spend the evening with Rob.

"Okay, you caught me. Anyway, I'm ready now. Where shall we go first?" Virginia asked, grabbing her purse and following Rita down the hall and to the elevator.

"Let's head toward St. Paul's. We should be able to buy a sausage pie along the way. If we walk quickly, we'll be able to get to Westminster today, too," Rita replied, getting a tight grip on the strap of her shoulder bag against the thieves that filled the London streets, just as they did in all big cities.

Walking down the street, they passed many little Chinese and Vietnamese restaurants. The delicious aromas of spices and cooking meats and vegetables wafted out to them as they walked by. Not stopping to linger over the enticing smells, Virginia and Rita pushed on through Piccadilly Circus and its teeming crowded streets to St. James Park, where mothers pushed their babies in carriages, secretaries lunched from brown paper bags, and schoolchildren played tag among the trees. As they exited the park on the way to Westminster Abbey, they stopped long enough to purchase their meat pies and cups of steaming hot coffee.

Chewing contentedly and warming their hands on the hot cups, they finally reached Westminster Abbey. To Virginia, this church and its connection with the monarchy was the true England of the history books. Its graceful spires and sweeping architecture symbolized everything wonderful about London and England. It was almost as important to her as the white chalk cliffs of Dover and the castle that over-looked the English Channel.

Standing on the sidewalk and looking up at the stained glass window on the front of Westminster Abbey's marble face, Virginia at last believed that she was in London. She would have visited there sooner, but Rita had made her promise that she would wait until she was free to show her the sights. She breathed deeply of the air off the Thames River, and blinked back tears of joy. Slowly, she joined the others as they entered the church for the afternoon service. She could feel the cool darkness enfolding her as she entered the quiet recesses. Inside, no one spoke above a whisper. Virginia and Rita walked silently among the gravesites and memorials that lined the walls. Stopping at the rear of the church, Virginia marveled at the tomb of Elizabeth I and her sister Mary. Although they hated each other in life, they had been buried one on top of the other and would spend all eternity together.

The rest of the afternoon passed quickly, and soon it was time for Virginia and Rita to return to the office to resume the day's tasks. Rita had plans to visit one of her group's biggest clients, and Virginia had to chair a division meeting. As she entered the conference room adjacent to her office, Virginia was overwhelmed by the warm welcome afforded by her division. She knew immediately that this would be a wonderful assignment.

Virginia stayed so busy at the office that the rest of the day whizzed by, giving her little opportunity to daydream about Rob. Even though they worked in the same building, they did not see each other all day. She had thought that being in the same building with him would be a distraction, but she was able to concentrate during her time on her job. She assumed that he felt the same sense of accomplishment at completing his work with her in the building.

However, when the evening finally came and Rob joined her in her flat, Virginia was extremely happy to spend her time with him. She loved having him all to herself. Both of them had made the promise to leave unfinished work at the office rather than bring it home with them.

The next morning, Virginia and Rita rose early to catch the first train to Ipswich. They boarded the train at eight o'clock and settled in for the hour and a half ride. Sipping tea and munching on scones served in the dining car, they watched as pastures, fields, and towns sped past their window. Green and yellow fields and woods dotted with the red of poppies flashed by as the train rolled through one little town or village after another. Quaint little stations with bright colors and pots of flowers welcomed them to stop in places with names like Chelmsford and Colchester. *Maybe some other day,* Virginia thought. Today nothing could sidetrack her.

Virginia and Rita gathered their briefcases and bags as the train slowed down for the station stop marked Ipswich. Pulling herself away from the lovely old architecture, she said to Rita before continuing on her way, "I would love to return here one day to enjoy the scenery. It's too bad that we have to rush back to London."

"I know what we'll do. We'll plan to spend the weekend the next time we come and tour the neighboring countryside. A bike trip would be wonderful fun," Rita said, pulling her along the long path that led toward the center of town.

"Great idea! I'm game for anything, Maybe we can talk Rob into coming with us. If not, we'll come after he leaves for Paris," Virginia responded as she studied the map that showed the direction from the station to the office.

Breathing deeply of the sweet, cold, country air, Virginia and Rita began their relatively short trek from the rail station to the office. The rolling hillsides of Ipswich reminded Virginia of her home in Towson, Maryland. She was not exactly homesick, but seeing the gentle sway of the brown grass in the meadows tugged at her heart a bit, and made her wonder how her parents were faring now that she was so far from home. She had only phoned them once since her arrival, and promised herself to do better. She would look for a postcard from the picturesque city to send to them.

Walking along the heavily trafficked road, Virginia thought constantly of Rob. She knew that he was busy in meetings all afternoon and late into the evening. She wondered if he thought about her as often as she thought about him. Virginia also wondered how her life in London would be after Rob left for France. Knowing that conducting a long-distance relationship would be tedious at best, she worried that the distance might prove too much for their new relationship. Being away from the office, she realized, afforded her the time to stew.

Rita sensed her friend's mood, and refrained from being her usual talkative self. She seemed absorbed in the beauty of the countryside, too, as they walked along the road. She knew that Virginia was worried about the future, and that there was nothing anyone could do to alleviate her concerns. Time and distance were the only factors that mattered.

The building buzzed with activity as Virginia and Rita entered. Sales representatives with earphones moved from one file cabinet to another as they filled orders. Supervisors spoke with the few disgruntled customers who wanted phone service yesterday, but called today. Mainly, the office functioned smoothly and well.

The receptionist at the door directed them to the hall on the left, from which they could gain access to the quieter marketing department. Stepping aside for them to pass, he wished them a good day. Thanking him, they quickly walked down the hall in the bright light of the building, peeking into offices as they passed.

Approaching the door, Virginia and Rita scanned the profiles of the many busy marketing representatives who carried on much more leisurely conversations with clients. In this office, no one rushed from one desk to another because the representatives handled certain accounts and kept the information in files on their computers. Here, although busy, they had time for coffee and conversation.

To Virginia's surprise, they were greeted by her old friend and dance partner, William Edwards. "Virginia!" he shouted with delight, taking her into his arms.

"William!" she gasped, too taken aback to say anything more.

When he released her, Virginia laughed at the sight of her old friend. She had been so busy getting settled and spending time with Rob that she had almost forgotten that William had also transferred to the British branch of the company. Seeing him in the bright light of the hallway with the usual boyish smile on his face reminded her of all their shared dances and their long discussions. She was so very happy to have found him.

"What brings you to England? Aren't you a bit far away from the farm in Towson, and the office in Washington?" William asked, escorting her to a chair inside the meticulously organized little office. He flashed a quick smile at Rita as he pulled out a chair for her, too. The small, sterile, industrial-gray office suddenly looked cozy now that the two beautiful women were there.

"I decided I didn't like the idea that you would be having all the fun in Europe, so I requested a transfer, and here I am," Virginia responded, flirting ever so gently with her friend as she scanned the room. Despite its cleanliness, the room had a hectic appearance, almost as if papers had been recently filed or swept into a desk drawer. The tidiness looked superficial, as if at any moment the file drawers would burst at the seams and the contents would spill onto the floor. This was definitely the office of someone who had much on his plate.

"Somehow, I don't think I buy that reason. I think you fell in love with another guy as soon as my back was turned, and you followed him here. I sure hope he's as good a dancer as I am," William teased as he studied her eyes in hopes of finding the real reason that brought Virginia all the way to England. When she looked away, he knew he had guessed right.

Remembering her manners as her cheeks flamed red, Virginia said, "William, I've been so rude. I haven't introduced you to my new friend. We met on the train from the airport, and became fast friends. Rita, this is my old dancing partner, William Edwards. William, meet Rita Timberlake."

As they shook hands and exchanged pleasantries, Virginia again scanned the office. This time she looked for photographs that might tell her the kind of life William had been living since his arrival in London. Her old friend loved to party, and she wondered if he had joined that kind of crowd in England.

William watched Virginia's furtive glances to the side of the room and immediately guessed her interest. Catching her eye, he commented with a chuckle, "I haven't changed a bit, Virginia. Almost as soon as I unpacked, I found the best club in Picadilly, and have been dancing my toes off. Only being out here this week has slowed me down. It's too quiet out here in the country. I've been going to bed early every night. I can't wait to return to London. I've got some serious partying to do."

Virginia and Rita joined William's hearty laughter as he described the clubs he frequented and the people he had met. His good looks, charming personality, and fabulous footwork had given him entrée to the party scene. William had met many of the lesser British young nobility, and entered their world of carefree living. He had already spent a weekend among some of the blue-blooded aristocracy on their yacht, sailing off the coast and partying all night.

"You must find it deadly out here," Rita offered as she smiled sweetly and flirtatiously at her new interest. "I'll have to show you some of my favorite haunts when you return to London."

"I'd love it, and I'll take you to parties that'll make everything you've ever done seem tame. I'll be back in town this weekend. I'll give you a call at the office, and make the arrangements. By the way, Virginia, I heard through the corporate grapevine that you're dating John Robinson. You just missed him. He left about a half hour ago."

"Oh, no!" Virginia cried, turning to Rita. "The man I saw standing on the platform must have been Rob. He was too far away for me to be sure, so I didn't call to him. I didn't know he was coming here today. He told me that he had meetings all day, but he never said where they would be."

Seeing the look of unhappiness on her face, William chimed in, "Sorry, Virginia, but it looks as if you'll be stuck with only me for the day. He was here for a hastily called morning meeting. We had some trouble with a prominent customer. That's why I'm staying here for a while. I guess he didn't have time to phone you. I'm not Rob, but I've been known to show a girl a good time or two."

William's face crinkled happily at the thought of having Virginia by his side once more. He had always been especially fond of her, even though she never showed more than a sisterly affection for him. Besides, with Virginia stranded here with nothing to do, he would have a chance to get to know her friend. He had sensed the same interest from her when their hands first met in a friendly handshake. Something in her eyes had told him that Rita would not be averse to spending some time with him.

"Well, I guess we could have it worse than with your handsome, dashing self. When will you be free to give us the grand tour of Ipswich? Let's take a break between meetings," Virginia said as she tried to look cheerful despite the heaviness of her heart at missing the opportunity to see Rob between meetings. She smiled into William's twinkling gray eyes and managed to sound almost happy

"I'm locking up right now," William responded, taking the office key from his pocket. "There's not much of real interest in this immediate neighborhood, but there are other sections of the city that have some lovely old homes and a couple of great churches. The botanical garden isn't too bad, either." He was always delighted to spend his off hours escorting beautiful women around the city of Ipswich. Having two on his arm at one time was a special bonus.

"Do you think we could stop to get something to eat?" Rita said. She was the kind of thin person who eats all the time and never gains any weight.

"I know a place where they serve the best steak and kidney pie you've ever tasted," William replied, turning himself into sandwich filling between the two beautiful women. With a huge happy smile on his face, he guided them from the building, past the stares of admiring and envious construction workers, down the winding lanes, and out into the heavily populated sections of town.

The little restaurant sat on a quaint back street. Despite the fact that it was not quite noon, it was already packed with people. Sliding into the last table, William, Rita, and Virginia settled in for a delicious meal.

"Order anything you want, ladies. Lunch is on me," William said grandly. He was as excited as a schoolboy to be with his old friend from the States, and with a woman that he hoped would soon be a new one. He was proud to be seen with such beautiful women.

The meal tasted as flavorful as William had promised. Unlike much of the English fare they had eaten in London, the food in this little town was uncharacteristically rich, and seasoned well. William explained that the husband and wife who owned the restaurant had spent much of their lives in India, and still relied on their favorite spices when they cooked. Although they felt stuffed after their meal, Virginia and Rita could not resist the chocolate *gateau* that called to them when the waitress showed them the dessert tray.

Licking the last of the cake from her fork, Virginia gazed out the window at the view of the fields, where sheep frolicked in the sunshine even on such a cold day. She wished that Rob were there to share this pastoral scene with her, and felt sad about missing him as she looked into William's sympathetic gray eyes. Bravely, she tried to return his smile. Her smile camouflaged the loneliness that filled her heart. She had come so close to Rob, and yet she still could not hold him in her arms or kiss his lips or look into his deep brown eyes.

Walking through the little town on William's animated tour of the sites, Virginia began to feel her spirits lift a bit as she watched children playing hoops in the playgrounds during recess and elderly women on the way to the grocery for their daily supplies. Businesspersons of all ages scurried from shop to shop on their lunch hour, running the errands that they needed to do before going home. The construction workers on the apartment across the street had taken their lunch break and sat on the curb, eating and watching people pass by.

As they entered the church, a little girl ran up to them with a bunch of violets in her outstretched hand. Her face was streaked and dirty, but her smile was perky and bright. She should have been in school, but Virginia assumed that the child was one of the many gypsies who roamed the European streets and either begged for money or sold flowers and odd and ends.

"Flowers, miss? Only a shilling," the child said in a sweet thickly accented voice.

"Yes, thank you," Virginia answered as she fished out a coin and placed it in the grimy little hand. The stem of the flowers had been neatly wrapped with tape to form them into a bouquet. The little girl dropped a polite curtsy and scampered off as Virginia rushed to catch up with Rita and William inside the dimly lighted church. They marveled at the splendor of the building in a small suburban town like Ipswich, which illustrated that major cities did not have the monopoly on ornate churches.

Strolling from the church and down the quiet lanes, Virginia noticed that something seemed to be happening between William and Rita. Although they still walked three abreast most of the time, William often did not notice when she stopped to admire a garden plot or study the carvings on a building. He appeared to find Rita's conversation very engrossing. She was happy for him, and relieved to see that he had found someone to make him as happy as Rob made her. She knew that Rita would be perfect for him. Of all her friends in the States or at the London office, Rita was the most kindhearted and thoughtful. In many ways, she was even a better companion than Edwina.

The trio returned reluctantly to the office, where Virginia and Rita conducted their necessary meetings, while William continued to unscramble the customer complaint that had brought an official of Rob's status to Ipswich. Although Virginia was not directly involved in the operation of the Ipswich office, she paid close attention to the details of the customer's case, the manner in which management had responded, and the continued dissatisfaction of the client. She wanted to be prepared should something of that nature happen in her organization. They arranged to meet later for tea before returning to London on the late train.

When they finally reached the train station, the sun had changed from the bright golden yellow of midday to the pale amber of late afternoon. As the train slowly approached the stop, Virginia kissed William lightly on his cheek as the cold air blew around their ankles. The train came to a noisy stop and waited for new passengers to board.

Giving her a big hug, William said, "It's been great seeing you again, Virginia. I was afraid that I'd have to wait until my return to the States to have our next dance. With luck, I'll be back in London in a week or so. We'll go dancing then. Maybe you can talk Rob into joining us."

"I'll give it my best, but he doesn't enjoy it as much as we do," Virginia replied as she climbed aboard the train for London.

"What is it my mama always says? Where there's a will, there's a way." He turned to give Rita's cheek a chaste kiss that lingered a bit on her soft brown cheek. Virginia could tell from the way Rita closed her eyes that she found the closeness of William very much to her liking.

"We'll work this out, Virginia, even if I have to install the customer's new service myself. Come to think of if, that's not such a bad idea," William called from the platform. Then he closed the compartment door, and the women settled onto the worn blue seats. He laughed and waved as the train slowly pulled out of the station and began its journey to London.

The streets had taken on the frosty glow of night as Virginia and Rita walked from the tube to their buildings. The fragrance of lovingly prepared dinners wafted down to them. They bade each other goodnight and entered their respective buildings with thoughts of the next day playing on their minds.

That night, for the first time since she had arrived in London, the sound of people leaving the neighborhood pub woke Virginia from a sound sleep. At first Virginia did not know where she was as she lay listening to the loud voices and happy laughter. Then, as she came fully awake and looked at the clock, she realized that it was midnight, and the close of the evening for pubs.

Easing her feet into her fuzzy slippers, Virginia

padded to the window and peered into the London night. Unlike at midnight at home, darkness had not claimed the city. Virginia watched as revelers staggered home under the effects of one too many pints of ale. Their singing voices slowly disappeared down the street, and quiet returned to the neighborhood. Their frozen breath hung heavily in the air.

Unable to fall asleep, Virginia turned on the television. Unlike the men and women leaving the pub across the street, the BBC had signed off for the night. Clicking off the test pattern, she pulled on her warm chenille robe. Clutching it close to her body, she walked through the cool flat to the kitchen. Remembering the warm milk her mother had prepared for her when she could not sleep as a child, Virginia poured a glass and zapped it in the microwave.

Taking her steaming cup to the window, Virginia stood in the darkness watching the parade of people on their way home. In the neighborhood in the States, local bars and restaurants closed at ten during the week. For the most part, life in the cities stopped fairly early so that people could go get ready for work the next day. With rush hour starting as early as six-thirty, there was little room for partying or barhopping on the weekdays. However, in London, people seemed to find entertainment regardless of the need to go to work the next day.

Remembering William's stories about parties, Virginia wondered how often he came to work tired from a long night of dancing. In discovering the London nightlife, he might have adopted that habit, too. From the dark circles under the eyes of many of her staff, she decided that many of them must be involved in the pub scene.

Draining the last of her milk and rinsing the cup, Virginia wondered if Rob had joined that crowd, too. Making a mental note to ask him the next time they were together, Virginia slipped under her covers and promptly fell asleep.

The next day passed at a snail's pace. Every minute Virginia hoped to hear something from Rob, but no call or E-mail message arrived. She knew that he was busy and would call as soon as he could, but the old insecurity returned to plague her. The lack of communication from him made her think that coming to England had been a mistake. She wondered if Rob really cared for her, or if he felt stuck in the relationship now that she had transferred to London. He might actually be looking forward to his next move, to Paris. She almost convinced herself that she should never have followed him. For the first time in her life, Virginia doubted a decision she had made.

That evening Rita left work early for a date with William, who had driven to town. He had been unable to bear the quiet of Ipswich any longer, and needed a dose of partying. She wanted to have time to fix herself up before he called for her later that evening. He had not told her where they were going, but Rita was so happy to be with him again that she really did not care. She had bubbled and gushed all day after his telephone call, and was almost unbearable as she sang and danced around her office. It seemed that they had really hit it off on their first meeting. Even in her gloomy mood, Virginia enjoyed Rita's happiness and the affection that blossomed between her two good friends. She would have to remember to write to Edwina and tell her that William had found someone to love in England.

By late afternoon, Virginia was the last to leave the building. Just as she was about to close her office door, the telephone rang. She ran to her desk and grabbed the phone. "Hello?" she called into the silent telephone. No one answered. "Hello?" she called again, but the only sound she heard was the empty line.

Slipping her purse over her arm and again snapping off the light on her desk, Virginia turned toward the door. Much to her surprise, she came face-to-face with a handsome man whose smile shone brightly in the dim light of her office.

"Rob!" she cried, rushing into his open arms and burying herself against his strong shoulders and chest. As his arms tightened around her body and his lips hungrily pressed her mouth, Virginia knew that she had not been mistaken in following him to London. The wild pounding of his heart told her that he had been thinking about her during his meetings, too. Rob was as happy to see her as she was to find herself finally in his embrace.

However, their happiness was short-lived. Rob had bad news to share, and had tried all day to think of the best way in which to break it. Clearing his throat and holding Virginia close, he decided on the direct approach. "Virginia, I have to leave for France tomorrow," he whispered in her ear. "The firm needs me in Paris. Now that the problems with Ipswich and the London offices have ended and the Paris office has been properly set up, it's time for me to go to France and open the new office there."

Sighing deeply, Virginia responded. "I knew we wouldn't have forever, but I was hoping for a little more time together. Well, it's been great while it lasted."

"I'll only be across the English Channel. It's really not that far away. We'll see each other every weekend. I know the nights in between will be lonely, but that's the best we can do for a while." Rob gently stroked her cheek and kissed her lips.

"I know. Don't worry about me. I have more than enough with my new job to keep me busy. The separation will only make us want to be together more," Virginia replied bravely as she straightened Rob's already neat tie.

Knowing the inevitability of the separation did not make the reality any less traumatic. Virginia and Rob decided that since this would be their last evening together, they would make the best of it. They dined out, took in a play in the West End, and stayed up talking all night. When the dawn broke, Virginia rode the tube with Rob to Heathrow Airport. She waited with him until the attendants called his flight, and waved bravely as he disappeared down the ramp.

It was not until she returned home that the loneliness hit her. Sitting in her living room with the curtains drawn, Virginia cried as she had not cried since she was a little girl and learned that there was no Santa Claus. Her mascara streamed down her cheeks and washed off the carefully applied blush. Virginia thought that her heart would burst. For four glorious weeks, she had held Rob and spent every free minute with him. Now, she was alone. London was suddenly dull and lifeless.

Seven

Virginia busied herself with writing correspondence, supervising her staff, and planning meetings as she tried to keep from focusing on her loneliness. In the evenings, she often volunteered at the Red Cross because she could not stand being alone in her flat. The only evenings that she did not appear were the ones on which she was too tired from work to do more than open a can of soup for dinner. As she worked, Virginia thought about the importance of her work at the Red Cross—providing service personnel on leave with tickets to West End shows, arranging the visits of entertainers, and helping with the annual fund-raising campaign. She refused to allow herself to think about the loneliness of being away from Rob. Regardless of what she did to occupy her time and mind, though, Virginia could not stop the pain that tugged at her heart.

As one Friday lengthened into evening, Virginia and Rita left the Red Cross office and walked home to their flats. Along the way, they stopped to marvel at the lovely spring flowers blooming in pots and window boxes. The owner of the little flower shop on the corner had set out buckets of colorful blossoms. Virginia stopped to buy an assortment of yellow, red, and orange blossoms with a few red poppies. As soon as she entered her flat, Virginia slipped them into a vase on the coffee table. Immediately, the flowers added color and sunshine to the living room, and a little bit of warmth to her life. Spring had finally come to London and begun to push away the gray cold and cloudiness.

After dinner, Rita came to visit. William was in Glouchester for the weekend on business and she was alone. They settled down in front of the television for an evening of movie watching. Almost immediately, the BBC news interrupted the showing of *An Affair to Remember* with a special report about an explosion linked to the IRA.

That night, the newscasters sounded strangely agitated to Virginia, almost as if they knew something big was about to happen. Everyone had been talking about the latest round of peace talks ever since Virginia arrived in London. It was the topic of discussion at every meeting, and on every street corner. But everyone knew that both sides had tried and failed to reach an agreement many times. Hearing their discussions, Virginia had been only slightly interested in the internal affairs of the British people. She had enough on her plate already. Still, that night, she worried about the undertone of tension she saw on the newscaster's face. "Rita, do you hear something different in the newscaster's voice?" she asked her friend.

"What? Oh, sorry, Virginia, I wasn't even listening. I was thinking about William. Does the newscaster sound different? I hadn't noticed," Rita answered, pausing to listen. "Now, that you mention it, I guess he does. Probably tired of relaying the same old news. I would be, if that's all I had to report every day."

"You're probably right. I'm sure it becomes quite wearing to report the same depressing state of affairs every night." Brightening a bit, Virginia continued. "Well, what should we do tomorrow? With both of our guys out of town, we have plenty of time on our hands. Hadn't we planned to visit the Tate Museum, Hyde Park, and maybe ride bikes out of town along the Thames?"

"That sounds fine to me. How about I come to get you around ten o'clock? We'll pack picnic lunches. The afternoon should be loads of fun," Rita chirped happily. She always loved spending time with Virginia. Now that they were alone again, they could engage in conversation without the guys listening and making snide comments about their interest in fashion and the arts.

Returning to their private thoughts, the women resumed their TV watching and talking. The voice on the television droned on, but neither of them heard him say that a splinter group of the IRA had taken responsibility for the bombing of a train station and that peace talks had once again stalled. They were both too preoccupied with plans and dreams of the return of William and Rob.

The next afternoon as they biked past Victoria Station on their way home, Virginia and Rita saw the aftermath of the explosion. The stately old building had been cordoned off by the police and closed to travelers. People lined the streets to gaze at the rubble that marked the sight of the bomb. Luckily, no one had been hurt, but one of the busiest tube stops on the system and a central train terminal would be out of commission for several days.

Feeling distressed and helpless as they returned home, Virginia and Rita settled into Virginia's flat in front of the television. They listened for any hints that might be in the voice of the television newscaster, just in case he had special updates to relay. Hearing nothing more than the usual reports about the IRA's actions, they reluctantly turned off the television, and Rita went home. There was little consolation in knowing that the rest of England felt the same tension and sense of foreboding.

Just as Virginia got settled in bed, the telephone rang. Thinking that it was Rita with more news about the bombing, she quickly picked up. "Hello," she almost shouted into the phone.

"Virginia, are you all right? I just got back to my apartment after a long meeting and heard about the bombing at Victoria Station. Is everything okay there?" Rob asked quickly.

"At the moment, everything's fine. We're waiting to see what tomorrow brings. There's also talk that the IRA might wait until Monday to do anything else. It seems that they love to disrupt rush hour," Virginia responded, feeling warmer and safer now that Rob had called.

"I was so worried about you. It's not easy being this far away from the woman I love," Rob added with a gentleness in his voice that Virginia had not heard before.

"Don't worry about me. I'll be okay. Rita has been through this scare a hundred times, and can tell me how to react. Besides, you'll be able to come for a visit soon, won't you?" Virginia asked, as she swung her legs over the side of the bed and sat up. She wanted her full attention on Rob rather than the comfort of her bed.

"Things are a little tight right now. I don't think I'll be able to make the trip to London next week.

I'm putting in fourteen plus hours each day. It seems as if I only return to my apartment to shower and change."

Rob did not like the separation any more than Virginia did. He had already been away from her far longer than he had anticipated. Work was just so demanding that he never had any free evenings or weekends.

"But, Rob, you're the boss. Take the time off. I really miss you," Virginia said, trying not to whine or put too much pressure on him. However, she wanted Rob to understand how lonely she was without him.

"I'm sorry, Virginia, but there's nothing I can do about it. If I get things wrapped up early, I'll take the Chunnel over. If not, we'll have to wait until the next weekend," Rob replied with sadness in his voice.

"I guess I'll just have to drag poor Rita around town a bit more. So far, she's being a good sport about it. However, I don't know how long her good humor will last. The good thing is that she's alone, too. Otherwise, I'd have to make the rounds by myself." Virginia spoke reluctantly, with a bit of teasing in her voice. She did not want Rob to feel pressured to be with her or to sense her disappointment in not seeing him.

"That's my girl! I knew you'd understand. Well, I gotta run. I'm exhausted, and need a few hours rest before the early meeting tomorrow. I'll call you if I get home before too late. I love you, Virginia. Sleep well." Rob sounded a bit more chipper now that Virginia had recovered from her disappointment.

"I love you, too, Rob. Good-bye," Virginia replied as she hung up the phone and returned to the comfort of her bed. She did not cry as the loneliness ate at her heart. Already she was working on a remedy for the unacceptable situation.

Virginia awoke early on Tuesday to the sound of shouting in the streets. The IRA had bombed a Piccadilly tube station at six-thirty that morning. This time, passengers on their way to work had been hurt.

Waving from the sidewalk, Rita indicated that she had purchased papers for both of them. Tucking them under her arm, she vanished into the building. In a minute, she stood knocking at Virginia's door.

A whirlwind of thoughts spun through her mind as she looked out of the window. All around were Londoners with copies of the paper, devouring and discussing the articles that spelled out what was known so far about the most recent IRA attack. After reading the news, people returned to their homes, wiping at tears, shaking their heads, wondering when and how the latest turn in the bombings would end. Along with the latest subway bombing had come the threat of attacks to the Chunnel and the intercity train systems.

Virginia's legs would no longer hold her, and she sank onto the sofa. Tears of worry and fear streamed down her cheeks. Beside her, Rita sobbed into her hands. So many people had been hurt, and so many might be in the future. She had known about the possibility of IRA attacks, but the reality was larger than she had originally thought. They had not realized that they would feel so devastated when the news finally came of yet another incident. So far, none of Rita's friends had been hurt, but they felt it was only a matter of time before someone they knew became a victim. Neither knew how to console the other, so they simply sat and cried until no more tears would come.

"This will never do," Virginia said, more to herself than to Rita. "I didn't come all this way to sit and feel miserable. I can't stand this on top of having Rob in France. There has to be some way that I can still see him. I can't handle the loneliness and the fear. I won't let this job keep us apart until I have absolutely no other choice. As long as he's in Europe, I should be able to figure out a way to be with him."

Pacing the room with a still tearful Rita watching her, Virginia thought through all of her options. The least pleasant was for her to sit quietly in London until Rob returned from France. Waiting helplessly was something that went against her nature. She never sat and waited for anything if she could help it. She always went out and worked for what she wanted. Her parents had raised her to believe that hard work always paid off big rewards. So far, she had always been successful. She was not going to let the IRA or anything else stand in her way now. She came here to be with Rob, and be with him she would.

Stopping her pacing, Virginia turned, looked Rita squarely in the face, and said, "I'm going to the Dover office. I should be able to find a room there somewhere for a few days. Despite the travel warnings, I should be able to buy my train ticket for the Chunnel once this quiets down. I know I can't leave for France from Victoria Station, but I shouldn't have any trouble from the coast. Now that they've closed the airports, there's really no other choice. I know this is a wild shot, because Rob might be too busy to spend time with me, but I have to try to be with him. I feel that he's my destiny. Have you ever felt that way? He's far too important in my life for us not to be destined to be together. Do you want to come with me? The Dover office is in my territory, but you could come along as an advisor. Besides, I understand that William is doing some troubleshooting there."

At first Rita was speechless. The thought of following William had crossed her mind briefly, but she had quickly rejected it as too risky. Also, her mother had always told her that a young woman from a good family did not follow a man. Rita had found the idea old-fashioned, but she had always listened to the little voice that repeated her mother's adage in her ear. She was certainly not the kind of woman who would seriously entertain such thoughts. She had raised enough eyebrows among the elderly matrons in her family by coming to London to work as it was. Many of them still waited for a knight to rescue them from the loneliness of life in their country homes. In her very proper family, young women did not live alone in the big city, but stayed closer to home. She certainly did not think it appropriate to do anything more. However, seeing the expression of determination on her friend's face, Rita found herself warming to the idea. Virginia was from a good family, and if she could follow the man she loved, surely Rita could, too.

"I'll go with you. We'll pack a few things and be on our way. I hope the trains won't be too full to take us," Rita said.

Virginia had not taken the time to think about the trains. Now her shoulders slumped at the thought that her plans might be ruined by the very source of transportation she counted on to take her to Rob. There was always the possibility that the IRA would shut those down, too, now that the organization had sabotaged Victoria Station. Well, that was simply a chance she would have to take. She was going to the man she loved with her best friend at her side, and that was all there was to it. Turning sharply, she left Rita to find her own way out and began packing a bag with the essentials she would need for her trip.

The train station was packed with people. Every woman, child, elderly person in London seemed to have had the same idea. They were all traveling away from the city in a press of bodies, suitcases, duffel bags, and boxes. Many of the older travelers had experienced massive bombings of London during WWII, and did not want to live through that again.

Seeing a woman busily trying to quiet three fidgety children, Virginia smiled.

"You're American, aren't you?" the woman said. "Don't you know, ducky, that the IRA is bombing all around us? This isn't a time for a vacation in England. You should go back home. Who knows what the IRA will do now? I'm not going to stay another night in London, if I can help it. I'm taking my children to Cotswold, where it's quiet, until the conflict ends. I don't care if they will miss school for a while. It's too dangerous here. Where are you going, my dear?"

"My friend and I are trying to go to Dover," Virginia responded. From the expression on the woman's face, Virginia could tell that the harried mother thought Virginia was out of her mind.

"Well, good luck, dearie. I think you're going the wrong way. I wouldn't want to be away from a major airport if I were you. Heathrow and Gatwick are closed today, but they'll reopen soon. Never can tell when something might explode, if you get my meaning. But you Americans have a bold way of looking at things. Take care of yourself," the woman called over her shoulder. Quickly, she herded her children toward platform number four, where the train to Cotswold was boarding.

"Do you still think this is a good idea? You heard what that woman said. You never can tell when something will happen. Shouldn't we stay in London, where we'll be closer to an airport in case things get out of control? In Dover we'd be close to the French coast, which is only ninety miles or so away and easily accessible by the Chunnel, but far from Gatwick Airport," Rita asked, looking as if she were losing her nerve.

"I'm going, Rita. I know I could call him, but it wouldn't be the same. I need to feel his arms around me. Nothing will make me change my mind. You can return to your flat, if you want, but I'm catching the twelve-fifteen to Dover. As it is, I won't get there until around five-thirty. I just hope I'll be able to use the Chunnel. The train might not even be running from there."

"No, I'm with you all the way. I wouldn't think of letting you travel to Dover without me. I'm just a bit nervous, that's all," Rita replied. She picked up her bag and trotted along beside Virginia, who was bearing down on platform number one. It was too late to turn back now.

The ride to the coast from London was long, but it offered beautiful scenery. Every seat on the train was occupied by people wearing worried expressions on their faces. As the train passed through one little hamlet after anther, Virginia and Rita gazed out of the steamy window at the countryside. The grazing sheep and cattle did not lift their heads as the train rolled past. Even the red poppies in the fields and along the track beds seemed undisturbed by the passing of yet another train carrying people from London.

"Isn't England beautiful?" Virginia sighed. "It reminds me of home, and of the farms in Towson. I guess that all sleepy towns look alike."

"I suppose," responded Rita, looking at her friend's dreamy expression, "but I've never seen an American farm. I've lived my whole life in the UK, don't forget. But this is lovely countryside. If Towson looks like this, you certainly have a beautiful home. I'll have to visit you there, or maybe ask for a transfer to the States one of these days."

They rode in silence for most of the five hours. Sometimes the gentle swaying of the train and the monotonous hum of the ventilation system mixed with the warm air inside the car to lull them to sleep. Whenever the train pulled into a new station, they were jolted wide awake and looked around to see if they had been observed. Finding most of the other passengers on the local to Dover also asleep, Virginia and Rita again drifted off, only to have the same pattern repeat itself over and over as the distance to the white cliffs shortened.

Finally, they drew near to Dover, the city that housed the lookout over the English Channel of Winston Churchill. From its cliffs on a clear day, Calais loomed on the horizon twenty-six miles away on the coast of France. Today, however, none of Dover's history mattered to Virginia. Today all she wanted was to see Rob. She would, too, if the IRA had not stopped the Chunnel from running.

"Oh, look!" Virginia whispered as the train slowed going around the bend. To the left rising high above the railroad tracks, stood the famed white cliffs of Dover in all their shining splendor. She could hardly believe that she was actually looking at the famous limestone hillside immortalized in the song. Suddenly the words flooded her memory: "There'll be bluebirds over, the white cliffs of Dover, tomorrow, just you wait and see. There'll be love and laughter, and peace ever after, tomorrow, when the world is free." She knew that the sparkle of the cliffs would represent England to her forever, even more than the flag or Buckingham Palace or Westminster Abbey.

As they stepped from the train, a flashing sign quickly confirmed what Virginia had been dreading. The transportation authority had decided to hold all of the high-speed Chunnel trains until further notice. For now, there was no way to reach France— only a few miles off the coast.

"I'll have to stay here until the trains are running again. I have plenty of business to handle, anyway. I'm disappointed, but I won't give up," Virginia announced resolutely as she clasped the handle of her briefcase more securely and followed the crowd that flowed into the city through the station's arch.

"That's my girl. I knew nothing would keep you down," Rita cheered as she brought up the rear.

Virginia and Rita stopped at a tobacconist shop in the train station to ask directions to the town's leading hotel. Stating that it had been filled to capacity, he directed them to a bed-and-breakfast at which they might be able to find lodgings. Following the directions from the station to the center of the city, they passed many boarded up and shelled buildings. Dover had not been spared IRA bombs, either. Much of it lay in ruins, waiting for the latest wave of terrorism to end and the repairs to begin.

Finally, they found the house with the tan painted shutters and a red wreath on the tan front door. Through the lace curtains blowing at the windows, they could see a floral patterned sofa and contrasting wing chairs in the living room flanking a fan covered fireplace. In the dining room, a long, sturdy, mahogany table surrounded by ten chairs spoke of happier times, when the family had gathered for dinner. Both rooms were filled with vases of roses.

A friendly landlady, Mrs. Vanessa Parker, smiled sweetly as she showed them to their comfortable rooms. They were small and cozy, about the same size as Virginia's room at home. The double beds looked very inviting, and the view of the main street was flooded with sunlight. The cheerful woman explained that before her sons left for college and then started their own families, the rooms had been theirs. She had replaced their brown plaid bedspreads with floral ones, and freshly starched white curtains adorned the windows. When the house proved too empty without them, she had converted it to a bed-and-breakfast. Her reputation as a great cook had led to constant bookings. The business was such a success that she'd had built a new wing and expand the capacity of her once humble home to ten bedrooms, some of which had private baths. In the summer months, she had to turn people away. The proximity of Dover to the French coast, the Chunnel connection, the historic nature of the city, and the delightful coastal waters all provided her establishment with a steady flow of customers.

Before the landlady left the room, Virginia asked

her if she had seen any signs of the IRA in the area. The kindly woman, seeing the anxiety on her face, responded softly, shaking her head. "Yes, dearie, but we have a wonderful group of reservists in the area. They came through early this morning. Around nine, I believe it was. They're on their way to Weymouth, you know, just a few miles from here. Those poor men looked tired. Must have been up since early morning. I bet they won't get a decent night's sleep until this latest turmoil quiets down."

Looking at their watches as the landlady hurried away, Virginia and Rita found that it was well past six o'clock. Even if the office were fairly close by in the downtown section of the city, it would probably be closing now. They decided to postpone the visit that would lend legitimacy to their visit to the Dover office until the next day. The warmth inside the train, the rocking of the car, and the gentle murmur of the other passengers had tired them out. Since no one would be in the office to see them, they decided to explore the town, instead.

As they ventured out into the streets, Virginia was struck by the absence of street signs. Unlike those at home and in London, the Dover city planners only positioned signs at the intersection of major streets. The only visible markings were on the sides of buildings, making it very difficult for strangers to navigate the ancient roads and streets. Virginia wondered if the absence of road signs was left over from WWII—when the British removed them to prevent the Germans from being able to find their way to London—or simply the work of teenage pranksters.

Through the thickening evening fog, Virginia could just barely make out the high walls of Dover Castle. She knew that it had once been off-limits

because of the base Churchill had built in the cliffs.
If she had time, she would tour the historic monument before she crossed the channel to be with Rob.
She promised herself that someday she would return
to Dover, as the bluebirds did, and explore all that
the quaint little town had to offer.

Growing even more tired from the strain and
travel, Virginia and Rita returned to their lodgings
and beds. Mrs. Parker had turned back the covers
and lighted small fires for them against the chill of
the evening and the remains of the storm that had
battered the coast for weeks. Pitchers of water and
clean glasses sat on the little tables beside the beds
in each room. Fresh towels and wrapped bars of fragrant soap lay on the dresser beside a jug of still
warm water in which rose petals floated. It was
mostly for decoration, but its presence added a
quaint touch. Between their bedrooms sat the bathroom that Virginia and Rita would share.

As she snuggled into lavender-scented, freshly
ironed, white sheets, Virginia thought about Rob.
He was so close, yet he was so far away. As sleep
overtook her, she promised herself that tomorrow
she would make the walk to the office to establish
her excuse for being in Dover before checking on
the Chunnel schedule. With luck, she would be in
Paris this time tomorrow. She had to hold him in
her arms once again. Virginia longed to feel the soft
stubble of his beard brushing against her cheeks as
he turned her lips up to his and possessed them in
a kiss filled with so much longing that it curled her
toes inside her shoes.

Glancing at the bedside clock, Virginia guessed
that Rita had fallen asleep in her room as soon as
her head hit the pillow. Her friend had told her that

she had little if any trouble sleeping, and had dozed on the train almost as soon as it left the London station. Smiling, she willed herself to fall asleep just as quickly, knowing that a busy day lay ahead of them tomorrow. Her last thoughts before dozing off were of Rob standing inside a train door waving good-bye as she ran down the platform toward him. As she reached out to touch his outstretched fingers, the train pulled away, leaving her standing alone on the platform. The image troubled her mind as she turned over to find a deeper spot in the incredibly comfortable bed. Pushing the image aside as the result of fatigue, Virginia slipped into a sound, peaceful sleep.

She did not hear the distant mournful whistle as the last train pulled out of Dover station on the way to Weymouth.

Eight

The sun shining into the room through the lace curtains woke them early the next morning. Looking down into the street below and then up into the hills, Virginia could not see any trace of the frozen mist that had covered the town last night. As she threw open the window, the sweet clean smell of an early spring morning greeted her nose. She wondered if Rob were inhaling the intoxicating fragrances of the season from his apartment window in Paris.

"I'm starving," Rita said as she opened the door to their shared bathroom. "I wonder what's for breakfast."

"I'd say it's toast, sausage, bacon, coffee, tea, tomatoes, eggs, and oatmeal, but I could be wrong," Virginia said pulling on her robe, grabbing up her towel and soap. From the water dripping from Rita's hair, she knew that it was her turn in the bathroom.

"Finished and dressed already?" a yawning Rita asked as Virginia knocked on her door. She had stretched out on her bed to wait for Virginia to take her shower and had fallen asleep.

"Yes, and you'd better hurry if we're to have any of that breakfast before we head for the office," Virginia answered, pulling the brush through her thick brown hair. The sunlight filled her with positive expectations for a day that offered so much promise. She sensed that everything would turn out all right, and that soon she would hold Rob in her arms once again.

As they joined the others around the long, stately dining room table, Virginia and Rita were surprised to see that the quiet little house sheltered so many. Along with the landlady, Mrs. Vanessa Parker, and her husband, Roger, there were Mr. and Mrs. Matthew Edgars and his unmarried sister, Miss Vivian Edgars, Mrs. Constance Stimple, and two elderly gentlemen, a Mr. Frank Kingsley, and Mr. John Brighton, who rounded out the assembly and made the count ten for breakfast.

Mrs. Parker was a short, round, red-cheeked woman who spoke with a thick coastal accent. Her husband was slender and tall, but slightly stooped and tanned from his years at sea on ferry boats and fishing vessels. Virginia learned that the Edgars had moved to Dover, hoping to retire from government work in peace and quiet, long before the IRA began its bombings of England's shores. During the latest surge, their house had been damaged. They lived as lodgers with the Parkers until they could rebuild. Unlike the other locals, the Parkers and Mr. Brighton, they seemed quite nervous and jumpy.

The other lodgers were on their way to other English cities and were using Dover as a stopping point on their journey. Reserve unit movement had kept them from booking passage on a train. Now that the troops were all engaged in guarding the towns, they planned to leave Dover that morning.

As Virginia's nose had told her, the breakfast was large and filling. Everyone ate heartily, with Mr. Edgars also eating noisily as he blew on his oatmeal and slurped his tea. No one talked as they devoured the contents of the heavily loaded platters and steaming serving bowls. When Mrs. Parker served the breakfast coffees and teas, conversation about the IRA's latest escapades filled the dining room. Mr. Parker produced copies of the morning paper for everyone. Its headline screamed the news of yesterday's latest IRA activity and the country's response to it. Reading hungrily, Virginia searched for any mention of any further transportation stoppages. So far, nothing more had closed, and the Chunnel was set to reopen. Finding nothing new, she sighed deeply, hoping that soon she would be with Rob again.

"Mr. Parker," Virginia began, trying to sound casual in her inquiry, "Has the IRA threatened to do anything to the Chunnel? Are the reservists still protecting it?"

"My dear young woman," Mr. Parker responded taking a break from lighting his pipe, "there are no troops in Dover any longer. They were among the first to head for Weymouth in the wee hours of the morning, I've been told. The Chunnel is scheduled to reopen around noon."

"That's wonderful news. I'm very interested in traveling to Paris as soon as I finish my business in town. With the airports closed, the Chunnel train's my only means of travel. My friend is there, and I'd like to visit him. Even if the airport were open, I'd prefer land transportation, for its views of the French countryside. As you know, Victoria Station was badly damaged in the latest IRA bombing. We couldn't leave from there, so we took the train down here. At least now, I'll be able to make my trip."

Virginia's voice barely disguised the joy she felt at being able to put her plans into action.

"Unfortunately, it'll take quite some time before Victoria is rebuilt. What a pity! At least things look a little better from here. However, the Chunnel is completely sold out for a few days. They're honoring all the old tickets before issuing any new ones," Mrs. Edgars chimed in. Then, seeing Virginia's sad face, she added, "Don't you worry. They'll be back on schedule in no time."

Virginia tried bravely to smile at the people, who all looked so kind and sympathetic. She managed something that was more of a grimace that a true lifting of the corners of her mouth. Her heart was too heavy to allow her to feel any consolation at the thought that her wait in Dover would be longer than she had expected. At least she would be able to finish her business and tour some of the historic city, although she'd been told the former Churchill headquarters was closed as a safeguard against IRA attack. No one wanted to give the IRA a chance to damage that symbol of English freedom.

After breakfast, Virginia and Rita left the peaceful house to mingle with the townspeople. The air seemed charged with a strange tension as everyone went along doing ordinary things with the IRA firmly in the forefront of their thoughts. Virginia could see the worry etched across the faces of everyone she passed.

Looking up into the hillside, she saw that the fog had lifted there, too. On the top of the lush green hill stood Dover Castle. Virginia longed to visit it, to see if it were haunted by the ghosts of the kings who had once called it home. She knew that Charles I had loved the castle more than any other. He only agreed to move away only when his bride Henrietta Maria spoke of her dislike of it, calling it an old outdated castle. He then settled into Whitehall, in London now part of the Parliament building.

One day, Virginia would return to Dover with Rob, and they would walk up that hillside to see the castle together. There were so many ancient buildings to see that even with having to wait for a seat on the high-speed Chunnel train, Virginia would not have time to tour all of the sights of Dover. There would be plenty left to share with Rob.

Breaking into her thoughts, Rita suddenly asked, "Now what do we do? There's no chance of getting to Paris for the next few days. Should we stay here, or return to London after we finish our business?"

With a shrug Virginia replied, "I guess there's really no point in staying here. At least in London, we'd be able to get our work done. Let's finish our tasks here, and then take the afternoon train back. Let's go back and pack our things. If I remember correctly, there should be a train to London at noon every day. We'll leave for London directly from the office." With Virginia guiding the way, they retraced their steps and headed back to Mrs. Parker's bed-and-breakfast house.

Mrs. Parker was not surprised when Virginia and Rita said that they would be returning to London immediately, with the Chunnel closed for perhaps days. Still, she would miss their cheerful faces and their youthfulness. They had added a sparkle to her dining room.

Virginia and Rita made quick work of their business. The head of the local customer service effort welcomed Rita warmly, and the chief of marketing bragged freely about his impressive sales figures to

Virginia. After spending time in his office and speaking with many of the staff, Virginia was convinced that the man's lively spirit helped to inspire his people to do their best.

As the train pulled out of the station for the return trip to London, Virginia and Rita felt a little sad about leaving Dover, as their visit had not turned out the way they had expected. Yet, there was something special about the town that pulled at their hearts as the train belched clouds of smoke into the air. Again the song, "The White Cliffs of Dover" flooded Virginia's memory. As the cliffs disappeared from view, Virginia knew that one day when she had more time, she would return to see them again. She was sure of it. Only when that time came, Rob would be seated by her side, and she would not be lonely anymore.

London was all bustle and noise compared to Dover as Virginia and Rita stepped from the train at five-thirty in the afternoon. They eased their way into the crowd and immediately headed for the company office. Everyone had left for the day by the time they arrived. Letting herself into the office, Virginia hunted through the day's messages for any calls from Rob and William. Finally, at the bottom of the pile of wire clips, she found an E-mail from each of them. According to the bulletin, Rob had chaired an important meeting between the company and the president of France, in the hope of teaming with the French telephone system to provide voice and data service throughout the country. Virginia knew that this meant that Rob would be difficult to reach for quite a while.

Rita had equal bad luck with locating William. According to the message, he was still in the south of

England, and up to his ears in system troubles. He would not be able to return to London for quite some time.

"Well," Virginia said, turning to Rita, "at least we know where they are now, for the time being. I guess I'll just have to wait for him to call. At least, he'll still be in Paris if and when I manage to catch the Chunnel train. You know, flying is beginning to look like a viable option. I could always rent a car and drive through the countryside once we're together—that is, if Rob can spare the time. I realize that his title and paycheck are bigger than mine, but it certainly looks as if he could benefit from time management skills. I don't understand why he's always so busy." She sank into the nearest chair, the strain of the last two days finally getting to her, making her knees weak and her mind tired.

"You'll have to sit him down and share some of your tips the next time you see him. Even successful people like Rob can use a helping hand now and then." Rita chuckled at her friend's irritation with the man she loved dearly.

Rita settled into a seat beside Virginia. She felt the tension, too, but not as much as Virginia. She could tell from the sadness in her friend's eyes that her heart was breaking from missing Rob. She wished there was something she could do or say to make her feel better, but she knew that nothing except their happy reunion would put the sparkle back into Virginia's lifeless eyes.

Taking Virginia's hand, Rita gently pulled her toward the door. It was time for them to return to their flats. Suddenly she was very hungry, and thought that Virginia must be, also. Virginia walked along beside her with an absent expression on her face. Her mind was miles away on the love she might not see for many more days, perhaps weeks. On the walk home, they stopped for some meat, salad greens, and bread that would serve as a quick supper. They decided to eat in one flat rather than mess up two. It seemed silly to them to use both when they spent so much time together, anyway.

Turning on the television, Rita worked quickly to assemble the meal as Virginia rested on the sofa. The BBC commentator reported that the IRA had struck once again in Belfast, and had sent a note to Parliament threatening to attack other subway stations and the airports. Placing a plate with a sandwich and some fruit in Virginia's hand, Rita watched as her friend absently munched the light meal. She hated to see Virginia looking so dejected and depressed. She hoped that in the morning, after a good night's sleep in her own bed, some of the old spring would return to Virginia's step. Rita patted Virginia lovingly on the shoulder as she stood at the door before leaving for her own flat.

"Oh, Rita," Virginia said, "I'm so worried that I'll never make it to France. Now, with the threats against the airports, the IRA will close England off from the continent. I won't be able to join him. I thought that I'd feel closer to him if I didn't stay in Washington. Now I know that it really doesn't matter where I wait for him. I still feel just awful. Being in England doesn't help one bit. You know, Rita, I had a dream about Rob the other night. He was running on a train platform, trying to hop on, to be with me. Just as he got close enough to leap, the train pulled away, leaving him standing all alone on the platform. He was so close that I could almost feel the warmth of his hand in mine. When I woke up,

I was all alone. I'm so worried. I'm so afraid I won't
see him for a long long time."

"You'll work out something. You finagled a transfer to the London office. You'll find a way to get to
France, IRA or not. I have faith in you. I've never
met anyone with more determination. This is simply
a little setback. Tomorrow, you'll have worked out
this little problem. I'll meet you at the coffee shop
in the morning, and we can walk to work together,"
Rita replied, waving goodnight as the elevator door
closed.

Rita had been right. Virginia's good humor did
return the next day, along with the news that Rob
was still heavily engaged in negotiations with the
French government. Virginia felt a bit stronger after
having a good night's sleep. Her mind had cleared
of the fog that clouded it, and the spring had returned to her step. She went through the day's work
of supervising her employees and attending meetings with her usual zeal as she mulled over her revised plans.

At lunchtime, Virginia e-mailed Rob and marked
it priority so that he would open it first. She doubted
that he would respond any time soon, but Virginia
had to let him know that she was thinking about
him. Something about writing the note and pressing
the send button made her feel more connected to
him than sitting in Dover and waiting for the return
of the Chunnel service. Virginia finally resigned herself to play the waiting game just as all the lovers of
important people engaged in heavy negotiations
did.

Virginia also decided that she could not return to
the States now. Not even the E-mail she received
from her mother that morning could change her

mind. Her parents worried about her safety in England, especially now that the IRA had become active again, and they wanted her to come home. Virginia decided that she would phone them later that evening and explain that her work here was important to her. She would try to make them understand why she could not leave England and Rob. Maybe hearing her voice would make them feel more comfortable with her plans.

Like many people whose hearts are far away, Virginia put all of her energy into her work. She attended meetings and contributed brilliant ideas. She soothed the ruffled feathers of customers and employees. She encouraged employees to offer suggestions to improve their jobs. Virginia drafted a plan for revising the function of the support staff, and won immediate approval for its implementation. She kept so busy at work that Rita had to drag her away for lunch, and to return home.

Rob was not the only one earning praise from his superiors. Virginia's boss was so enthusiastic about her ability to assess a situation and produce a workable solution that he recommended her for a position on the regional senior vice president's staff. She would still not be of the same rank in the company, but the new position would afford her more opportunity to travel throughout the offices in Europe. She might even find herself in Paris.

Virginia e-mailed Rob the news, and, as always, waited for the response. She was confident that he would be proud of her accomplishments, but she wanted to hear him express it. Her parents had been beside themselves when she phoned to tell them. She had remembered the time difference, and managed to catch them before they became busy with their activities. Her father had remarked that this had certainly been the year for change in Virginia's life. He wondered what would happen next.

Virginia was so excited about the new assignment that she could barely sleep. She longed for the travel and the responsibility of the new position. She looked forward to the opportunity to contribute to the company on a broader scale. Mostly, she was thrilled about turning the job into her ticket to Paris.

One night, when she finally fell into a restless sleep, Virginia dreamed about the train in the railroad station again. This time Rob was the one on the train as it pulled out, and she was the one who ran to catch it. In her sleep, she wondered if they would ever be together again.

Nine

During the long days of waiting, Virginia often wondered what it was about Rob that she found so attractive, other then his incredible deep brown eyes, slender hips, soft brown skin, long athletic body, and resonant voice. Those were all physical things that were good for luring someone, but not for keeping them. She carefully considered the aspects of him that made her follow him to England when she could have been at home, listening to the world news from thousands of miles away. Instead, she sat in a foreign city threatened by rebellious factions waiting for a man she hardly knew, but wanted to spend the rest of her life with, to find a way to come to her.

Suddenly, she knew why she had followed him to England, and would continue to follow him for the rest of her life. It was the tilt of his head, the slight forward leaning of his body when he gave his full attention to her conversation, the touch of his hand on hers, the taste of his lips, and the salty tears that mingled with hers when they said their good-byes in Washington. All of those things made her want to be his forever. She really was not the hopelessly romantic type. Growing up on the farm with brothers had cured her of that. Yet, somehow, Rob was King

Arthur, her father, all the poets she had ever read, and even her beloved brothers, all rolled up into one man. She loved him, and that was enough of a reason to last a lifetime.

That night, when she returned to the flat from an exceptionally grueling day at the office, Virginia was too tired to eat or sleep. Instead she sat in front of the television listening to the BBC tell of the latest news. As her eyelids became heavy, she dozed in her chair and dreamed that Rob sat at her side in a little house somewhere in the States. Outside the air was clean and peaceful, with only the occasional twitter of the last birds to disturb the silence. Inside, the fire crackled gently in the fireplace. A large golden retriever slept at Rob's feet, and a cat bathed itself while sitting in her lap. Their jobs no longer separated them by miles of water and hours of travel time. When the workday ended, they returned home to each other and happiness.

The jingling of the telephone broke the reverie. Opening her eyes, Virginia found that the crackling fire had merely been the static on the television. The twittering birds had been the whistling of the teakettle. Rob was gone, and so were the dog and cat. She was not at home in the States, but in England waiting for her lover to return.

Rising slowly and walking through the dining room and into the kitchen, Virginia squared her shoulders. She knew it was Rita calling. Each of them had been so busy with meetings that they had not been able to eat lunch together. It would not do to worry Rita with her concerns and dreams. She had problems of her own—and she had not heard from William for several days, and was wondering if the new relationship had already hit a snag.

As she often did, Virginia prepared her plate as she chatted with Rita. Even when they did not dine together in the same apartment, they often ate while talking on the phone together. That way, neither of them had to eat alone. Rita's animated conversation usually helped Virginia to relax, and momentarily put Rob out of her mind.

Virginia was not the only one alone with thoughts of better times. Rob sat in his office, putting the finishing touches on his day's work and thinking of her and their life together. His memory of the fragrance of her perfume mingled with that of the beautiful brandy-colored roses that his secretary had placed on his desk. She replaced them several times a week, saying that his office needed a little extra color. She had no way of knowing that the lovely blossoms only made him feel melancholy.

Rob seldom had time to think of anything except work, but when he did, his mind was always on Virginia and the home they would make together. His imagination conjured up pictures of him sleeping in their big warm bed under a thick fluffy comforter with Virginia lying in the crook of his arm with her head on his shoulder. His hands felt the softness of her skin under his fingertips as he slowly lifted the hem of her cotton batiste nightshirt to reveal her warm thighs. He envisioned the exploration of her curvy thighs and the thatch of hair above. He imagined tasting a sweet nipple that hardened and stood erect as his tongue drew teasing circles around it. Then he captured her lips and tongue with his until she moaned and drew him over her. Rob saw himself perched above her on his knees, looking down on the expression softened by love on Virginia's face. Gliding into her, he felt her match his movements with her own as they enjoyed each other in slow careful lovemaking that took them away from everyday cares. Spent, he turned onto his back and once again pulled her into his arms. In his imagination, they were always the perfect couple.

Shaking off the arousing thoughts, Rob returned to the last of his work. If he did not stop thinking of Virginia he would never get out of the office, and he needed to sleep. He had spent the day running from meeting to meeting, and felt exhausted.

However, Rob found it difficult not to think of her constantly. The E-mails and company memos were filled with accounts of her accomplishments. She had in very short order moved her division into the position of being the premier units by which everyone measured success. Everyone copied her practices, and immediately saw results. Rob often had to keep himself from crowing with pride at her success.

Yet, it was Virginia's success that prevented Rob from asking her to come to him in Paris. As much as he wanted her at his side, he could not ask her to give up her position in London for a lesser one on his staff. She had earned the position she currently held. Rob would not ask her to give it up for him.

So he waited, knowing that their separation could not last forever. Rob spent long hours at the office to fill the loneliness. He jogged along the paths in the parks so frequently that mothers with their strollers now waved, and vendors shouted greetings at him as he passed.

As Rob turned out the light, he listened to the silence of the deserted office. Shrugging his shoulders, he headed for the elevator and the empty Parisian streets. The grandfather clock in the hall struck ten as the elevator door closed behind him and he began his descent. Pulling the collar of his cashmere coat tight around his neck, Rob trudged home to the nothingness that awaited him.

The next morning, Virginia threw wide open the windows of her flat as the first true warmth of springtime hit London. With it came the news that the IRA had been driven back, and had announced a cessation of further attacks against major attractions and the transportation system. People breathed sighs of relief that they would not have to look suspiciously at everyone. Still, they knew that they must remain vigilant against unattended briefcases and packages. The IRA had promised peace many times, only to return to bombing as soon as people let down their guard.

The airwaves were filled with stories of happy Londoners who rushed out of their houses to embrace the warm air and sunshine. Children could once again play games in the streets without fear of menace. Passengers on subway and commuter trains could anticipate making their trips without interruption or detour to other stops. Those in line for admission to tourist attractions like the Tower of London or galleries could enter without having to read the almost constant reminder that England had been a country at war within itself.

And Virginia started making plans. The warm weather gave her new determination to pull some strings, play some chits, and, in general have her way about ending the separation from Rob. Virginia's heart skipped a beat at the thought that she might soon be with Rob once more. She had not seen him in more days than she cared to count, and missed him more each day. There were so many things she wanted to tell him, so many thoughts and dreams left unspoken, that she grew more and more impatient for his return with every day that passed.

After their long hours at the office, Virginia and Rita often took walks around the city instead of going straight home. In every neighborhood the sight of rejuvenation greeted them. Even on the blocks where IRA bombs had done their worst, people had banned together to clean up the streets now that the threat of further attacks had ended. London was no longer held prisoner.

The energy of the office increased with the temperature and new freedoms. Every salesperson had increased success with contacts. Formerly bogged down researchers found ideas flowing freely. Managers spent time in the field with salespeople, rather than in the office solving problems. Everyone could sense the company's revenues rising.

Virginia marveled at the positive affect of a little sunshine. She, too, felt rejuvenated as she sprinted from one meeting to another. She breakfasted and lunched on black coffee, but was so happy with the pace that she did not mind. At least, she was too busy to feel the nagging pain of missing Rob.

She worked such long hours at the office that her community service time faded away. Virginia missed going to the Red Cross, but there was no way that she could volunteer her time there when she had so little of it. She worked from seven until close to nine every night. The walk home with Rita provided her only exercise. She had not turned into a workaholic; she simply enjoyed the challenge and the results. Besides, with Rob away, she had nothing else to do.

One night as Virginia returned, the jangling of the telephone broke the silence of her usually silent apartment. Quickly closing the door, she rushed into the kitchen. Answering breathlessly, she waited until a familiar voice replaced the faint static.

"I'll be in London tomorrow, Virginia," Rob said happily without hesitation. "I have a meeting at the office about revenue figures and positioning in the morning, but I'll be free all afternoon. In fact, I'm taking a few days off to do some sightseeing, if you get my meaning. Do you think you can free your calendar?"

"You bet I can. If I'm not mistaken, I'll be at the same meeting. I have a meeting with one of my people over lunch, but I can arrange to be free after that. I can hardly believe you'll be here." Virginia smiled as she slipped out of the tennis shoes into which she had changed for the walk home.

"It's been a long time, Virginia," Rob said huskily.

"Much longer than I expected, Rob, much longer. I thought being here would give us time to see each other, but it hasn't. Well, at least we'll have some time together before you return to Paris," Virginia said softly. She could barely speak over the wild beating of her heart.

"It's only five days, but we'll make the most of every one of them. I'll see you tomorrow, Virginia. Goodnight," Rob replied gently.

"Goodnight," Virginia whispered as the phone hung heavily in her fingers.

Suddenly energized and far from tired, Virginia had much to do and only a few hours in which to do it. Virginia decided that she would dust and vacuum before going to bed, even though the cleaning lady had visited on Saturday. She did not want Rob to find any dust on the tabletops.

As she hurried around the rooms, Virginia hummed for the first time in months. Rob would soon be here. She would soon hold him in her arms again. These would be the best five days of her life.

Ten

Sitting in the cluttered office at seven o'clock the next morning, Virginia tried to contain her nervousness. She had hardly slept, and had finally given up the tossing and turning at four. She had spent the rest of the night finishing the presentation she would deliver on Monday, and had planned to write during her usual lonely weekend. With Rob in town, her plans had changed drastically. She had to complete all the activities with which she usually busied herself in his absence before his arrival.

"Janet, hold all of my calls, please. I have to finish these reports before the meeting this morning," Virginia said, pressing the intercom button without taking her eyes from the papers on her desk.

"Sure thing, Virginia. I'll keep everyone away," her secretary replied.

The meeting that they would both attend would not start until eleven. She had four hours in which to finish her week's work, but she could not focus on any of the tasks on her desk. Virginia's mind kept rehearsing what she would say and how she would act when she saw him. Rob was only hours away. They would soon be together for five days. Virginia could hardly wait.

Virginia forced herself to concentrate on the

notes of her meeting with her employee, Jeff, later that day. He had asked for her help with one of his projects, and she needed to familiarize herself with the results of his research prior to his arrival. She prided herself on never appearing distracted, or less than completely professional.

The time lagged as Virginia worked or at least tried to concentrate on the papers that littered her desk. After finishing Jeff's report, she moved to another study that required her attention. Finding that one deadly dull, she had put it aside in favor of one on the benefits of local area network services versus those of fiber optics. Glancing at the small clock on her desk for the twentieth time in as many minutes, Virginia decided that the fault was not in the reading material, but in the person doing the reading. She could not keep her mind on the reports, knowing that Rob would arrive very shortly.

At ten-thirty, Virginia pushed aside all pretense of work. Placing the complete projects on the left of her desk and the ones still needing her attention, she was surprised to find that so little remained for her to handle. Despite her anxiety about seeing Rob, she had managed to clear up all but two very thin folders, neither of which required more than a quick scan and a signature.

Yet, as the minute hand barely moved, Virginia rose and checked her makeup at the mirror inside her closet. She wore only blush and a touch of lip gloss, both of which needed only a light refreshing. She ran the pick through her hair to lift and separate the curls, and adjusted the lapel of her taupe-colored suit, under which she wore a tailored silk blouse with a matching scarf at her neck. She had dressed with more than her usual care that morning, knowing that Rob would soon be with her. She wanted his first sight of her after so long an absence to set his heart pounding.

Picking up the file that she needed for the meeting and a pad of paper, Virginia left her office for the conference room down the hall. She controlled the urge to rush, but took her time. She wanted to look contained and composed, not frazzled.

"Well, I'm off," Virginia announced as she passed Janet's desk.

"Enjoy the meeting. I understand that John Robinson from France will be making a very informative presentation today." Janet smiled at her young boss.

"I can hardly wait to hear him," Virginia commented while hiding the true meaning of her words. "The chairman's memo said that Rob has great news to share with all of us."

Walking down the hall, Virginia wondered at her skill in keeping the nature of her relationship with Rob a secret. On the few occasions that they had been in the office together, they had been very careful about maintaining purely professional posture. They had not looked lovingly at each other or gazed longingly in the other's direction. Their fingers had not strayed and touched. Their voices had not betrayed the depth of their affection. In short, no one in either office knew that they were lovers. Virginia and Rob wanted to keep it that way. They both loathed office affairs that had a way of spilling over into the work ethic of both parties. They would keep their private lives to themselves as long as possible.

Carefully, Virginia opened the door and peered inside. The usual assembly of mid and upper levels of management had assembled around the confer-

ence table. Each was chatting amicably over a steaming cup of coffee or tea. Some clutched pastries and
muffins as late morning snacks.

Virginia, however, was too nervous to touch any
food. Instead, she accepted a cup of tea in a delicate
china cup. Taking her customary seat to the left of
the chairman, she tried to show interest in one vice
president's conversation about the new account he
had landed, and the golfing that he would soon be
able to do if the good weather continued. Her eyes
constantly wandered over his shoulder to gaze at the
door. She stifled a sigh every time she saw it open
and Rob did not enter.

As the gavel to open the meeting fell, so did Virginia's heart. Her first thought was that Rob's plans
must have changed. Next, she worried that something had happened to the train, and Rob on it.
She quieted her pounding heart by telling herself
that bad news would have arrived ahead of the chairman and his call to order.

Virginia listened attentively as the chairman,
George Nelson, praised the various vice presidents
for the revenue increases in their departments, the
quality of the research in the special groups, and
the superior customer care in the liaison specialties.
With each compliment, bursts of applause greeted
his words. He would stop and smile graciously until
the staff of the thriving corporation again became
silent. Mr. Nelson would not speak until the only
sounds in the room were his voice and the occasional clicking of silvers spoon on china cups.

Taking copious notes to share with her staff, Virginia smiled at each compliment. Her group had
worked hard since her arrival, and deserved the
praise. The only thing that would make her happier

than having her work recognized would have been sharing the triumph with Rob. Since he was now an hour late for a meeting that had been delayed for his benefit, she assumed that he would not arrive.

A great flurry of activity erupted in the hall outside the conference room. They strained to listen to the conversation, but could hear only animated voices. Even the tussle at the door was muted. Virginia used the momentary break in conversation to pour herself another cup of tea from the server in the kitchenette at the back of the room.

Virginia took a few deep breaths and tried to calm her pounding heart. Her knees were so weak from the closeness of Rob after so long that Virginia feared she would not be able to make the walk to the conference table. Her hands shook so violently that Virginia was surprised that no one had noticed. She was grateful for the shadows created by the recessed kitchen. At least Rob could not see her lack of composure.

She wanted so desperately to call out to him, to fly to his arms, to bury herself in his warmth. However, in that place and at that time, Virginia had to maintain a totally professional demeanor. She had to regain her composure.

Setting the full cup on the counter, Virginia adjusted her jacket and squared her shoulders for one of the longest walks of her life. She would have to return to her chair without the help of her failing knees. If only Rob did not turn his gaze on her, she would be able to return to her seat unnoticed. Luckily, her chair was diagonally across from his.

Rob had turned his attention to George Nelson, who spoke proudly of Rob's accomplishments in Paris and did not see Virginia approaching the table.

He did not see her slip into her seat and turn her attention to the chairman's introduction of the new arrival. He did not observe the smile of pride that played at the corners of her very composed lips with each word of praise that George Nelson uttered.

It was not until the respectful applause from his peers began that Rob turned his attention to his colleagues assembled in the conference room. As his gaze swept theirs, he looked into Virginia's eyes. His face lit up at the sight of her. With all the control he could gather, Rob forced himself to stay in his chair. He would not allow his desire to pull Virginia into his arms to make them a spectacle in front of all their associates.

Virginia, too, resisted temptation. Instead, she only nodded in greeting as their eyes held for a long second, then Rob pulled his gaze away from her. Now that he had finally arrived, there would be time for lips to touch, hands to explore, and voices to declare their love.

Rising, Rob grasped the remote control for the large screen television. With the click of a button, he darkened the room and activated the picture. Immediately, the room filled with music and the sight of people biking through famous French parks, strolling down long quiet lanes, and chatting in secluded restaurants. Smoothly, the scene changed to hospitals in which busy nurses and physicians rushed to treat patients, offices where workers labored over projects, quaint shops in which merchants sold their goods to happy customers, and home offices where people worked alone. Making one last shift, the focus changed to families at rest in front of the television, teenagers talking with their friends, younger schoolchildren hunched over their books, and par-

ents engaged in conversation and dinner prepara-
tion. In each scene, items from the telecommunications industry were always close at hand. From cell
phones to cordless phones, from computer hookups
to satellite transmission, the signs of technology
making life more enjoyable, work more productive,
and leisure more fun filled the screen. In an adver-
tisement with universal appeal, happy French people
showed that telecommunications had become an in-
tegral part of their lives.

To save Rob from appearing less than humble,
the projector began to crank out informational
slides that disclosed the total revenue that would
be generated by the DC corporation's partnership
with the French telecommunications company. The
expense of the ad, the cost of renovating and maintaining the new office on the Champs Élysée and
its sales force, and Rob's astronomical salary were
quickly forgotten as the bottom line profit figure
flashed on the screen. Ecstatic applause filled the
room as the lights came up once again.

Rob did not shrink from accepting the praise. Instead, he stood tall and surveyed the group. Many
of them had said that working with the volatile
French would be impossible. They warned him that
he would never be able to make them commit to an
alliance to which they would contribute funds, let
alone time.

Rob had done the impossible, but it had not been
easy. He had spent long hours working on the deal
adapting the particulars of the arrangement to suit
first one government official and then another.
Agreement gained one day was rescinded or modi-
fied the next, and he had to start over, to gain the
confidence of people who had initially been in favor

of the arrangements only to change their minds and join forces with those against it. Finally, Rob had overcome all of their objections, and the president of France had signed the deal.

Rob had quickly begun the ad campaign before new objections could arise. Within hours of the first airing, the telemarketing group had been swamped with orders. It seemed as if everyone in France had been waiting for the products to become available.

Simultaneously, the American installation crews had begun the construction of the offices that would provide the services. They had worked around the clock to be ready the day the commercial first aired. With the press of a button, the computerized totally digital telecommunications office had become operative and ready to provide voice and data services to anyone in the vicinity of Paris who might want it. With the success of that office, the French government had agreed to allow the company to expand. That success and expansion had earned Rob accolades from across the Atlantic—and had robbed him of time with Virginia.

Nodding his head in recognition of the appreciation, Rob darted a glance at Virginia. Hers was the praise that really mattered to him. He wanted her to understand that his absence from her side had, at least, justified his reputation and salary.

Virginia felt incredible pride at his accomplishments. She regretted the time that they had missed, but she understood that he had been transferred to Europe for the purpose of establishing business relations with France and opening the office. He'd had to be successful, with all eyes on his efforts. Failure would have been unthinkable and incredibly humiliating.

No one had really expected success, despite Rob's reputation. However, corporate memory would have forgotten that he worked against the odds, and that the French government was a tough customer that more than one senior vice president had not conquered. No one would have said that he failed because of his race, although the thought would have lurked behind their words of regret. Rob had known when he accepted the position that he had to succeed.

In the corporate world in which the glass ceiling still existed, Virginia had taken a similar risk in following Rob to England. She also knew that all eyes would be on her performance. The reason for her promotion had been quickly forgotten as the need to prove herself had once again raised its head.

As their eyes met, Rob and Virginia shared a brief moment of triumph. Both had been successful in the tasks that they had set for themselves. Now, they would be able to steal a few days for themselves. As soon as their meetings ended, they would steal away from the prying eyes of the corporate world and devote all of their energy to making their relationship as successful as their corporate affairs.

When the meeting ended, George Nelson guided Rob from the conference room and out into the teeming London streets for a private lunch at an exclusive men's club in the Kensington section of the city. As Virginia watched him leave, she felt disappointment at not having him to herself, and then relief. She would be able to concentrate on her afternoon meeting without Rob's presence and the unfulfilled promise of intimacy hanging over them. Although she knew that the weekend would pass too quickly, she could not allow Rob to interfere in the work that still lay ahead of her that afternoon. There would be plenty of time for quiet conversation and snuggling that night.

Virginia set her mind to her work, and managed to accomplish all that she had set out for that day without interruption by thoughts of Rob. She ate a quick lunch of Caesar salad and tasty French bread at her desk while putting the finishing touches on a presentation that she had to give the following week. She briefed her secretary, as usual, on the calls she expected and the meetings that she would have to attend. By sheer force of will and determination, she did not think of Rob more than a dozen times.

Her afternoon meeting turned out to be an encouraging session for Jeff. He was simply feeling overwhelmed by his work. Jeff left her office with a confident smile, his self-esteem bolstered. Virginia had honestly been able to say that his report had been very carefully prepared. She had made only the smallest of suggestions for additional research.

Noise in the hall outside her office broke the spell of her concentration at five o'clock. The day had ended uneventfully, despite Rob's presence in London. Big Ben had managed to sound every hour, Parliament had conducted business, and Virginia had finished all of her work.

Once Virginia had thought that she heard his voice in the hall as a group of men passed by. However, she had refused to rise and peek outside. After a few minutes, the silence had returned, and with it her concentration.

Now, Virginia allowed the sounds of employees wishing each other a good evening to wash over her as she packed her briefcase. She had promised herself that she would not take home any work, but, out of habit, she tossed her calendar and laptop into her bag. Virginia knew that she would not touch either with Rob in town.

As she reached the lobby on the first floor, Virginia scanned the departing faces for signs of Rob. When she did not see him waiting for her, she slipped through the revolving doors with the other workers. Once on the sidewalk, she followed the current of humanity that flowed toward the subway and home.

While gripping the leather overhead strap, Virginia took a mental inventory of her closet and decided on her attire for the evening. They had made no definite plans for dinner, leaving the choice open. She would suggest something simple, so that she could wear slacks and a light sweater. She had bought a special red-and-black checked cashmere and soft wool slacks for their first evening together.

As she unlocked her door, Virginia felt the first waves of excitement begin to sweep over her. She had been so composed all day that the sensation felt alien as it coursed through her body. She was surprised to see that her hands shook ever so slightly.

Even though she had thoroughly cleaned the apartment, Virginia found herself looking at it as if it were new to her. She saw the teal blue area rug that picked up the dominant color in her sofa and drapes. She gazed at the accessories and wondered why she had ever thought the reproduction Ming vase attractive. It contained the correct colors, but its shape was so plain and ordinary. Only this morning, she had enjoyed its simple lines, which now appeared dull and almost boring. If time had allowed, she would have rushed to Harrod's for a replace-

ment. The celebrated department store would have
had something with more pizzazz.

Looking at her hands, Virginia wished that she
had stopped for a manicure yesterday. Her cuticles
were a little ragged, and it was almost time for a
change in color. Glancing at herself in the hall mirror, she thought that her hair could use a little trim,
too. If she had time, she could have had both of
those done tonight.

However, Virginia only had time for a quick
shower and a change of clothes. Rob would arrive
at seven-thirty. The subway had been so crowded
that she'd had to wait for the fourth train before
she could board. The florist's shop had been
crowded with customers, and the service slow. She
only had time to place the flowers she had purchased in a vase before dashing to the bathroom.
Suddenly, the clock on the mantel struck seven, and
her hair and nails did not seem very important.

Rob arrived precisely on time, and carried a large
box containing two dozen red roses. He watched silently as Virginia lovingly placed each one into her
best vase and set it at the center of the dining room
table. They chatted about the day's meetings as she
went about this simple domestic task.

As soon as Virginia's hands were free, he pulled
her trim body into his arms. Allowing his lips to taste
the sweetness of her mouth and the softness of the
skin of her neck, he breathed deeply of her fragrance. His arms had ached to hold her that afternoon at the meeting, and now there was nothing to
keep them apart. His body remembered every curve
of hers, and his hands went out to check the accu-
racy.

Settling into the comfort of his chest, Virginia felt

warm and safe in Rob's arms. The nearness of him made her body tingle with wonderful sensations. Her fingers played gently at his skin above his sweater. Her lips nibbled on his earlobe when not engaged in tasting the pleasure of his lips. Her hands caressed the thick muscles of his shoulders and back, while her thighs rested heavily against his. Rob had been working out while in Paris by himself, and Virginia loved the hardness of him.

As Rob led her in the direction of the bedroom, Virginia remembered that she had not put away the shoes she had worn to the office. Somehow, that little chink in her otherwise perfect housekeeping did not matter as Rob's fingers fumbled with the tiny mother-of-pearl buttons on the front of her sweater and an oath of frustration escaped his lips. Chuckling, she slipped her hands under his and finished the job.

As they stood in the hallway, Rob's fingers deftly rose to the task of unzipping and removing her slacks. Dropping them onto the pile of clothing on the teal area rug, he unfastened the hook on her black lace bra and slipped off her lacy panties. He moaned softly as he allowed her to pull off his sweater and trousers. His briefs quickly joined the pile of their attire.

Bending down and picking her up in his strong arms, Rob carried Virginia into her bedroom and deposited her on the bed. Lifting her up with one hand, he quickly stripped off the comforter and decorative pillows with the other. Reaching beneath her, Virginia pulled back the blanket and sheet.

As their naked bodies pressed hungrily together, all thought of work, London, Paris, vases, manicures, and haircuts floated away. All that mattered was that they were together again, and in each other's arms. They did not hear the clock on the mantle as it struck the hour—and the next, and the next.

Eleven

Virginia awoke the next morning to the aroma of freshly brewed coffee and toasted scones. While she had been sleeping, Rob had slipped out of the flat and purchased the necessary items for a quick breakfast. He had even remembered the marmalade.

"Wake up, sleepyhead!" came the boom of Rob's baritone. "We have a lot to see. It's time to hit the streets."

"I was under the impression that you came to London to see me, not Big Ben. I guess I was wrong," Virginia retorted as she pulled the robe over her still naked body. For the first time in ages, she had slept in the nude, with only the warmth of Rob's body next to hers to keep her warm.

"I saw plenty of you last night, and again this morning, if I remember correctly. I'll save some for dessert tonight," Rob commented, entering the bedroom with a cup of coffee for Virginia in his hands. At the sight of her with standing in the middle of the floor with open robe and tousled hair, he immediately rose to the occasion.

Placing the cup on the nightstand, he slipped his warm hands under the terry cloth of her robe and caressed the velvety smoothness of her body. Nuzzling her sweet neck, Rob whispered hoarsely, "I guess the Victoria and Albert will have to stand without me."

As he carried Virginia back to bed, they forgot about the coffee that chilled on the nightstand and the scones that waited on the kitchen counter. Nothing mattered except being together as they allowed the nearness of each other and the heat of their kisses to blot out the sounds of London and the chiming of the clock. All thoughts of everything except pleasing each other vanished from their minds.

Virginia had never known love until she met Rob. She had known that because of Rob's gentleness the first time, every time would be wonderful. She enjoyed his hands exploring her body under the soft, white, cotton batiste nightgown. She loved the feel of the closeness of their bodies. She tingled when he helped her slip her gown over her head.

Rob was awestruck by Virginia every time they made love, as he was now. Rob marveled at her thin trim body, and pulled her hungrily into his arms. His hot lips burned her skin as he kissed her eyelids, cheeks, nose, neck, breasts, and downward. Aflame, she teased his body with her lips and fingers until he pulled her under him and joined with her.

Her body arched to meet his, and her rhythm matched his until they reached the pleasurable crescendo. Then they held each other and slept undisturbed through the night. Their love cradled them as they slept in gentle warmth.

The spring afternoon sunshine felt warm on their faces as they mingled with the Saturday traffic. A few tourists with maps made their way along the crowded streets as the residents of London did their weekly shopping. Virginia and Rob eased into the foot traffic and headed toward the central section of the city.

Taking his hand, Virginia led Rob toward St. Paul's Cathedral through the sunny streets. As expected, the cathedral was crowded with visitors enjoying the day, students studying its architecture, and tourist snapping photographs.

Virginia and Rob managed to find standing room in the south transept just as evensong began. The cathedral was ablaze with candlelight, awash with the smell of incense that rose in wispy clouds to the domed ceiling above. Acolytes and crossbearers in black robes with white tunics and ruffled collars led the procession of choir boys and clergy down the center aisle to where they took their places. A hush fell over the worshipers and visitors as the lay reader read the first lesson from the lectern.

From where they stood, Virginia and Rob marveled at the play of lights on the ornate gold carvings, dark-paneled wood, and glittering white statues. Looking up at the dome, they were impressed by its height and majesty. The massive windows captured light on this day and illuminated the colorful mosaic-tiled ceiling.

As the voices of the combined men and boys' choir soared to the heavens singing the hymns and the Benedictus, Virginia looked up to see Rob's reaction to this beautiful cathedral, the home of the diocese of London. Finding him deep in thought, she was surprised to see his forehead lined with furrows. His fingers played slowly over his knitted brows. She wondered if thoughts of his return to France were already dragging at his heart.

Sensing her eyes on him, Rob looked down into her concerned face and tried to smile. He did not want to ruin their time together. He squeezed her hand and smiled as he pushed aside the thoughts of work that had crept into the day.

"Rob," Virginia whispered, "isn't this the most glorious cathedral?"

Nodding, he replied, "Yes, but just wait until you see Notre-Dame. You might agree that its beauty is greater. I can hardly wait to show you Paris in all her splendor."

"Sounds as if you're bragging. I think Paris would have to go some to beat London," Virginia responded as the press of visitors began to move around the cathedral once more. Now that the service had ended, everyone felt free to speak in subdued tones once again.

"No, I wouldn't say that I'm being unnecessarily proud. There's just something incredibly impressive about a cathedral sitting on a little island in the middle of a river, that's all. You should see the flying buttresses and the bell tower . . . impressive," Rob retorted as they stepped into the sun once more.

"You sound like an engineer," Virginia chuckled as they strolled along holding hands.

"Well, I guess I do," Rob conceded with a laugh. "I would have majored in engineering or architecture if international business hadn't sounded more lucrative. Anyway, one of these days I'll show you my designs. In my spare time, I've been known to sketch a fair house or two."

As they walked toward St. James Park, Virginia asked as she pointed to across the street, "Do you think we should continue our sightseeing? I wouldn't mind having some hot chocolate and tea cakes at one of those little shops."

"No, let's go on. I'm looking forward to seeing

St. James Park and Westminster Cathedral. They're both very famous, and a necessary part of any tour of London. Besides, there's time for refreshments later. Let's keep going while the sun's still shining. I hope you have good walking shoes." Rob smiled as he dragged an almost drooling Virginia along.

"All right, but I do want a cup of chocolate before we head back. That shop has the best in London. Every time I'm in this neighborhood, I treat myself. I'm not going to miss an opportunity." Virginia looked longingly across the street.

"I promise that on our return trip we'll stop there. I'd hate to be the one who deprived Virginia Summers of hot chocolate. Stop pouting. Let's enjoy our sightseeing together. Onward to St. James Park!" he said, pulling her through the streets as if he were the resident of the town, and Virginia only the visitor.

When they arrived, they found the park blissfully empty except for the old men and women who regularly fed the assorted birds that called the pond their home. Virginia extracted a bag of bread crusts from her purse, and immediately pigeons, sparrows, larks, and the occasional duck flocked to her. Rob laughed as she shooed away squirrels that threatened to eat all of the treats. He cleared the discarded newspapers from one of the benches and sat down to watch her as she frolicked with her feathered friends.

Joining him in his tranquil surroundings after she threw the last crumbs to the squabbling birds, Virginia again found Rob deep in thought. He did not seem to notice when she slipped her gloved hand in his, or planted a kiss on his cheek. He was far away, with furrows lining his brow once again.

Shaking himself, Rob commented, "I know I promised not to let work interfere in our weekend, but it's difficult putting it away. Strange, when I'm in Paris I think about you constantly. I wonder what you're doing, who you're seeing, and how you're reacting to the little stresses of life. When I'm here, the job follows me everywhere I go. I left the office in the capable hands of my secretary, who has my number should something happen, but I still can't keep the business out of my mind."

"I think you're doing wonderfully. Don't try so hard. I've been thinking about work, too. I guess it just gets under our skin. However, I do have a solution to our problem," Virginia said, trying to comfort him.

"Really? What is it?" Rob demanded as a squirrel darted away with the last of the large crusts of bread.

"I can transfer to Paris. Not right this minute, of course, but as soon as I can work it out," Virginia replied with a broad smile.

"I'd like nothing better than to have you in Paris with me, but you know how difficult it is to work out those transfers. You were lucky to get this one. If it hadn't been for the company's desire to expand the European market, you'd still be in DC. You've become a vital member of the London office. I don't think you'll see a transfer any time soon," Rob commented as he pulled Virginia to her feet.

"Maybe not, but it's worth a try," Virginia replied as she matched her stride with his.

"I guess you're right. Let's not talk about work anymore. What's the next stop on our tour, Miss Virginia Summers? By the way, do you plan to feed me at some point? I'm getting hungry," he asked, making playful growling noises. "You were right about stopping for hot chocolate."

"Ladies and gentlemen—or should I just say gentleman—our next stop is a little shop for the best sandwiches you ever ate, and then onward to Westminster Abbey for more statue gazing." Virginia said, pretending to speak into a megaphone as she picked up his sudden change to a bright sunny mood. "I'll accept this as a compromise."

As they walked along the sun shone on them, making everything a soft yellow. Stopping in the doorway, Rob chuckled as he looked into the little, brown wood-paneled shop with its dark grained counter. The fragrance of the meats and cheeses made his mouth water, reminding him of solo lunches in Paris. He could not remember the last time he had savored the aroma of food and a leisurely lunch. He usually only had time to grab a sandwich on the fly before hurrying back to his office. When he dined with someone, it was always over business. He barely tasted exquisite meals while making sure that the deals progressed smoothly.

"Make mine cheese on whole wheat with mustard to take out," Rob ordered contentedly. Then he added, from instinct gained from closeness, "And the lady will have a turkey on a roll with lettuce, tomato, and low fat mayonnaise."

"How did you know?" Virginia asked as she looked at him, puzzled.

"I didn't. I just guessed. Don't all women eat low fat food? At least, all the women in my office do. With all that great food and those delicious pastries in the bistros and restaurants of Paris, they still barely eat anything as they watch their weight. I say eat, drink, and be merry." Rob laughed as he lightly placed a kiss on her forehead.

"Yeah, and buy a girdle at Harrod's," Virginia

quipped as she accepted her neatly packaged sandwich.

Eating her lunch as they walked, Virginia pointed out little churches and towers along the way. When they reached Parliament, Rob stood with his mouth open looking at its glory. The sight of Big Ben made the greatest impression on him.

"Ever since I was a little boy this building and this clock tower have been England to me. It gives me chills to stand here with London's sounds, sights, and smells surrounding me. If you hadn't followed me to Europe, I would have flown here for the meeting and left immediately afterward. I never would have allowed myself the opportunity to enjoy the city. Seeing the sights has never been my style. See the good influence you've had on me?" Rob had a touch of nostalgia in his voice.

"Dover and its white cliffs are England to me. One day, we'll travel there together. I know a great little bed-and-breakfast where we can stay. It's at the foot of the hill, just below the castle," Virginia added, resting her head on his shoulder.

"Sounds great to me!" Rob replied, taking her hand and guiding her across the street to Westminster Abbey, where people milled about between services.

There, too, Rob felt oddly familiar with the surroundings as he led Virginia straight to the burial site of Sir Francis Bacon. All his years of study and pouring over history books were finally paying off. He found that he knew London even without the help of his wonderful guide.

"Bacon was buried standing up, at his request. That's why his space is so small," Rob proclaimed, like a child showing off newly acquired knowledge to his proud mother.

"You've done some research since your last trip." Virginia chuckled as he continued to point out other tidbits.

An expression of youthful pride flooded his face as Rob added, "You aren't the only one who's fascinated by London and things English. I bet you don't know what's behind those gates . . . the tomb of Elizabeth the First and her sister Mary. And over there is—"

"I do," Virginia interrupted, waving her hand to silence him, "but I'm impressed. Let's wander through SoHo before we head back."

Walking through the busy streets, Virginia and Rob continued to try to one-up each other by pointing out well-known and obscure sights. Her months of living in the bustling city gave Virginia the advantage over his college memories of pages read in order to pass required tests. Finally, laughing, Rob called a truce as they headed for the crush of people in the subway station.

The underground teemed with people making their way home. Everyone pushed and shoved to enter the already full trains, on which people sat in every available seat and stood shoulder to shoulder grasping the overhead straps and railings. As the door closed and the bell signaled their departure for the next stop, the American lovers blended into the crowd.

Returning to Virginia's flat, they set about preparing dinner. As Rob chopped vegetables, mixed the dressing, and tossed the salad, he pushed all intruding thoughts from his mind. He was determined to enjoy this evening with Virginia without interfer-

ence. There would be time enough to let them monopolize his life when they were hundreds of miles
apart.

As the afternoon lengthened into evening and the
dinner dishes had been placed in the dishwasher,
Virginia and Rob settled into the pattern that would
become their evening routine. Turning on the television and settling down on the sofa next to Rob,
Virginia felt relieved that she had not planned any
activities. She had originally thought of inviting Rita
for dinner or to take in a show, but, at the last minute Virginia had decided that she wanted to have
him all to herself. She eased her head on his shoulder as he pulled her closer. Despite the warmth of
the evening, they had built a fire. The flames in the
fireplace sparkled and danced, warming them with
their energy.

"What'll we do with this nice long weekend?" Virginia asked. She pulled her legs onto the sofa and
sank even deeper into his chest.

"I don't want to think about anything except the
here and now. I'm holding the woman I love in my
arms, the funniest show I've ever seen is on the TV,
dinner was delicious, and the fire mixed with the
wine I consumed during the meal is lulling me to
sleep. There's nothing better than this. So why try
to plan anything?" Rob's answer was in a drowsy
voice.

"I couldn't agree more. Just having you here
rather than on the other end of the telephone is
enough for me," Virginia whispered, snuggling
closer to him as the warmth from the fire soothed
and comforted them.

For a while Virginia took her cue from him as the
silence enfolded and warmed them. She had

dreamed that their weekend together would be wonderful, and it was. Now, with her arms around Rob and her head on his chest, she was in paradise. Listening to the deep gentle purr of his heart and the soft puffs of subdued snores coming from his slightly parted lips, she knew that Rob was right. Nothing could ever change this from the wonderful closeness she had imagined it would be.

Suddenly, Rob sat up. "I thought you said that a swing band would be performing at one of the local clubs tonight. What are we doing sitting here when we could be out dancing?" he demanded, suddenly completely awake and ready to go.

"I'd love to go dancing, but are you sure you can handle it? You've put in horrible hours on this project. I didn't think you'd have the energy." Virginia searched his face for signs of fatigue.

"Don't worry about me. You know I'm a fairly decent dancer—no Fred Astaire or Gregory Hines, mind you, but pretty good. Let's go," Rob said, pulling Virginia to her feet. After teasing her lips with a gentle kiss, he gave her a little shove toward the bedroom so she could put on her shoes.

"Just let me brush my hair, and I'll be ready," Virginia called, fairly dancing her way to the bedroom. A night of dancing would add more magic to the already heavenly day.

The night air carried just a hint of a chill as they made their way through the darkness to Blues Guitar, one of the most happening clubs in London. Purple, magenta, and lemon lights decorated the entrance. A bold neon sign flashed its name. People lined up to enter in a queue that stretched around the block. Inside, the music was blasting, and people of every description were dancing and mingling, making it difficult for the waitstaff to deliver the drinks that added to the loose atmosphere of the club.

Virginia and Rob mingled with the other laughing couples on the dance floor. They matched so perfectly that it looked as if they had always been together. They chuckled when he stepped on her toes, and congratulated each other on being well-matched when they executed their steps flawlessly.

"It certainly is nice having you in my arms again, Virginia. Reminds me of home," Rob said as he pulled her close.

"I'd begun to think that we'd never get the chance to do this again. Our schedules have kept us so busy. At least we have this weekend. Let's make the most of it," Virginia replied as she leaned her head on his shoulder.

"All that's missing is the confetti, champagne, and the countdown to New Year's," Rob commented with a happy smile.

"Let's order a bottle of champagne and toast our weekend together," Virginia offered as the band changed the tempo to something more leisurely.

Nestling in his arms as the band began to play an old slow number, Virginia remembered the first time she had danced with Rob at the company New Year's Eve party, how she had not liked his arrogance then, and found him too self-confident. She had hardly contained her impatience to be away from him as his arms enfolded her. Now she would do anything in her power to keep the music playing forever.

As they eased around the floor, Rob gazed deeply into her eyes and smiled happily. For the moment, work and the distance that separated them seemed unimportant. Neither wanted to think about the papers that filled their office in boxes.

"We'll have to do this more often," Rob commented as he spun Virginia in a graceful turn.

"Let's not talk and break the spell," Virginia answered. "This night was made for dancing. I want to remember the feel of your arms and the sound of the music when you return to Paris."

"You're right. I won't say another word," Rob replied as he pulled her still closer and nuzzled her soft neck.

For the rest of the evening neither spoke of work or the distance that separated them. They were happy to be together and in each other's arms. All too soon the need to return to their offices would separate them.

Instead of turning on the lights as they entered the apartment, Virginia and Rob headed straight for the bedroom. They were tired, but wonderfully happy as the sounds of music and laughter echoed in their heads. The evening had been a wonderful respite from their usually hectic lives.

However, sleep was not their first priority. The perfection of the evening and the closeness of their bodies had awakened thoughts of love that pushed aside the need for sleep. As he captured her mouth with his, Rob's hot breath burned into Virginia's skin, and she wrapped her arms around his neck. She clung to him as if that night were to be their last.

Their hands raced over each other's bodies, searching for pleasure spots and memorizing them for the future. Their lips trailed kisses along eyelids, mouths, ears, and cheekbones. Their fingers caressed tender recesses and stroked burning flesh.

Their tongues tasted sweetness beyond belief as they moved in concert with each other.

Separating from her ever so slightly, Rob looked deeply into Virginia's eyes and guessed at the emotions that filled her just as they swirled through him. They had so much living to do in such a short time that every moment became precious. After this weekend, they might be separated for months if their jobs became hectic again.

"Virginia, I love you more than my own life. I don't know how . . ." Rob did not know how to continue.

Sensing the direction the conversation would take, she said, "I know, Rob. I'm concerned about the same things. I love you so much, and our time together is so limited. I don't know what to do."

"We'll have to find a way to make the days pass quickly between visits. We won't let work keep us apart. Spending time with you this weekend only makes me more determined than ever to manage my life rather than allowing the job to do it," Rob spoke so sincerely that Virginia's heart almost broke with the knowledge that in only a relatively few hours they would be separated again.

"Let's make the most of the time we have," Virginia replied as she studied Rob's tortured face. She could tell that he was making mental notes of the contents of his in box, the items that he would delegate, and the appointments the he would rearrange so that he would have more time to spend with her. She had already gone through the same exercise.

Burying his face in her warm neck, Rob responded, "You're right. I have much more enjoyable things to do now than think about work."

For the next hour, they only thought of pleasing

each other. London and Paris, Big Ben, Notre-Dame Cathedral, and travel in the Chunnel were far from their minds as they lost themselves in each other and found that their love transcended the distance that separated them.

As the clock on the mantel struck three, the slightly rowdy voices of the last pub crawlers floated up to greet them. Looking sleepily at each other, Virginia and Rob nestled more firmly together against the darkness outside their window. Outside, the air had taken on a nighttime chill. Inside, the apartment held a rosy glow.

Turning Virginia's face up to his, Rob smiled down at her and said, "Why don't we do a little shopping tomorrow? I think I remember a little shop around the corner from Harrod's that just might have a ring in your size. That is, if you'll have me."

"Is this a proposal?" Virginia asked as the haze of leisurely lovemaking cleared.

"I know that we haven't known each other that long, and our jobs keep us apart, but I'd like to know that we have that level of commitment to each other. I love you, Virginia, and I want you to be my wife," Rob replied very seriously.

"I feel as if I've known you forever. I can't think of anyone I'd rather spend my life with. Yes, Rob, I'll marry you. I want the permanence, too. We'll just have to work harder on the logistics of our living arrangements," Virginia responded as Rob gently kissed the corners of her mouth. The afterglow of sex mingled with the immense happiness caused by her love of Rob.

As the streets once again grew silent, Rob looked into the eyes of the woman he loved and wondered how they would be able to solve the problem of distance. With an involuntary shudder, he pushed the thought from his mind. That night and that weekend were meant for love, not for worrying. He would not let anything interfere with his enjoyment of holding Virginia in his arms.

Virginia sighed as she sank a little deeper into his strong wide chest. With firm resolve, she promised herself that on Monday she would put into motion the plan that had been lurking in the recesses of her mind. However, for now the only thing that mattered was the nearness of Rob and the need for sleep. They had another big day scheduled.

Suddenly very tired, she sank into a deep sleep disturbed only by the train dream. This time she could feel her fingers tightening on his only to have him slip away at the last minute, leaving her alone and lonely. Involuntarily, Virginia tightened her grip on Rob's hand as the night grew deep, and London slept.

Twelve

The next day, Virginia and Rob slept late, something neither of them had done in years. Their schedules were always so hectic that they never had time to enjoy a leisurely morning or to relish the aroma of freshly brewed coffee. As the sun streamed in the window, they sat at the kitchen table making plans for the day. Virginia felt surprisingly at peace with herself and the world. She knew that she loved Rob with all of her heart, and that he felt the same way about her. She did not stop to question what could go wrong when two people cared so deeply about each other.

The impatient jingling of the telephone interrupted the tranquility of their second cup of coffee and conversation. As Virginia rose to answer it, she only briefly thought about the possibility that work might intrude on their weekend. However, as she heard the voice on the other end ask for Rob, she grew tense.

"For you," Virginia said as she handed Rob the phone.

"Yes, I understand. Right. What's the flight number? Four o'clock? Fine, I'll be there. Thanks, Jeanette," Rob responded as he hung up the phone.

From the sudden droop of his shoulders, Virginia

knew that their time together had come to an end. She did not wait until he broke the news. Instead, she spoke first to ease the gloom that had suddenly overshadowed the room.

"Well, let's get going. If you have to catch a four o'clock flight, we can still visit the London Dungeon, and even the Tower," Virginia said as she began cleaning up the remnants of breakfast.

"No, Virginia, I have a four o'clock meeting. In Paris. Something's come up that couldn't wait until tomorrow. We'll have to cut our plans short. There's an electronic ticket for the twelve-thirty flight to Paris waiting for me at Gate thirty-five at Heathrow. We only have time for a quick but necessary stop at the jewelry store for your ring, and then I'll have to take the tube to the airport." Rob began to help stack the dishes in the washer.

"I'll ride out with you. That'll give us a few more minutes together," Virginia said as she tried to put on a brave face. She had hoped that nothing would intrude in their stolen moments. However, in her heart, she had expected that the world of corporate business would not leave them alone.

Doing his part to lighten the gloom and to make the most of the little time left to them, Rob brightened and said, "I'd love to have you with me, but it'll be a solitary ride back for you."

"I don't mind. I might take the bus back and see some of the countryside. Or maybe I'll go to the flower show at Kew Gardens. I'll be fine. Let's go," Virginia said as they linked arms and left her apartment. Despite the pressures of his job, nothing could dim the glow of their love and the excitement of spending time together.

They talked the entire forty-five minute ride to

the airport. The train gradually emptied of riders as it passed the city limits. Soon it seemed as if they were the only ones making the trip to the airport on that beautiful morning. Alone in the car, they kissed and held each other close. Virginia's new three-carat diamond ring sparkled on the third finger of her left hand in the sunlight.

Heathrow was packed with travelers arriving at and departing from London. After Rob checked in at the first class passenger gate, they found a remote corner away from noisy children and irritated parents to await the call of his flight. Checking the board, they discovered that flight 6234 to Paris would be leaving on schedule.

As she rested heavily against Rob's shoulder, Virginia already missed him. The last minutes were bittersweet, at best, and a reminder of the reality of their lives. It would be months before they could have time alone together. She would have to savor the memories of this weekend until they could be together again.

"I'll call tonight, but probably not until after midnight," Rob promised as the flight attendant made the last call for passengers.

"I'll be waiting," Virginia responded as they kissed one last time.

"I love you," Rob stated simply as he looked into her eyes one last long time.

"I love you, too, Rob." Virginia clung to his fingers.

As he handed the flight attendant his boarding pass, Rob looked back, smiled, and waved. Walking down the ramp, he disappeared into the bowels of the big airliner bound for Charles de Gaulle Airport in Paris. Their weekend had ended.

Virginia wrapped her arms around her body. The warmth had suddenly left the sunny London sky as the airliner taxied down the runway and lifted into the bright clouds. Although Rob was no longer with her, she could still see him in her flat, and feel him in her arms. She could taste his sweet kisses on her lips and smell his sensuous body. She could hear his voice as he whispered her name and words of love. Every memory of the last days flowed through her mind. Every word echoed in her heart. She retraced every step they took and revisited every building, conversation, or silent moment. The memories would have to last until they were reunited.

Looking at the brightly shining diamond that wold have been the envy of all of her girlfriends at home, Virginia knew that at that moment she would gladly trade it for a simple band of gold for more time with Rob. Rather than its bright light of unfulfilled promises, she would rather have the reality of meals together, washdays of mixed laundry, and evenings at the theater or in front of the television. Setting her shoulders and walking toward the entrance to the subway, she decided that she would have to find a way to make their time together more permanent.

Knowing that she could not return to the city immediately, Virginia took the train to Kew Gardens. The vast botanical complex on the outskirts of London teemed with people enjoying the warm weather and the beautiful displays of flowers. She smiled at elderly couples who seemed to know exactly when the other wanted to stop and look at flowers. She chuckled at little children as they chased butterflies. One day she and Rob would be there.

Sitting at tea in the aviary, Virginia gazed out the

window at the gaily blooming beds. Flower heads bobbed in the breeze as birds searched for bugs and worms. The sun shone brightly on the rainbow colors of columbine, freesia, and roses. She wished that Rob could be at her side, and share the beauty of spring with her.

Finally, that night, Virginia forced herself to return to her empty flat. The day that had started with so much promise for the lovers had ended with separation. Too exhausted to even think of eating, Virginia settled into her bed with an unfinished book and a cup of tea. Looking at the clock, she saw that Rob would not phone for at least three hours.

As the mantel clock struck one, Virginia turned out the light. With a shrug of resignation, she snuggled into her pillow with the knowledge that she would not hear from Rob that night. Work had once again succeeded in separating them. She fell into a deep dreamless sleep almost immediately. When she opened her eyes again, it was morning and time to go to work.

The office was bustling with people. Monday morning always seemed to be the busiest time. The tube was more crowded than usual, the line at the coffee shops was longer, and the atmosphere in the office was more somber, as everyone returned to work and put thoughts of leisure behind them. Virginia did not have time to feel sorry for herself, or to miss Rob. As soon as she walked in the door, her secretary handed her a pile of callback slips and her updated calendar. As she gulped her first cup of coffee and rushed to the first of three meetings, she wondered if Rob's day had begun, too, even after their late night.

At lunchtime, rather than go out with the others,

Virginia finally read her E-mail. Quickly reading through the morning's messages, Virginia saw that the latest IRA activity in the suburbs had put a communications office out of business. Fortunately, no one had been injured, but thousands of customers in the Gloucester area were without telephone service. The company had already dispatched emergency crews to make the repairs.

Opening the next folder, Virginia read the usual list of appointments, promotions, and transfers. Many of the names of people in the States were familiar to her, and some of the European ones she remembered from meetings she had attended. She added her congratulations to the growing list of messages.

Moving to the list of personal announcements, Virginia saw that several of the women had posted announcements of their engagements and weddings. One of the grandmothers on the staff had used E-mail to announce the arrival of her first grandson. She decided against adding her own news to the messages, since she had not asked Rob about making a formal announcement. As a matter-of-fact, she had not even told Rita. For now, Virginia would remain silent and content herself with gazing at the rock that glittered on her left hand.

By afternoon, she had managed to whittle away a large portion of the projects in her in box. When the tea wagon arrived, Virginia stopped for a much needed break. Stretching her tired back and shoulders, she joined the others in the conference room for tea and little sandwiches.

The afternoon tea breaks served as social functions. Managers of every level mixed with the staff and exchanged information about projects and deadlines, upcoming organization changes, and morale. Top management encouraged all levels of supervision to spend relaxed time with employees in order to hear their concerns and effect change, if they could. Virginia always attended the teas when she was in the office. She enjoyed getting to know her people in a more relaxed atmosphere.

As Virginia accepted a cup of tea, Rita appeared at her side. Her friend looked happy to see her after the long weekend. As usual, they would have considerable gossip to share.

"Well hello, stranger. How was your weekend?" Rita cooed as she placed two cucumber sandwiches on her plate beside a slice of cake.

"Perfect until Rob received a call yesterday morning, and had to cut his stay short. He hadn't planned to leave today. How was yours?" Virginia replied as she nibbled on a huge chocolate cookie. Whenever she needed consolation, as she did now with Rob's return to Paris, she reached for chocolate. Something about the richness always made her feel better.

"Uneventful. I didn't do much. Why didn't you call me? We could have gone to a movie or something," Rita said between bites.

"I guess I wasn't much company after he left. I went to Kew for the flower show and stayed there until they closed the gates. It's one of the most restful places in England. I strolled around for a while, grabbed a light meal, and then I came home. It's not easy being in this long-distance relationship."

"You still should have rung me up. I would have liked to have kept you company. Besides, I haven't been to Kew since I was a little girl and my mum took us to the show. I would have liked to have seen the gardens," Rita replied with only slightly hurt feelings.

"Sorry. I guess I just didn't think." Virginia handed the waiter her dishes and gave her full attention to Rita.

"The weight of that rock on your hand must have drained your energy. I'm surprised that you're not wearing your arm in a sling," Rita teased as she looked nonchalantly around the room.

"Ah, so you noticed." Virginia chuckled gaily.

"I'd have to be blind not to see it. I'm tempted to pull out my shades, it's so bright," Rita teased as she studied her friend's hand.

"Stop that! Other people will see you! I don't plan to make a general announcement about our engagement. So far, you're the only one who knows about it," Virginia stated as she pulled her hand away and stuffed it into the pocket of her suit coat.

Growing somber, Rita commented, "I guess the ring and the commitment make it even harder for you to be apart now. When will you see each other again? Are you going to Paris any time soon?"

"I don't know. Rob hasn't called since he returned. As soon as I hear from him, I'll be able to make plans. I hope we won't have to be apart as long this time," Virginia replied as Pamela and Catherine joined them. The two women were colleagues of Rita's, and managers in the adjacent unit. The four of them had lunched together, but neither of them exactly considered the women friends, although they were about their ages and very friendly.

"Hi, Virginia. I saw you at the Victoria and Albert Museum over the weekend. You were with John Robinson. I guess you were showing him around town, huh?" Pamela demanded, being the more inquisitive of the two.

"We were doing some sightseeing. He was here for a meeting and the weekend," Virginia replied honestly.

"You looked as if you were enjoying each other's company," Catherine added with a big smile.

"We're old friends from the States," Virginia replied without divulging any additional information.

"Oh, we thought it might have been more than that. Anyway, you certainly had good weather for showing him around London," Pamela replied as she began to lose interest in the discussion. Now that she had failed to uncover any information, she no longer cared about Virginia's weekend.

Virginia and Rita exchanged a furtive glance as teatime ended and everyone returned to their offices. When she was ready to make the announcement, Virginia would shout the news to everyone. Now, however, she wanted to keep the relationship to herself. She had plans to make, and was as yet uncertain about her direction.

"She certainly is nosey," Rita commented as they stood outside Virginia's office door.

"She means well. I'm just not ready to let people know. I don't know Rob's feelings about a public office relationship. Someone's bound to notice the ring. I'll deal with it then." Virginia returned to her desk.

"You could always let his identity remain a mystery. That way, you'd be not only a Yank, but a woman of intrigue, as well," Rita offered with a raised eyebrows.

"You've been reading too many mystery novels." Virginia laughed with a shake of her head. "Let's eat out tonight. I'm not in the mood to stay alone in my apartment."

"Sounds good to me. Pick me up when you're ready. See you," Rita replied and waved.

The rest of the day passed in a flurry of activity, for which Virginia was very grateful. When she and Rita finally reached home, they changed and then walked to their favorite restaurant down the street. From the crowd in the little place, it seemed as if the warm, late spring weather had brought everyone out for dinner. Finally, after standing in line for thirty minutes, they slipped into a booth.

"Have you ever seen so many people? It's as if they're giving away food here. A little warm weather, and all of London turns out," Virginia quipped as they looked around at the crowd.

"Hard to believe that this is our sleepy little place, isn't it? We'll have to find another restaurant if we want to escape the crowd from now on," Rita replied over the happy laughter of the diners.

"It's not so bad. At least everyone's happy. It wasn't so long ago that the whole city looked devastated from the IRA attacks. I'll take this any time." Virginia studied the familiar menu. To celebrate the warm weather, the proprietor had added a light salmon mousse to the usual steak and kidney pie, fish and chips, omelets, and bangers.

As the waiter took their order, Virginia looked around the room at the happy faces. Families chatted gaily about work and school. Solitary men and women devoured their meals, along with their "Do not disturb" novels. Couples linked fingers and gazed at each other in the particular way known only to lovers. Feeling lonely for Rob, she turned her attention to Rita's conversation.

"So, what are your plans? Will you request a transfer?" Rita repeated with irritation still lingering in her voice at all the commotion in their usually sedate restaurant.

"Strange you should ask." Virginia replied with a nod of her head that made her earrings jiggle. "My boss stopped by to see me this morning. He wanted to know if I'd like to throw my hat into the ring for a newly created position in the Paris office. It's basically the same job as the one I'm doing here. The company wants to expand, and needs people with expertise to lead the charge. I'm seriously thinking about it."

"I'll miss you, but I think you should go. I wouldn't leave my handsome lonely fiancé in Paris by himself. Sounds like trouble to me. However, going there would mean starting over professionally and socially. With the exception of Rob, you wouldn't know anyone. I wouldn't be there to teach you the city." Rita smiled as she stirred her iced tea.

"Don't worry about me. I didn't know anyone here, either, and look at the great friend I've made. I'll tell him that I'm interested in the transfer tomorrow. I got the distinct impression that there really isn't a pool of applicants. He made it sound as if he were only feeling me out to see if I'd be interested in a job that already has my name on it. You know how people act when they're only asking to be polite, but really planning to do something that involves you, anyway?" Virginia munched contentedly on the succulent meal.

"I know all too well. That's how I got this job three years ago. My boss mentioned it casually over tea one afternoon. I wasn't against it, but I didn't jump at the opportunity, either. The next day, the announcement appeared that I'd been promoted. At least, you have a reason for wanting to transfer. I was perfectly happy in York." Rita smeared butter on her toast.

"Why don't you see about coming with me? We'd have a great time together. Rob's always busy. We could take a working vacation. There's probably a position like yours waiting to be filled in that office, too. Ask around and see," Virginia urged as she poured another cup of tea and added half a packet of brown sugar.

"To Paris? Well, I hadn't really thought about it. Virginia, this is too sudden. I have my flat to sublet. I just don't know how I'd do it," Rita said, trying to convince Virginia that this part of her plan was half-baked.

"The company will take care of the sublet. You know that. I've already looked at the relocation package from here to Paris, and it's wonderful. You can sublet, or the company will cover the rent if you're only on temporary assignment. Think about it," Virginia added encouragingly while looking at Rita over her cup of tea.

Studying the dessert menu, Rita replied, "Okay, you've made your point. Besides, an assignment to the Paris office, temporary or not, will look great on my resumé. Not many people have the opportunity to work in a new location with exciting scenery and stimulating people, and also help grow the company."

"You're too good. I'm sure your sacrifice for the good of the company will not go unnoticed." Virginia chuckled as she watched Rita pretend to be insulted. "Paris, here we come!"

The next day Virginia and Rita spoke with their

respective bosses and set the temporary transfers in motion. Virginia's boss was very pleased that she had taken his hint and willingly agreed to head up a similar division in Paris. Since she had kept her relationship with Rob a secret, he did not suspect that her acceptance of his suggestion was in any way linked to romantic involvement. He simply thought that he had done a masterful job of selling her on the idea. Virginia only smiled, and allowed him to feel smug about his role in her decision. She did not see any reason to disabuse him.

Rita's boss was initially shocked at her request, but he quickly decided that she was indeed the perfect person for the position. He knew that she had moved reluctantly from York to London, and had missed the country setting. However, she had proven herself an immensely capable manager, and would certainly be an asset to the Paris office. Rita had the right mix of personality and charm teamed with professional acumen to inspire subordinates to give their best.

By the end of the day, the company's relocation office had made all their plans. The company would cover their rent while Virginia and Rita worked in Paris. The travel representative had purchased train tickets from Victoria Station that would take them to Dover and the connection to the Chunnel. Once in Calais, they would board a high-speed train that would whisk them to Paris. The Chunnel and its speedy connections had become the chosen method of travel for many people, who considered them faster than flying from Heathrow or Gatwick to Charles De Gaulle and then taking a taxi into the busy city. Once in Paris, Virginia and Rita would report to the designated personnel office that had arranged for their use of company-owned apartments. All Virginia and Rita had to do was to pack their personal belongings and go.

Virginia's phone call to her parents had not been as smooth. Although they were thrilled by her engagement news, they did not like the idea that she would follow Rob to Paris. They were of the old school, and thought a woman should be married before following her lover. However, when her parents realized the depth of her affection for Rob and her determination, they conceded. After all, Virginia was a grown woman who had to follow her own destiny.

For Virginia's part, she would not be swayed from her course regardless of the criticism, and no matter how firmly it was delivered. Even if her parents had not agreed on her course of action, she was going to Paris to be closer to Rob, and nothing and no one could stop her. She had already left her homeland, crossed an ocean, and traveled more than three thousand miles to England to be near him. Certainly a little thing like the English Channel was not going to stop her now. She had learned the truth of the old adage: "Home is where the heart is." Her home was with Rob in France, or wherever work took him.

Virginia had reasoned that this assignment would also be beneficial for her career. The company thought so highly of her work that it encouraged her to take the risk of working in an untested environment. Her bosses knew that she had the management skills and the savvy to be able to handle any situation. Her education and professional training had placed Virginia among the brightest and best in the United States branch of the company.

Since arriving in London, she had proven that she deserved her reputation by becoming one of the stars of that office. Now, she was off to Paris, to prove herself once again. Even if she were not going to Rob, Virginia would have been extremely excited about the challenge of the unknown.

Rob could hardly wait until Virginia arrived. Although she had not told him that she was coming, he had heard through the company grapevine that her transfer was in the works. However, he did not phone her to spoil the surprise. When Virginia appeared in Paris, he would act appropriately surprised. Still, he found it difficult not to say anything that would spoil her plans during their nightly conversations. Rob simply expressed regret when Virginia told him that she would be unavailable for their Friday evening call because of tickets to the theater with Rita. As they hung up, he promised to phone her early on Saturday, knowing that Virginia would be securely in his arms by then.

Now that Rita had committed herself to following Virginia, she was ready to go, and equally unwilling to change her plans. She had always dreamed of seeing Paris one day. She had not planned for the opportunity to arrive with so little preamble. However, she was always game for an adventure.

Every night after work, Virginia and Rita poured over books about France, especially Paris, until their vision grew blurry, their heads began to roll forward, and sleep overtook them. Finally, too exhausted to turn another page, they closed their books and bid each other goodnight. The next day over lunch, they began their preparations again. They were as excited as vacationers going on a trip to exotic foreign lands, and did not want to miss a single sight.

"The Louvre has one of the most impressive art collections in the world," Rita said. She read the information about the arts in Paris as she munched her Caesar salad.

"Yes. Did you know that the French resistance movement smuggled many of those same paintings and sculptures out of the city before the Nazi occupation began? If it hadn't been for those brave people, the paintings might have been stolen," Virginia said, showing off her knowledge of French history.

"Or worse. The paintings might have been hidden by Nazi generals, and among the many lost items. I can hardly wait to see the Arc de Triomphe, the Champs Élyseé, the fabulous gardens, Notre-Dame de Paris, and Sacre Coeur. It'll be nice to walk the streets of the city in which Josephine Baker bared her all—or, rather, almost all. I'm dying to go shopping at the Baccarat store." Rita turned the pages to see more beautiful photographs.

"I want to take in a show at the Folies-Bergères. I've heard so much about that dance hall that I just have to go. Somehow, I don't think I'll have any trouble convincing Rob to go to that theater with me. He might object to a Shakespearean drama in the West End, but I don't think he'll say anything against seminude women dancing the cancan," Virginia laughed heartily as she finished her soda and signaled for their checks.

Virginia and Rita were still laughing when they returned to the office. Their departure could not come soon enough. Both of them were already wearing the last of their unpacked clothing.

However, the best laid plans often hit snags. First, Virginia's transfer was held up because of problems that suddenly developed in the London office. For weeks she labored to settle the dispute between several employees. Once that was finally done, her boss—with a few words of apology—assigned her to work on a major presentation to a newly signed corporate client. While Virginia was making the last presentation, the managing partner of the Paris office phoned to say that he had been optimistic in thinking that her division would be ready for operation so soon. He wanted to delay another month.

Realizing that she would never be able to surprise Rob by simply appearing in Paris, Virginia shared her plans with him as she grew more frustrated by the delay. Rob, of course, was delighted at first, and could hardly wait until she joined him. However, as the days dragged into weeks and then into months, he began to question the possibility of putting their dream into reality, too.

In the months that passed, Virginia and Rob consoled themselves with weekend visits when work allowed, and middle of the night phone calls. They communicated more by E-mail than long distance, because each of them always had time to read the contents of their in box. They cherished each message, reading it repeatedly. The most precious times were those spent holding hands.

Thinking that Virginia would arrive any minute, and that they would soon share an apartment, Rob had moved out of the company's apartment and into one of the most prestigious gentlemen's clubs in Paris. He did not see the point in maintaining a two-bedroom apartment with den when he was hardly ever at home. Besides, another member of the organization had arrived with his wife and two children, and needed the space.

Rob was content living in the club. He took the

few meals he ate there in the dining room with the other single businessmen. Maid service kept the large comfortable room perfectly clean. The only problem with his new living arrangement was that women were not allowed. When Virginia visited, they spent their nights in a hotel near the Louvre that he had arranged for her.

Since she did not wish to go to Paris alone, Rita postponed her relocation each time that Virginia put hers on hold. Her boss was very happy to accommodate her. Besides, Rita was only going on this adventure to be with Virginia. She had every intention of returning to London after a few months of the temporary assignment.

Finally, on a hot summer day in June, Virginia and Rita locked their apartments and headed for the train station. Rita chattered constantly on the train ride about the sights she would see and the people she would meet, forgetting the fact that she spoke only hastily learned French. Virginia let her ramble, knowing that the reality of miscommunication would temper her enthusiasm soon enough. The first time Rita tried to follow instructions based on her improperly formatted question, she would realize that she was not in London anymore, and that Paris was not always the friendliest of cities.

As soon as they cleared the London city limits, the meadows and rooftops looked surprisingly out of place compared to the hectic city. Virginia discovered that the beauty of the English countryside impressed her as being more splendid and majestic now that everything was green and lush.

Almost immediately the gentle swishing of the train's wheels taking them closer and closer to Dover put Rita to sleep. Although she loved her friend dearly, Virginia was all too happy about the peaceful quiet escape from Rita's excited chatter. She relished the moments for quiet thought.

Gazing lovingly at the diamond that glittered on the third finger of her left hand, Virginia leaned back in her seat and thought of Rob. So much had happened since she decided to transfer to Paris to be with him. She had made plans to leave London, turned over the care of her apartment to the company, phoned her parents about her change of address with a promise to phone often, and managed to keep Rita from becoming totally hysterical with joy. She had shared each delay with her parents until she could call with her final plans.

There was no turning back now. The adventure had begun for all three of them. Virginia wondered where it would end.

As the train sped to Dover, her eyelids became heavy. She crossed her arms over her chest and allowed her eyes to close. As usual, she dreamed of riding on a train that was leaving the station. Usually, Rob was seconds too late to join her as the train pulled out. This time, however, he managed to touch her fingertips with his. In her sleep, Virginia could feel the warmth of his hand on hers.

In a few hours he would again be at her side.

Thirteen

The trip to Dover seemed to take forever. Every farm they passed and every village through which the train sped brought Virginia closer to Rob. However, the ride seemed it would never end. The train was perfectly comfortable, and Rita was a delightful traveling companion when she was awake, but Virginia could take little comfort in either. She would not feel relief until she was finally in Paris and in Rob's arms. Too many delays had already interfered with her happiness.

When they arrived in Dover at noon, Virginia and Rita immediately tried to transfer to the Chunnel, only to find that it had been closed. The IRA had finally done what everyone in London had feared; it had issued a bomb threat against the rapid transit tunnel laid under the English Channel that connected English with Europe via the French port of Calais.

"Now what?" Rita asked as she stood knee deep in bags. The other displaced passengers appeared to be asking the same question.

"We'll take the ferry. It's notoriously rocky, but we'll survive," Virginia replied as she led her friend toward the rapidly filling bus that would take them to the ferry.

"I'm not much on small boats," Rita stated with a worried expression on her face.

"You'll like it," Virginia stated as she settled their bags around their feet and gripped one of the last two dangling leather straps on the overcrowded bus.

"Maybe I'll just stay here until the Chunnel train's running again. Dover's a lovely city," Rita said as she tried to leave the bus, pushed forward by the mass of people entering behind her.

"Too late. We're on this adventure together," Virginia said as the bus jerked forward.

"Oh my," Rita groaned, already envisioning the crossing.

Virginia and Rita joined the other travelers as they lined up and entered the ferry. Rita said nothing, but bit on her bottom lip constantly.

Once underway, they found the crossing rough, and hard on the stomach. The choppy June hurricane season had angered the water in the channel, causing it to batter the ferry and toss it around. The waves were almost dangerously high. The wind was hard and hot. As the white cliffs vanished in the distance, Virginia and Rita moaned and leaned overboard for the third time.

Calais brought very welcome relief from the pitching and rocking. Clutching their suitcases and trying to smooth their wind-tossed hair, they made their way to the train station and boarded the waiting express to Paris. Settling onto the cushions, Virginia and Rita felt safer and healthier now that they were once again on dry land.

"I hope the next time we cross the channel the water will be calm. That was horrible!" Rita groaned, still very aware of her sick stomach.

Virginia, faring a little better, said, "It was rough,

wasn't it? But at least we saw the white cliffs from the channel side."

"I didn't see anything except black water. I'll fly, or take the Chunnel back. No more ferries for me." Rita was not her cheerful self.

With a chuckle Virginia said, "One day, something will make you change your mind."

"I wouldn't count on it," Rita replied sullenly.

By the time they reached Paris, Virginia and Rita felt much better. A rosy color had returned to their cheeks and lips, replacing the greenish tinge from seasickness. Once again, they were excited about the prospects of beginning a new life in a city far from home or friends.

As soon as the train slowed in the station, they spotted a man from the travel division of their office, who held up a sign bearing their names. Taking their bags and leading them to the waiting car, he introduced himself as Jacques Duval. It was his charge to meet all arriving employees of Virginia and Rita's status and transport them safely to their accommodations. Paris was no more dangerous than Washington, DC, New York, or London. However, for people who did not speak fluent French, it could be expensive. More than one tourist had paid more than necessary for a taxi ride from the airport or the train station.

Bowing gallantly as he shook their hands, Duval explained in heavily accented English, "I have the pleasure of taking you to your new apartments in a fashionable section of Paris near the Cathedral of the Sacre Coeur. On our way, I will drive you around town on a brief sightseeing trip. Since it is much too late in the afternoon for you to consider working today, I will stop briefly at the nearest grocery for you to pick up a few necessities for tonight. If it is all right with you, I will pick you up tomorrow around noon, for a complete orientation tour of the city to help you learn your way around prior to Monday's workday."

"Mr. Duval, you've been most kind, meeting us at the station. Please don't feel obligated to be our tour guide, as well. Besides, I have a friend in town who will show us the sights, and I've been here many times." Virginia knew she would like his company and the tour, but she did not want to be a burden to him.

"But *I* haven't. Mr. Duval may take *me* around tomorrow," Rita interrupted as another must-see statue passed quickly by her window.

"Very well, it's settled. Who better to show you the sights of Paris than someone who has lived his whole life here? I will hear nothing more about it. You are guests in my country, and valued clients of my office. It is the duty of my office to serve. I am at your disposal. If you and your friend decide to join us, there's plenty of space for two more," Duval answered as he ushered them into the air-conditioned limousine.

Immediately, Virginia and Rita felt relief from the oppressive heat of June in Paris. Driving from the station down the Champs Élysée, Mr. Duval pointed out the Arc de Triomphe, the shopping district, and the Louvre. Turning left away from the Seine, he moved toward the Paris Opéra, the Madeleine, and finally the Cathedral of Sacre Coeur in all its glory, sitting on top of the hill.

"Where is everyone? Is this a holiday?" Virginia asked as she scanned the almost empty streets.

"Oh, no. It's June. Everyone who can leave Paris

does so in the summer. It'll get worse in August. You'll find that the Opéra has closed, as well as many of the restaurants. The ones that are open this week will probably close next. That's the way it is here in the summer. It's too hot to work," Duval replied happily and with pride.

"I certainly hope that the museums won't be closed. I've waited my whole life to see Paris. I'll be very disappointed if nothing's open. Where are the tourists?" Rita almost whined as she stared out the window at the virtually empty avenues. She had imagined that Paris would be as busy as London, and filled with visitors.

"They are here. Don't despair. Remember that this is afternoon, and many people are inside resting from the heat. The museums and most of the shops will reopen later this evening. There's still more than enough to see. Now is a wonderful time to take a trip to Versailles, too. It'll be hot, but magnificent," Duval replied as he pulled to the curb.

Duval soon stopped at a little grocery store and then at their lovely, red brick, apartment building with balconies, two blocks away. Virginia and Rita strained their necks to see everything the city of light had to offer. They could hardly wait until he picked them up in the morning for the daylight tour.

As Duval deposited their bags on the sidewalk, he said, "I'll pick you up early tomorrow. I suggest a walking tour of your neighborhood tonight. *Bon soir.*"

To their delight, Virginia and Rita found that each of their apartments provided a fabulous view of the city spreading out before them at the foot of the hill. Running between apartments, they compared sights as they stepped onto the balconies and inhaled the rich aromas of Paris. The perfume of freshly baked bread rose to greet them from a bakery down the street.

Rita was so stunned by the splendor of the city that she did not notice as a large cockroach casually strolled past her foot on its way toward the bag holding her supplies. Virginia saw it and, with one carefully placed foot, removed it from Rita's apartment forever. The splat was almost deafening in the silent apartment.

"What was that?" Rita asked, pulling herself away from the view at the crackling sound.

"Only a cockroach, your first visitor. I wonder what else we'll find waiting for us," Virginia answered, strolling into the bedroom. Rita's apartment was slightly smaller than her corner unit, and it did not have as many windows.

"Oh, no! I hate bugs of any kind, but especially cockroaches. Let's hope that's the last one," Rita moaned as she scooped up the remains in a thick paper towel.

"I wouldn't count on that, if I were you. This building's very old. All kinds of bugs have had the opportunity to move in here." Virginia directed Rita toward her apartment next door.

The company-owned apartments were spacious and comfortable, homey though not luxurious. Virginia was pleased with what she saw as she studied her kitchen. It had recently been renovated, and still smelled of paint. It was not very large, but it was clean, with plenty of counter space and a table and two chairs.

The bedroom was also tastefully furnished, in heavy mahogany furniture. Two nightstands flanked the queen-size bed. Each held a lamp with twin, milk-white, glass globes. There was an armoire, a dresser, and a vanity table with a little floral uphol-stered chair. Much to her delight, Virginia found the bathroom spotlessly clean, shining, and very modern. The decorator had even installed a bidet.

Returning to the large living room from which the dining room branched, Virginia discovered the same care in decorating. She had missed the com-fortable elegance of the apartment when they first entered, being attracted by the view from the mas-sive double doors that opened onto a lovely balcony. Virginia decided that as soon as she could find the local flower market, she would turn the balcony into an oasis for flowers.

After Rita returned to her apartment next door, Virginia walked into the kitchen and put away her few purchases of bread, cheese, cereal, milk, coffee, and fruit. She was suddenly very tired, ready to get some sleep. The day had started early before the first birds began to sing. Now, looking at her watch, she discovered that it was already almost nine o'clock. The long days of summer and the beauty of Paris had made her forget the time. She could not go to sleep until after Rob called. His secretary had said that he would be tied up until late. Virginia was not surprised that she had not heard from him.

Padding next-door in her slippers, Virginia knocked at Rita's door. A sleepy Rita answered. She had already brushed her teeth and put on her night-gown, and was unpacking the last of her bags when Virginia arrived.

"I didn't realize I had so much stuff. It didn't seem like so much while I was packing it, but now I see it's incredible how much I've accumulated. I'm beat, and I'm going to bed as soon as I finish this. I just can't let these bags sit here overnight. I know that it doesn't make sense, but it's one of my little quirks." Rita returned to her bedroom, with Virginia following her.

"Sounds like a good idea to me." Virginia answered with fatigue heavy in her voice. "I'll probably do the same thing. I want to get up early, too, so that I can finish my shopping before Mr. Duval arrives. I'm only still awake because I'm waiting for Rob to call. I brought my new cell phone with me."

"We'll have to return one day when we don't have to work. I know we'll see many of the sights while we're here, but I'd like to be a real tourist in this town, too," Rita said as she tossed the last of her things in the dresser drawers and closed the door. Stacking her suitcases in the close, Rita indicated non too subtly that she was ready for bed.

"See you tomorrow," Virginia said as she walked toward the door.

"I hope Rob calls soon. I'm really tired, and I'm sure you are, too. Goodnight," Rita commented as she walked Virginia to the door.

"Bye," Virginia said as her friend closed and locked the door. Virginia could hear Rita's loud yawning as she walked toward her apartment.

Virginia sat in the living room and watched the stars for as long as she could. Her head fell forward and her eyes closed while the air-conditioner hummed in the silent night. She awoke jerkily as the bells of Sacre Coeur intoned midnight. Rising, she walked to her bedroom, turning out lights as she went. Rob had not called, and she was too tired to stay up any longer. Slipping under the light duvet

cover, Virginia slipped into an immediate and
dreamless sleep.

A loud chorus of birds greeted her as the morning
dawned bright . . . brighter than any Virginia had
ever seen at home or in London. No wonder people
loved Paris and called it the city of lights. The city
sparkled more brightly than any she had ever seen.

Looking from the balcony door toward Sacre
Coeur, Virginia almost gasped at the splendor of the
view. The sun radiated off the white marble of the
glorious cathedral with its three terraces, statues of
saints, small and large domes, and gold lions. She
had never seen anything so gorgeous. She hoped
that Duval would include a tour of the cathedral on
the itinerary. If he did not, she would stop there
herself later in the day.

Rita arrived just as Virginia finished brushing her
hair. They had both dressed casually and comfortably against the heat of Paris in June. They had
taken Duval's advice and unpacked their umbrellas
as protection against the burning sun, too. Despite
its many parks, Paris was a city of large expanses of
open treeless areas.

Quickly slicing some bread and cheese and making a hasty pot of coffee, Virginia pulled together
their light breakfast so that they could step out into
the city that was now their home. She and Rita ate
hungrily of the sweet crusty bread and devoured velvety cheese tasting of honey.

By the time they left the apartment, the streets
were already congested with cars and pedestrians
who appeared to be in a hurry to go nowhere in
particular. They pushed past with loaves of unwrapped bread under their arms and net bags containing meat, cheese, and fruit swinging from their

hands. Few people spoke to each other or even ac-
knowledged that they were aware of each other—unlike in London, where everyone smiled or nodded
greetings. The French seemed to be content being
alone in a crowd.

Virginia and Rita eased their way into the traffic
inching its way down the hill and away from Sacre
Coeur. They passed several small grocery stores on
their way to the main outdoor market a few blocks
south. Mingling with the other shoppers, they purchased fruit, more cheese, vegetables, and a small
piece of ham. Virginia also purchased pots of flowers
for the balcony. Everything was terribly expensive,
but the vendors carried abundant supplies, so that
anyone who could afford the prices would not have
to go away empty-handed. As Virginia peeled off
francs from the money she had changed from
pounds before leaving London, she wondered how
the poor fared, and decided that they probably did
without meat and made most of their own cheese
and baked their own bread. The cost of living in
Paris was very high.

By the time Virginia and Rita had made their purchases and wandered around their neighborhood a
bit, it was almost time to meet Mr. Duval at their
apartment. Hurrying along with the flow of traffic,
they followed a previously unexplored wide flight of
steps that led upward past the little shop on the corner and beyond their building to the Sacre Coeur
itself. Climbing higher and higher with their purchases growing heavier with each step, they finally
found themselves in a wide plaza at the rear of the
cathedral, where vendors sold paintings, religious artifacts, and clothing. They were swept along by the
tide of people until they reached the front of the

cathedral, where they managed to step aside for a look at the imposing structure rising high above them, up still more steps leading to the front doors.

Having known the sober red of St. Patrick's Cathedral in New York and the understated, soft, off-white marble of Westminster Abbey, Virginia found Sacre Coeur, with its gleaming stark whiteness and gold ornaments, dazzling beyond belief. Even the heat of the summer morning could not outdo the radiant warmth given off by the cathedral. Virginia and Rita stood open-mouthed, admiring it, until finally, without speaking a word to each other, they were drawn by its magic into its dark interior. In its stillness, they found the true spirit of the church. Elderly worshippers, younger women and men, and children knelt in prayer.

Kneeling beside an old woman in tattered clothing whose soiled hands shook as she prayed the decades of her rosary, Virginia and Rita offered up prayers for family and friends. Looking up into the domed ceiling with its elaborate design, Virginia watched the smoke from the candles that lighted the cathedral rise upward, taking her prayers with it.

Leaning close to Rita, Virginia whispered, "I wish Rob could be here. He would love the carvings and the oil paintings. We haven't taken the time to visit here on my weekend trips to Paris."

"If he ever stops working long enough to return your call, he certainly would enjoy it here. This is stunning. I thought St. Paul's was breathtaking, but this cathedral is really out of this world." Rita could hardly express herself, having been struck silent by the glory of the cathedral.

Once outside again, they hurried along the winding streets back down the hill to their apartments. They only had time to put their purchases away before Mr. Duval's limousine pulled up. Jumping out, he rushed around to the passenger side to open the door for them. The sun played in his graying hair and mustache, causing him to appear quite dashing.

The stately vehicle glided down the hill and caused quite a stir among the children while Mr. Duval pointed out the local sights along the way. They passed the Moulin Rouge, drove through Montmartre, and circled the imposing Paris Opéra. They stopped at the Madeleine for a closer look before continuing onward to Notre-Dame Cathedral, which sat on an island in the Seine. They lingered until he reminded them that there were other stops to make before the afternoon sun disappeared.

Next they motored around the Left Bank and made a leisurely circuit through the neighborhoods, pausing here and there for a quick peek down an alley or interesting side street. They drove past the university buildings until they reached the Eiffel Tower. Standing high above the city on four stout legs, the tower built for the World's Fair of 1889 rose above the city. Straining her neck to see to the top, Virginia silently vowed to return to that very spot with Rob as soon as she could find him and drag him away from his office.

Although Virginia had visited Rob in Paris, she had spent most of the time in her hotel with him and had seen little of the city. Rob did not want to spend the little time they had together in seeing the sights of the city in which he lived. He preferred to study her face and body. He reasoned that they would have plenty of time to spend looking at statues and paintings once they were together in Paris.

Checking the power supply on her phone, Virginia resigned herself to another day without Rob. His job kept him so busy that she wondered if she would see more than his sleeping form once they started living together. She certainly hoped that she would get more from moving to Paris than just the sound of Rob snoring in her ear at night.

Their last stop before Mr. Duval returned them to their apartment was the Louvre. On the way, they drove past the Arc de Triomphe and down the Champs Élysée, where pedestrians busily rushing here and there clogged the wide sidewalks. Although prices were high, the restaurants along the boulevard seemed to be doing a brisk business. All the people they had not seen on the streets when they first arrived were out in force, despite the horrible heat and humidity.

The Seine bordered the Louvre on one side, and impressive stately homes stood on the other. In front of it spread the Tuileres Gardens, an immense expanse of breathtaking lawns and trees with fountains that invited hot sweaty visitors to stop for a few minutes. Vendors sold ices to cool down perspiring people as they strolled in the shade of overarching trees.

Before returning them to their apartment, Mr. Duval took one side trip to the office. He wanted them to be able to find it on Monday morning without any difficulty. Driving the route they should walk that morning, he showed them the shortcuts from their apartment building to the office. Phoning Rob's office and receiving no answer, Virginia decided against making the trip to the tenth floor. She would go home and wait in the cool apartment. Rob could not possibly be tied up all day, not on a Saturday.

When they finally reached their new home, Virginia and Rita were exhausted from the tour, but very grateful for Mr. Duval's efforts. Waving goodbye, the driver eased the enormous car into the traffic and vanished in a cloud of heat vapors. Virginia made a note in her pad to write a thank you to Duval as soon as she rested from the heat for a few minutes.

Her apartment was especially inviting as the sunset shone through the balcony doors and the cool air circulated through the rooms. Virginia stood for a long time looking down on the city that was to be her home for the next few months before returning to London, or the States. Living in Paris would definitely not pose a hardship. Already Virginia loved her new city.

A gentle knocking at the door broke the silence and Virginia's reverie. Turning away from the beauty of Paris and the flowers that brightened the balcony, she opened the door. To her surprise, the visitor was not Rita.

"Rob!" Virginia exclaimed as she rushed into his arms.

"I thought I'd never get out of meetings. I'm so sorry that I wasn't here to meet you," Rob whispered as he buried his face in Virginia's neck and breathed deeply of her sweet fragrance.

"That doesn't matter anymore. I'm so glad to see you. Where are your bags? You're moving in, aren't you?" Virginia asked as she stood on tiptoe to peer over his shoulder into the hall.

"We'll have to delay that for a while. I have to go out of town," Rob replied with a sad shake of his head.

"Out of town! I just arrived, and you're leaving?

What is this?" Suddenly the bright room looked dismal, and the thrill of their reunion died all too suddenly.

Taking her hands and leading her to the sofa, Rob pulled Virginia into his arms and they sat together and looked into the sunny city. Slowly, he allowed the words that almost stuck in his throat to flow. Virginia listened carefully as he spoke, and refused to allow the tears of disappointment to fall.

"It can't be helped. We're opening a new office in Rome, and it's my job to do the groundwork. Remember, that's what brought us to Europe in the first place. That's my job. It's what I do. I leave Sunday night for a few weeks," Rob explained slowly as he struggled with the continued separation.

"You know as well as I do that few weeks can quickly turn into months. Well, I guess I'll just have to enjoy Paris without you. I'll certainly see a lot of Europe this way. Me in London, you in Paris. Me in Paris, you in Rome. What's next?" Virginia replied with a sulky tone in her voice.

"Let's hope that we'll go home after this. The company only has plans to open one more office, and that's in Greece. Let's not ruin the time we have. I'm game for an afternoon of sightseeing, and I'm all yours for most of the day tomorrow," Rob offered as he pulled Virginia to her feet.

"Greek, ha? Well, that's another country I've always wanted to visit. Maybe you should volunteer for that job after you finish setting up the Rome office," Virginia replied as she gathered her purse and sunglasses. She was almost serious.

"We'll see. I'm not sure that I want that assignment. You're adjusting too easily to our long-distance romance. You might not want to settle down with me if I don't put down roots soon." Rob smiled with relief that Virginia was coping so well with the unfortunate turn of events.

"I haven't adjusted at all, Rob, but there's no point in pouting. You do have a job to do, and you're good at it. I'm good at what I do. Fortunately, we have at least managed to get us on the same continent. I don't mind flying to Rome. It's only a short trip. Weekends in the shadow of the Vatican sound great to me. I just hope that we'll find a cure for this travel bug before we're too old to have a family." Virginia heard sarcasm creep into her voice again.

They spent the rest of the weekend seeing all the sights that Rob had refused to visit during his short residency in Paris. Now that he was leaving again, he did not mind waiting in lines with other visitors. Even the heat and humidity of the end of June could not put a damper on the enjoyment they felt in simply being together.

That night, Virginia and Rob enjoyed the sweetness of each other with the same hunger that they had devoured the city. Lying spent on damp sheets, they talked about their future and their return to the States some day. They both knew that Rob's immediate involvement in the plans of the company would eventually diminish as the expansion ended. In the meantime, they would be content with the time they had together.

As Virginia drifted off to sleep, the old dream returned. As she waved good-bye from the train, Rob stood on the platform surrounded by luggage. As the dust cleared and she looked down the track, he had vanished.

One of these days, nothing would keep them apart.

Fourteen

Virginia did not believe it was possible, but, on Monday the streets were even more crowded, and the pedestrians were even pushier. What had been a manageable crush over the weekend was now bedlam as people scurried to work, men sold newspapers from corner stands, and minimarkets sprang up everywhere. The workday Parisian crowd pushed and shoved more than that of London by a mile.

When Virginia and Rita arrived at the office after being propelled through the streets by the throngs of people, they were greeted by their new secretaries and shown into their new offices. With a sigh of relief, Virginia dove into her work and pushed thoughts of Rob's latest absence from her mind. One day the separation would end, but, until it did she had work to do. Rob was not the only one whose reputation was widespread throughout the company.

Virginia found herself being caught up in a feeling of euphoria and the scents of summer in Paris. She realized one evening on her way from work that she did not drag up the hill, but walked with a lightness to her stride as the beauty of the city filled her senses. All around her, the flowers were in bloom and the birds were singing. She found it was hard to be gloomy when everything was so bright and cheerful. Despite the heat, humidity, and predictions by the locals that it would only get worse, Virginia was very happy in her new home. Besides, if she could survive the summers in Washington, DC, where steam rose from the Potomac River, she could live comfortably in Paris.

Rita's sense of humor had returned as she became more comfortable with her ability to communicate in French, and she kept everyone laughing with her jokes and stories. To their surprise, she found that she remembered her college French without even trying. To Virginia, for whom learning a new language was never a problem, speaking French daily soon came easily. They were not Parisians, yet they were certainly comfortable living in Paris. Rita especially found the Left Bank enjoyable, so they visited the area of poets, artists, and scholars often. Virginia enjoyed walks in the gardens on both sides of the river, and spent many weekend hours in the sunshine. She always carried paper and pens with her so that she could write to Rob about all the things she saw. She shared everything with him, preferring letters to E-mails for personal reflections.

June lengthened into a full-fledged Parisian summer. Flowers bloomed in every garden and every window box. Children played in the streets, lovers strolled the parks and filled the bistros, and older couples clucked their tongues at the antics of the young. The flowerpots on Virginia's balcony echoed the enthusiasm for the warm weather by overflowing with blossoms of every imaginable color. Everywhere the feeling of expectation filled the air. No one knew exactly what would happen, but they all waited for it. No one wanted to miss it when it came.

And then one day, it did . . . the thunderstorms

of summer. Virginia had never seen such rain. It soaked through her umbrella and her raincoat, leaving her drenched and dripping. Everyone sniffled from the dreaded summer cold, and good humors changed overnight to bad. Galoshes were the footwear of choice for men and women. Any thoughts of looking fashionable were pushed aside as the wind and the rain pelted faces, streamed down windows, flooded gutters, and flattened the blooms on the flowers. Shopkeepers in doorways used papers to protect their heads, and finally gave up and went indoors to await customers who never arrived. It rained for two weeks without letting up.

And then, one day, as quickly as it had started, the rain stopped and the sun came out. Flowers lifted their soggy heads, children again ran wild in the parks, lovers strolled the gardens, and old people returned to commenting on the outrageous behavior of anyone not of their generation. Church bells that had appeared hushed and somber in the rain rang out joyously through all of Paris. The happy sound was deafening as Notre-Dame, Sacre Coeur, and all the smaller churches simultaneously rang their bells.

With the lightening of the weather and the moods came July and Bastille Day. Rob had said that he would come for the event. Since his departure for Rome in June, they had not been able to coordinate their weekends, and had spent almost a month apart. They were both looking forward to having time together.

Virginia busied herself preparing for Rob's return. She cleaned the apartment and bought extra food, knowing that Rob would be ready for meals at home after living on hotel food for a month. She bought a bottle of wine to toast their reunion, and flowers for every table.

Virginia was not the only one making preparations. The city of Paris was polishing its brass, hanging banners, blowing up balloons, and tuning instruments for the big parade down the Champs Élysée and onward to the Bastille. The gold and brass decorations on bridges had been polished to their original glory. They sparkled so brightly now in the sunshine that they were blinding. For the first time since coming to Paris, Virginia saw the warm side of the usually tight-lipped French. Everyone smiled and shouted greetings in the street as the excitement of the huge annual celebration filled their hearts with joy and happiness.

Virginia waited anxiously. Their plans had been thwarted so many times that she tried not to build up her hopes. However, she was swept up in the excitement of the city, and could not help herself. Virginia imagined meeting him at the airport or the train station and throwing her arms around him. Sometimes, she saw him at her front door. Always, Virginia faced the reality of an E-mail or phone call saying that his plans had changed. She was ready for any scenario.

Rita had heard from William, too. She had not seen him in months, although they had kept up a steady stream of E-mails and calls. A very warm relationship had developed between them. He had promised to come for the Bastille Day celebration, too.

The morning of the parade arrived brighter and louder than any Virginia had ever experienced. Everyone in Paris seemed to own a horn, and blow it all day. Car horns honked, bicycle bells tinkled, and church bells rang. Streamers and confetti floated everywhere, and covered the sidewalks of the Champs Élysée with multicolored spots and ribbons.

Virginia and Rita took their places on the curb. Every office and restaurant in town had closed for the day. Everyone in Paris lined the streets, hung from balconies, stood on steps, and peeked through crowds for glimpses of the parade participants.

As the bands struck the first notes, the crowd joyfully broke into "The Marseillais," the French national anthem. Tears flowed unashamedly down the cheeks of women and men alike. Handkerchiefs waved, flags unfurled, and hands clapped as the soldiers marched down the boulevard. People dressed in period costumes danced and sang along the route. They waved as they laughed and marched. It was almost like watching troops return from war. Only now, they were parading for the enjoyment of the spectators.

Virginia and Rita cried and held each other as they sang with gusto and shared happiness. Standing on tiptoe and looking as far down the Champs Élysée as she could, Virginia tried to see the end of the parade, which stretched for miles. Studying the faces in the crowd, she tried to see Rob's.

The music swelled as tanks rolled by the viewing stand. The crowd roared as a flyby of the combined armed forces filed the sky. Balloons rose skyward when the marching bands of each division paraded by in perfect drill order. Faces shone with pride in the brave men who were so often called to keep peace.

"Virginia, look!" Rita shouted over the music as she pointed to the third battalion to appear. "That's a precision drill team. Have you ever seen such skill?

They're wonderful! And look! Isn't that William in that limousine?"

Following Rita's pointing fingers, Virginia saw William riding in the first car, which carried the logo of the corporation. He looked much thinner than she remembered, but happy and proud to be in the spotlight. He waved to everyone along the route.

"Let's follow them to the Place de la Bastille. We'll be able to speak with William there," Virginia suggested, holding Rita's hand to keep her from charging past the police barricade into the street. She scanned the faces for sight of Rob, but she saw no one else that she knew. If Rob had planned to join the parade, he had missed his opportunity.

"Let's hurry before everyone else has the same idea," Rita said, pulling Virginia through the crush of people.

A huge crowd of people with happy faces had already beaten them there. Swarms stood mingling with the uniformed soldiers and costumed participants who had just finished the long march up the Champs Élysée and onward to the Place de la Bastille. They looked tired but happy, and ever so proud. Their families, friends, and the citizens of Paris, and all of France, could not stop hugging and kissing them. Bastille Day brought out the best in everyone.

Easing their way through the throng, they approached William's limousine. He was engaged in conversation with a pretty young woman, and did not see them walk up. Impatiently they waited until the crowd of admirers cleared, and then Virginia and Rita called to him. At first he did not believe his eyes as he looked from Rita to Virginia. Then, with a whoop that would have scared the pigeons if the Place de la Bastille had not been so noisy, he threw his arms around Rita and smothered her in kisses. Releasing her, he pulled Virginia to him for a loud kiss on the cheek.

"I didn't expect you two to find me so soon in all these people. What a great surprise! Wow! I've really missed you two. It's been too long. We're all finally in the same city again." William opened the car door and slid to the ground on one leg, using a crutch.

Neither Rita nor Virginia spoke, staring at the cast on his leg. They did not know what to say. He was so brave about the injury. He had not mentioned it in any of his letters. Immediately Rita wanted to take him in her arms and hold him close, but she feared he would think her reaction was from pity rather than love. Not knowing what to do, she did nothing, and he pulled his other crutch from the back seat and placed them both under his arms.

Balancing himself just right, William turned to them and said good-naturedly, "It took me a while to get used to them, but I'm good to go now. I'll be as good as new in no time. That'll teach me to stay on the ground. I don't think I'll do any more parachuting."

Rita slipped her arm lightly through his and beamed into his eyes. "I'll just bet you get around pretty well now, too. You're going to be hell on wheels when you finish physical therapy."

He grinned like a kid on Christmas morning and planted a kiss gently on Rita's lips. His future wife, although he had not asked her yet, had passed her test with flying colors. Now it was his friend's turn.

"May I still have the first dance when we return to the States?" William asked as he remembered Virginia's promise from their last corporate party on New Year's Eve.

"My dance card is rather full, but I think I can give a grounded jumper the first, the last, and any in between that Rita will share. It's great being together again. How much longer will you be in the cast?" Virginia queried as she joined in the fun despite missing Rob.

"Another two months, I think. I shattered it pretty well. Remind me never to do anything that dangerous again. I almost lost my dancing legs," William replied as they eased through the crowd, moving slowly toward the sidewalk.

Searching the crowd again for signs of Rob, Virginia turned to William and asked, "Where is he? I don't see him anywhere. Why didn't he join you in the company limo? As late as yesterday morning Rob promised to be here."

"You know more than I do. I haven't spoken to him in weeks. He's probably just lost in the crowd. I've never seen so many people. Not even the Fourth of July fireworks in DC draw this many people." William scanned the crowd for Rob.

"I'm going to the office to see if he's there. He might have gotten stuck in an emergency meeting. I'll see you two later," Virginia said, kissing her friends on the cheeks and walking away from the crowded avenues. She could not stand around waiting for him to appear. He might held up on meetings for hours. Worse still, he might still be in Rome.

The streets were so crowded that Virginia decided not to try hailing a cab. Instead, she would walk to the office. Maybe she would see Rob along the way.

The July sun was hot and the air thick as Virginia crossed Rue St. Honore, walking in the direction of

the Opéra and Sacre Coeur. She passed lovers sitting
at open-air cafés, children playing in the streets,
women waving from balconies. French flags flew
from every house and building. The fronts of cars
were draped with red, white, and blue tricolors. Love
was in the air as men and women walked hand in
hand through the streets. With a wistful look, Virginia wished she were one of them. Even the old
people smiled at the sight of happy people falling
in love all over again.

Virginia looked in every doorway as she rushed
up the steps to the office. The halls were empty and
silent. She found no one as she peered into the
semidarkness of each conference room and the office of the president. Not finding Rob among the
shadows, she quickly scribbled a note and taped it
to her office door. In it, she instructed him to meet
her at Sacre Coeur at four o'clock, where she would
wait until six before returning to her apartment. She
gave him directions there, too, just in case he had
forgotten in the weeks of separation.

Rushing from the building and up the hill toward
the cathedral and her apartment, Virginia stopped
at a little park where children's toys nestled among
wooden benches. Sitting near the swing set, she
rested, trying to think of what to do if he did not
meet her at the church or come to her apartment.
Her heart grew sick with worry, and her mind became quite troubled as the possible reasons for
Rob's absence flooded her thoughts. Maybe he had
been detained by unavoidable meetings, and would
appear at her apartment later. The worst and most
frightening thought was that he had stopped loving
her, and would not appear at all. It was always possible that a man capable of running the affairs of a

major corporation might break off his engagement with a woman he hardly ever saw. Distance did not always make the heart grow fonder.

Nothing in his conversations or E-mails would lead her to believe that their relationship was not on firm ground. However, Virginia had heard too many stories of women left at the altar by men who had simply decided not to wed and did not have the courage to break the engagement. She did not want to think that Rob was one of those men, but he might be. After all, he had left town as soon as she arrived. He claimed that the job required his constant change of address, but he might be using that as an excuse. Whatever was the reason for his absence, she would have to wait patiently until he explained things to her.

Covering her face with her hands, Virginia finally let the stress—of waiting for Rob to return, of being far from home, of his absence and the worries it caused—to take possession of her. She had been brave and strong for so long. She could not keep up the front, even to herself, any longer. Her shoulders shook as she sobbed, not caring who heard her or how foolish it made her look to be crying on a day of celebration. Bastille Day was not the time for tears.

Through her tears, she felt a hand resting gently on her shoulder. Wiping her eyes with her fingers, she looked up as the last of the afternoon's sun silhouetted the figure of a tall man in a black suit. She could tell from the width of his shoulders and the tilt of his head that it was Rob.

Rising, Virginia rushed into his arms. She threw her arms around him and held on as if her life depended on it. She showered his cheeks and lips with kisses, laughing and crying at the same time. Rob's strong arms crushed her to his chest as he buried his nose in her sweet fragrant neck.

Easing back to look into Virginia's eyes, Rob said, "Sorry I missed the parade. I had a meeting this morning in Rome at the Vatican, of all places, and couldn't get out of it. I caught a flight as soon as I could. I'm sorry I disappointed you. But I'm here now."

"I was so worried. Since you hadn't called or E-mailed, I didn't know what to think," Virginia replied, looking into his eyes for signs of lost love.

"Nothing and no one can keep me away from you, Virginia. I might arrive late, but I'll always be here. Don't ever think that I won't show up. It's funny, but I knew I should look for you at Notre-Dame or Sacre Coeur. I looked at Notre-Dame first, because it was closer to the parade route. When I didn't find you there, I came up here to search for you," Rob concluded as his fingers brushed the last of the tears from Virginia's cheeks.

"You mean you didn't stop at my apartment, or the office?" Virginia asked, still reeling from the good fortune of having her arms around Rob once again.

"No, should I have? I didn't think that you'd be there. I knew you'd be somewhere in the Bastille Day crowd. Somehow I just knew that you'd be in one of the two great churches of Paris, and you were," Rob answered, kissing the end of her nose.

"I'm certainly glad you found me. I left notes on my apartment and office doors, just in case you stopped at them. I had looked all over for you, and was afraid you might have forgotten all about me,"

Virginia said as new tears of relief glistened on her lashes.

"There's no way possible that I could have forgotten you. The memory of you, the smell of your hair, the feel of your skin, and the taste of your kisses, are what keep me going when I'm lonely and missing you. You're my stability. You're my love and my life and, if you'll still have me, you'll be my wife," Rob responded, silencing any further comments from Virginia by sealing her mouth with his. They melted together as the late afternoon sun spread its rosy warmth over them.

"You know I'd love to marry you here in Paris right now, but let's wait until we return to the States. I guess I'm an old-fashioned girl, but I'd like to get married with family and friends standing around me. However, I'm so happy to have you with me today that I might just change my mind and drag you into the nearest church," Virginia said with a sigh as she eased away from Rob's strong arms.

Silent, he took her hand and allowed her to guide him up the last of the steep steps that led to the cathedral on its perch overlooking Paris. From the top, they surveyed the city that lay at the foot of the hill. Thousands of people still mingled in the streets. The sound of auto horns and band instruments rose to meet them.

Reaching the terrace, they stopped and looked at the city below. Paris in all her summertime majesty lay open before them. In the rays of the afternoon sun, they were two people in love with each other, life, and the view of the world's most romantic city. In the center of the city stood Notre-Dame, alone on her island in the Seine as a tribute from man to God. To the right rose the Eiffel Tower, a monument to man's building ingenuity. And to the east sat the Arc de Triomphe, a tribute to the unknown soldier who gave his life in World War I.

"I knew you'd manage to get me up here somehow. I've resisted this walk, but you've managed to drag me here," Rob retorted as he followed her, panting from more than just the exertion of the climb.

"Just give me time, and I'll show you the heavens," Virginia teased as she leaned against his shoulder.

"Wait a minute. Let me catch my breath. Besides, I have something to tell you." Rob chuckled as he paused on the steps.

"What? You're just stalling. I remember that you told me that you'd only visit the cathedral as a sign that you'd leave Europe and return home. Since that's not likely, I know you're just trying to stop me from dragging you inside," Virginia teased as she waited for Rob to gain his composure from the climb.

"That's what I want to tell you. I am returning to the States, and you with me, if you'll go. I've had enough of this life. I loved it when it was all I had. But now I have you, and our life together. We can't make plans with one of us living in one country while the other one is in another. Long-distance isn't the kind of romance I want. I'm an old-fashioned kind of guy. I want to wake up with you in my arms every morning," Rob stated seriously, holding Virginia's hand tightly in his.

"You're really serious about this, aren't you? What about your career, and mine? How can we simply drop everything we're doing?" Virginia asked as she tried to absorb his news.

"Of course I'm serious. You know that it takes the company months to work out transfers. We'll put in our papers on Monday. By the time the transfers come through, we'll have finished the work we came to Europe to do. We're going home. This is my last trip to Paris," Rob stated resolutely.

"Well, then, I guess it's time to enter the cathedral," Virginia said as she linked her arm in his.

Turning around, they gazed at Sacre Coeur. The sun had changed the white structure to rosy red as it bathed the hill in its last glory. Slipping their arms around each other, Virginia and Rob climbed the last steps and entered the coolness of the smoky interior, where they found the same old woman kneeling in prayer and fingering the same well-worn rosary beads. They lit a candle and added their words of thankfulness to hers.

When they left the cathedral after looking at the altars and windows, the sun had set. On the way back to Virginia's apartment, they stopped to buy a loaf of bread, some fruit and cheese, and two bottles of wine. They would all have plenty to celebrate tonight. There were so many plans to make, and so many loose ends to tie up. Virginia and Rob were anxious to return to the States and begin their life together. Their plans had been postponed long enough.

As they pushed open the door of her apartment, the aroma of roasting chicken greeted them. Rita and William had already set the table for four, made a salad, and started turnips and parsnips. A bottle of wine had been decanted, and four glasses sat ready for a toast. They broke into happy smiles as Virginia and Rob walked into the apartment.

Rita cried and kissed Rob on his cheek. "Happy

Bastille Day!" she said with more meaning than the simple words could convey. She was overjoyed that Virginia and Rob were finally together again.

"Hey, big fella, where were you this morning? Why didn't you come with me today?" William asked. "The company wanted to put on a big show, and needed its top dog, you know."

"I couldn't get away until this morning. Business! Anyway, I'm here now. Let's not talk about work at all this weekend. This is a time for celebration, not work," Rob replied without letting go of Virginia's hand. There was something comforting about being loved so completely that he did not want to release her even for a minute.

"Well, you missed a good one! I bet no parade in Washington was ever bigger," William said, sitting on the sofa and pouring the wine for the first toast. His crutches lay on the floor nearby.

Taking his glass, Rob offered the first toast saying, "I'm sure you represented the company just fine . . . crutches and all. Here's to us . . . to health . . . happiness . . . our futures . . . our friendship."

William, adding his toast, said with a hitch in his voice, "To the women whose love keeps us going through the tough times . . . Rita and Virginia."

The women looked at each other, and then at their men. Never had either of them felt so alive, and so happy. The hardship, the waiting, and the worry were worth it, knowing that they were so completely loved.

"Before we sit down to this wonderful meal, we have an announcement," Rob said as he stepped slightly forward.

"Oh, really? You mean you've finally decided to

explain that rock on Virginia's hand?'' William teased a little drunkenly.

"No, it's even bigger than that. We've putting in our transfer requests and going home. It's time Virginia made an honest man of me,'' Rob stated with a happy smile.

Suddenly realizing that they were starving and had not eaten since early morning, they dove into the wonderful dinner Rita had prepared and gobbled up fruit for desert. Then, throwing the sofa pillows onto the floor with the two bottles of wine between them, they sat in the dark with only the glow of the candles as they watched the stars flicker in the night sky.

As they grew sleepy, Rita and William left for her apartment a few doors away. They arranged to meet for lunch the next day at noon on the Champs Élysée, near the Arc de Triomphe. From there they would tour the city and make their plans for the return trip home. There was so much Virginia and Rita wanted to show them, and, as usual, so little time.

But tonight, all thoughts of anything besides each other were pushed far away as they closed and locked the door. When they turned out the lamp, the dazzling glow from the bright stars flooded the room. Virginia and Rob stood gazing out at the streetlights of Paris below. His arm lightly rested on her shoulder. For the first time in their relationship, he had taken his destiny into his own hands and decided to lay down roots. He could devote his full attention to Virginia.

Virginia melted against Rob's chest as his arms encircled her. Gently, he kissed the top of her head and then her forehead. Lifting her chin slightly, he

lightly pressed his lips to her eyelids and the tip of
her nose. With a feathery touch, he brushed her
cheeks and chin. Looking deeply into her eyes, he
allowed his lips to come to rest on hers as she slid
her arms around his neck and rested her fingers in
his hair.

His hands slowly caressed Virginia's shoulders and
back before coming to rest at her waist. Softly he
cupped her buttocks in his hands before pressing
her firmly against him. She sighed when she felt the
pressure of his desire against her thigh. Her fingers
wandered leisurely from his hair to his neck, and
downward to his shoulders.

As their hands memorized each other's bodies,
their tongues tasted the sweetness of their shared
kisses. Their breath came in quick puffs as the need
to consummate their love increased. First pressing
his cheek against hers and then nuzzling his face in
her neck, Rob held her tightly. He could feel her
heart pounding against his. They had spent so many
nights apart that he could not bear the thought that
she might not really be in his arms when he awoke.

Looking into her sweetly smiling face, Rob knew
that he did not have to explain his feelings to Virginia. He took both of her hands in his, and slowly
led her to the bedroom. He could hear the song of
a nightingale through the window as he kissed her
goodnight and closed the door. As soon as their
transfers came through, they would never be separated again. As for the moment, they thought only
of each other.

Virginia lay in her bed listening to the mingling
of sounds of Paris and the sound of Rob's soft snoring. Her heart felt light with his arm resting over
her stomach. As she drifted off to sleep, she

dreamed about the train once again. This time their hands held tightly as the train picked up speed. In her sleep, Virginia sensed that all was well.

Fifteen

The morning broke to splendid sounds and smells. The sun shone with unparalleled splendor. The promise of a life together had a way of making everything look fresh and renewed. Hope for a brighter tomorrow swept away the fear of separation and loneliness. The songs of birds and the joy of living filled the air as the city began to right itself and return to normal after the Bastille Day celebration.

"Good morning, sleepyhead!" Rob beamed, greeting Virginia as she emerged from the bedroom at nine o'clock dressed in a navy blue skirt, white blouse, blue flats, and matching cardigan. "I hope you like a big breakfast. I'm starved."

Laughing, Virginia rushed into his outstretched arms. She never ate more than a piece of toast in the morning, but today she knew she would devour the feast he had spread before them on the dining room table. She had not heard him stir and leave their bed. She had been sleeping so peacefully.

"You must have gotten up pretty early. It smells great!" Virginia cried, surveying the brioche, hard-boiled eggs, fruit, juice, and steaming coffee with hot milk.

"I hope I didn't wake you when I took my shower.

I tried to be as quiet as possible, but living alone so much has dulled my senses a bit. Let's eat. There are so many places I want to see today, and we have to meet William and Rita at noon on the Champs Élysée," Rob said, seating her at the table. A vase filled with roses and forget-me-nots added color to the festive table.

"You remembered," Virginia whispered as her eyes misted.

"I remember most things, Virginia . . . the walks in St. James Park, the flat in London, your apartment in Washington, the red dress you wore the first night I met you at the company's New Year's Eve party, the tears in your eyes as you waved good-bye to me, and the smell of your perfume. I remember everything, but, like most men I don't always tell you how important you and the memories are to me. Even when I've refused to visit the tourist places in this town, I've pictured us there. I guess I didn't want the pain of remembering while we were apart. Now, I'd like to visit the places where I've pictured us, and some of the places that I wouldn't go. Do you think we could do that?" Rob asked, studying her face for understanding of the love that overflowed his heart.

"I'd love to see all of our favorite spots again. The only thing I won't do this time is wave good-bye. I won't ever do that again," Virginia answered firmly as she lay her small soft hand over his large one.

As the sound of Mozart floated through the apartment, they ate their breakfast without speaking. Both of them enjoyed being able to sit together without having to make small talk. They had shared enough so that silences did not bother them.

"What should we do first? I'm ready to get

started," Rob stated as they stacked the dishes in the washer.

"Let's head down the hill toward the Seine. Along the way, we'll stop at the Paris Opéra, so you can see its fabulous structure. We can linger a bit at the Palais-Royal, then go to the Louvre, to see if it has reopened. By the time we do all that, we'll be ready to meet Rita and William."

"I'll be ready for a nap if you drag me around Paris like that!" Rob jokingly complained.

"You said you wanted to see everything, and that's only a beginning. There're still the Eiffel Tower, the Arch of Triumph, and the Latin Quarter to visit. We've only just begun. There's so much that we've never seen," Virginia responded, locking the door and taking his hand.

"I might not have seen the sights of Paris, but I certainly examined every curve of my most precious sight. Those days we spent together were special," Rob added as he picked up his camera.

Watching him pick up the necessary tourist accoutrement, Virginia said with a chuckle and a slight blush, "I'm not complaining about our days and nights alone. I'm just suggesting that it's time we broadened our horizons a little."

"I'm game for that, as long as we leave time and energy for the basic necessities," Rob teased as they entered the crowded elevator for the ride to the lobby.

With her leading Rob into the sunshine, they began their journey through the streets of Paris. All the visitors from other French cities seemed to have had the same idea. The sidewalks were filled with people gaping at the sights of the city of Napoleon, Richelieu, and Marie Antoinette.

When they reached the Champs Élysée, they found Rita and William waiting for them at a quiet little café that offered a good view of the Arch of Triumph. From the way Rita wiggled her bare toes, Virginia could tell that they had walked a bit, too.

"What have you seen?" Virginia asked, anxious to begin the tour again. She was so excited about having Rob at her side that she wanted to do everything at once. She could barely sit still and sip her coffee.

"Take it easy, Virginia. Paris survived the Nazi occupation, but I'm not sure it's ready for you," William pleaded. He knew that Rita was tired of walking, and wanted to give her more time to rest. He needed a break, too. He had abandoned the crutches in favor of a wheelchair, which made his arms ache from propelling it along the crowded streets.

Sensing her friend's disappointment, Rita said, "Why don't you go on without us? We'll meet you back at the apartment around six. The first one back should start dinner. Or, if we're too tired, we'll go out."

"Great! We'll see you there," Virginia responded, finishing the last of her coffee. She looked over at Rob who sat looking at the Arch of Triumph at the top of the block.

"Let's go there," Rob said in a commanding voice.

Taking Virginia's hand, he led her up the slight hill to the famous arch, where the Unknown Soldier of World War I was buried. The majesty of the site was only slightly marred by the traffic circling it. In time, they forgot that they stood in the middle of a busy crossroads and looked only at the splendid monument.

Later, walking around the Latin Quarter, Virginia and Rob sampled the wares of little cafés and bakeries. They were thrilled to see so many ethnic groups represented and an abundance of black people, many of whom were expatriates, living there and in the artistic section of Montmartre. They felt at home as streams of jazz and soul music floated from the windows.

As the afternoon shadows lengthened and clouds blocked the sun, Virginia and Rob headed back to the apartment. They had seen so much that Paris had to offer the awestruck tourist. As they climbed the hill leading to Sacre Coeur, the skies suddenly opened, and hail the size of golf balls started pelting them on the head and shoulders.

"Quick, in here!" Rob shouted over the claps of thunder. He pulled Virginia into the doorway of a deserted shop. The owners must have left Paris to escape the heat, and had not yet returned. The blinds were closed tightly against prying eyes, and a "Gone to Lyon for Vacation" sign hung on the door.

Standing huddled together, Virginia and Rob watched the lightning flash in the charcoal gray sky. The wind wrapped her shirt around her body, revealing her shapely legs. It stung their faces, and tried to dislodge Rob's hat. Virginia shivered in the sudden change of temperature, and pulled her cardigan closer. Rob wrapped his arms around her to keep both of them warm. The day had changed from scorching to freezing in a matter of minutes.

As they protected each other from the elements, Rob found himself responding to the closeness of Virginia's body and the vanilla sweetness of her hair. As if involuntarily, his hands began to caress her shoulders and back. He lifted her chin and planted a hungry kiss on her willing lips. His tongue possessed her as her arms glided around his neck, and she pressed herself against him. The wetness and the wind were forgotten.

"Let's go home," Virginia whispered, intertwining her fingers in his as she clung to him and his lips burned against her neck.

They ran up the hill and the steps that led to her apartment. Her fingers trembled as she struggled with the key in the lock. Rob's labored breathing brushed the hair on the back of her neck, causing her to shiver as he reached around her to help unlock the door. She leaned against his chest and closed her eyes as he pulled her hair away from her neck to kiss the soft skin at the nape.

Looking into each other's eyes, they pushed the door open and stepped inside. "Hi, we beat you! Good thing you gave me your extra key," Rita chirped, coming from the kitchen with a plate filled to overflowing with pasta and sausage. William followed with a basket of baguette pieces and two bottles of wine.

Virginia and Rob glanced at each other, shook their heads, and broke into gales of laughter. Falling onto the sofa, they tried to compose themselves as their puzzled friends stood watching them.

"What's wrong with you guys?" William asked. He had never seen Rob act so seemingly out of control before.

"Nothing," Rob answered, gulping for air. "We're just happy to be home. The weather got to us, that's all."

"Well, get yourselves together. Dinner's ready," Rita said, looking at them as if seeing both of them

for the first time. This was certainly a new side to
the usually serious Virginia.

All through dinner, Rob and Virginia smiled at
each other as if hiding a secret. Under the table, his
leg rested against hers with a firm comforting pressure. His hand held hers whenever he didn't need
it to feed himself. She occasionally touched his
cheek or shoulder. Rita and William could clearly
see that they were much in love . . . and in need of
privacy.

As they cleared the dishes, Rita said, "We're thinking of leaving for London tomorrow. William wants
to take the ferry, rather than the Chunnel. I'm nervous, but I'm going to do it. I know we haven't
worked out the transfer arrangements, but we'll just
take our chances. There's a train to Calais at eight
in the morning. If the weather holds, we could be
in London for dinner. I've already phoned ahead,
and both of our apartments are still unoccupied, if
you're ready to come, too. What about you? Are you
ready to start back to the States?"

London . . . Virginia longed to see the Dover
white cliffs once more. She was determined to climb
the hill to Dover Castle this time. She wanted to
walk the streets of London and hear the vendors in
Charing Cross Road. The pigeons in Trafalgar
Square and the birds in St. James Park needed to
be fed. She was suddenly lonely for her old flat, and
the sound of English accents.

The States . . . she wanted to dance one last waltz
with Rob, and fill her card with William's spirited
tangos. Virginia could hardly wait to inhale the smell
of clean straw in the barn, enjoy the playfulness of
new kittens in the loft. The taste of her mother's
apple pie called to her to come home. Home! Mar-

riage! A life together. She hesitated, concerned for her future. She wondered how the corporation would react to her sudden departure from Paris and Europe.

Rob thought for only a few minutes and decided that a few phones calls were the order of the moment. If he could reach the right people, both of them could be on their way home. Home . . . a new life with Virginia. No more traveling . . . no more hotels.

Virginia, Rita, and William waited as patiently as possible as Rob placed the calls to the directing managers of their respective divisions. Since he was one of them, it only seemed appropriate that he would make the contacts, feel out the company's reaction, and determine the climate. They tried not to listen as Rob conferred from the bedroom.

"What if the timing isn't right?" Rita asked as she sat clenching her hands. "Rob hasn't been on his new assignment long. It's easier for you to transfer on the spur of the moment, since you've worked through the complications in the office that brought you here in the first place. We knew from the beginning that our assignments were only temporary. My director told me yesterday that my time was almost up. But what about Rob? He's only just started in Rome."

"Don't worry about him. Rob knows his way around the company politics," William offered with more confidence in his voice than he felt.

"Let's hope you're right. I'd love to return to the States, but I won't leave here without Rob. There's no way that I'll put that kind of distance between us. I'm not that fond of taking risks," Virginia added as she paced the length of the living room.

After thirty minutes of conversation, Rob emerged from the bedroom. The others studied his face as he joined them. He did not look any the worse for the calls, yet he was not smiling.

Taking Virginia's hand in his, Rob looked deeply into her eyes and said soberly, "I don't know how to break this to you, but we're going home."

"It's okay, Rob, you tried . . . wait a minute—what did you say?"

"I said we're going home. The boss agreed that your time here has run its course, and he found someone to implement my plans in the Rome office. We're going home," Rob repeated as he pulled Virginia into his arms.

The room erupted with gleeful celebrating as the dream of returning to the States became a reality.

That night, Virginia gave all of her plants to the old lady who lived next door. Rob watched from the sofa as she gathered the trinkets she had purchased to remind of her of Paris, carefully wrapping a porcelain figurine of the Eiffel Tower and a Limoges box in newspaper before placing them inside. She quickly threw her clothes into her bag. She left her beret on the table next to her purse, to wear on the trip. She wanted to look particularly Parisian as she left the wonderful country.

Standing on the balcony, they looked down on the city one last time that night. The lights twinkled out one by one as Paris went to sleep. Paris would live forever in their hearts, had finally decided to rest.

"I'd like to see Sacre Coeur again before we leave," Virginia said as she rested against Rob's broad chest.

Taking her hand, he led her out of the building

and up the hill. The cathedral that had become so important to them glowed a white silvery color in the moonlight. Inside a little outdoor alcove, they lit candles one last time. Virginia smiled at the sight of the same old woman kneeling in the back pew saying the decades of her rosary. Some things in Paris never changed.

As they walked back down the hill to her apartment, they stopped at the little children's park. Sitting on the same bench in the glow of the moon, Virginia and Rob held hands. Neither spoke as they sorted through their very different experiences of France. She would never be able to share with him the loneliness and the worry she had felt at his absence. There was no need to try. They understood enough already.

They returned to the apartment. The silence in the once lively room was deafening, and almost sad. As Virginia reached for the light switch on the wall, Rob took her hand in his.

"No," Rob whispered. "We don't need that."

Cradling her in his arms, he took her to the bedroom. The moonlight fell across the bed as he slowly undressed himself, and then Virginia. She trembled as he removed her blouse and slacks, leaving her standing in her white cotton underpants and bra. His fingers seemed to burn her flesh as he fumbled with the clasp. Finally, he cupped her breasts in his hands and kissed each one. Then he pulled her nakedness against his, and held her so tightly that Virginia felt as if she would never be able to separate from him again . . . and she liked the sensation of their oneness.

Pulling down the sheet and spread in one motion without releasing his hold on Virginia's shoulders,

Rob eased her down onto the bed until they sat together on the cool sheets. Their hands lovingly explored each other, first their faces and ears, and then their necks and shoulders. He allowed his hands and eyes to trace patterns on her nipples as she massaged his shoulders.

Easing his hands down her body, he leisurely stroked her thighs and lower abdomen as his tongue tasted hers and his lips pressed hotly against her mouth. Virginia groaned as his fingers explored her warm interior. Her fluttering fingers trailed down the length of his body, stopping along the way to tease his hard nipples. Rob moaned softly as her fingers found his organ and gently caressed it, slipping the condom over its rigid form.

Leaning her backward onto the pillows, Rob slowly lowered himself over her until their lips touched. Kissing her mouth and cheeks, he tenderly began to enter her moist recesses. As Rob moved slowly and lovingly into her, she began to relax and let the love they shared block out the tension of her hectic life.

Virginia started to move her hips in rhythm with his. Her hands clung to his shoulders, arms, and back. She arched her body to meet his as the waves of passion washed over her. Looking into her half-closed eyes, Rob could tell that she was enjoying their coupling as much as he was. The joy of being together had completely erased the pain of their separation.

Seeing Virginia so satisfied, Rob increased the pace of his thrusts. Responding to his soft moans, she again matched his movements. When he slowed down, so did she. Sometimes he quickened the strokes. At others, he lengthened them until she felt she would catch fire from the heat generated by his motions. Then she moved her hips away from his throbbing member, as if trying to escape from flames. He moaned and lifted her buttocks upward until he could once again reach her most pleasurable inner recesses.

As the pleasure became unbearable, their pace quickened, and the motions became more urgent. Virginia clawed at Rob's thighs and buttocks. He called out her name as he thrust madly, straining to release both of them from the desire that held them prisoner.

Arching her body to meet his feverish thrusts, Virginia cried out as the bubble of passion burst inside her. Never had she experienced a feeling so close to pain and yet so completely pleasurable that she wanted it never to stop.

Clinging to Rob's shoulders, which were moist with perspiration, she chased the vanishing feeling, matching his furious rhythm in her quest. He groaned through tightly clamped teeth and shuddered as he achieved release from the desire that had tightened every muscle and nerve in his body. Collapsing in a heap of legs and arms, Rob and Virginia lay in each other's arms, the world reduced to the area of their bed.

Rolling onto his back, Rob pulled Virginia against his chest and cradled her in his arms. For a long time, neither spoke as their breathing returned to normal and their hearts stopped pounding. Slowly, as if awakening from a deep sleep, Rob lightly kissed her damp forehead. Lifting her chin so that her eyes were level with his, he kissed her smiling lips. They belonged to each other fully. Nothing, not even the separation of work, could part them.

Snuggling against him once more and pulling the sheet over their shoulders, Virginia listened as Rob's breathing deepened and slowed. Kissing him lightly on the cheek, she closed her eyes and went to sleep in the security of his arms, knowing that he would still be there in the morning. Nothing could separate them now.

The morning that dawned was even brighter than usual. Birds fluttered past the window and perched on the sill to sing. Summer's lush beauty lay ahead.

"Wake up, sleepyhead!" Rob coaxed, giving Virginia gentle shakes and planting feathery kisses on her cheeks and lips. "We have to meet William and Rita at the train station. Wake up!"

"Not yet. It can't be morning yet. You make such a good pillow that I don't want to get up. What time is it?" Virginia said, rubbing the sleep from her eyes.

"It's early, only six-thirty, but we have to shower, dress, and eat before we leave. I'll hop in now while you get yourself together. I'll be out in five minutes. By then you should be completely awake," Rob answered, pulling the sheets around her shoulders as he slipped from the bed.

Lying there listening to the water pelting the shower curtains, Virginia felt more at peace and happier than she had since she was a little girl, when she woke up on her birthday to the aroma of her favorite breakfast of omelets and fresh biscuits. She stretched every muscle, and looked out the window. They were going home.

Frowning for a moment, she vaguely remembered having her train dream. Although not as frightening as it had been, Virginia remembered that she had stood on the steps watching as Rob struggled to pull himself onto the moving train. He succeeded in getting one foot up, but had to stop as they approached a tunnel. She watched sadly as he faded from view.

Shrugging her shoulders, Virginia dismissed the dream. Rob was with her, and everything was going well with them. That silly dream did not matter any more.

Slipping her feet onto the floor, she padded to the bathroom. "May I come in?" Virginia shouted through the closed door.

"Sure. Would you mind washing my back?" Rob answered, handing her his soapy sponge.

"Not at all, and any other part you'd like," Virginia teased as she came in and began the pleasurable task.

"The back's enough. I can handle the rest myself. You're certainly in a good mood this morning." Rob chuckled.

"We're together, and we're going home. Of course, I'm happy," Virginia replied as she added more soap.

As she scrubbed, Virginia admired the muscles that rippled down his back and across his shoulders. She had seen her brothers as they worked on the farm, but their bodies did not look as well-toned as Rob's. They were thin lean men, with long muscles that bulged when they lifted things but were invisible at other times. Rob's body was more substantially built and heavily muscled.

"Hop in and I'll scrub yours before I leave. Damn, I wish we had more time. I'd love nothing better than to take you back to bed," Rob said in a husky voice as he lathered her. His manhood hardened from the nearness of her beautiful body.

"There'll be time for that when we arrive in England, sir. Now control yourself. We don't want to miss that train. Go away. You're being a pest!" Virginia laughed, pushing him from the shower and drawing the pink-and-blue floral curtain.

"Yes, ma'am. I can already see who'll wear the pants in this family, "Rob responded, giving her soapy body one last peek before leaving.

When Virginia joined him in the dining room, the breakfast was already spread on the table. They ate in silence, giggling and casting sideways glances at each other like schoolchildren as they munched their toast. They had to run to catch up with Rita and William, arriving at the platform as the last whistle sounded.

The trip to Calais on the packed train was more fun than the ride to Paris had been. They laughed, talked, and played bid whist the entire time. When they got hungry, Virginia produced some cheese and a baguette to accompany the fruit that William had purchased before leaving Paris.

The sun shone brightly the entire way, promising a calm crossing to Dover. From the shore they could see the smooth stretch of water between the coast and England's shores. Rita looked relaxed as the ferry purred across the channel. Everyone on board seemed to be enjoying the weather and the crossing.

When the white cliffs came into view, Virginia shouted, clapping her hands like a little girl, "Look, everyone! There they are. We're almost in Dover."

"And to think I almost didn't make this crossing. Look at the view I would have missed if we'd used the Chunnel. Thanks for convincing me," Rita added, smiling at William as she shaded her eyes and looked in awe at the impressive hillside.

"The cliffs are so beautiful, especially with the sun shining on them. I didn't notice them on the way over. Actually, I don't remember much of my first crossing. This one, I'll remember forever," Rob said as he pulled Virginia tightly against his chest.

When they arrived at the Dover port, they discovered that a massive strike had stopped the trains. Rather than rent a car, they decided to spend time exploring Dover. There was no need to rush; their lives together lay ahead of them.

They registered at the best hotel in town. Selecting adjoining rooms, they quickly unpacked their bags and rushed out to do some sightseeing. Dover was a town that held much appeal for all of them.

Much to Virginia's delight, the castle was once again open to visitors, who flocked to see its building and grounds, and to the underground defenses of the British Army. The corps of engineers had carved headquarters out of the soft chalk cliff, from which they had a clear view of the channel and the coast of France. Standing on a balcony where Churchill had stood, Virginia and Rob looked out across the clear water to the coast of France, to Calais on the shore ninety miles away. Resting her head on his shoulder, Virginia thought of how much had happened to them in the past months. She wondered if she would ever be satisfied with a routine life again after all this excitement.

The castle was an imposing structure with high walls, deep wells, and large public rooms. Even on this warm day, the interior was very cool and quite dark. As Virginia strolled from room to room, she could almost see the ghosts of long dead English kings roaming the halls. Often she looked behind her, to make sure that only Rob was following her.

Stepping out into the sunlight, Rita exclaimed with a shudder, "Boy, that was creepy. I know I saw someone in the king's bedroom. Just for a second, out of the corner of my eye, I saw a shadow moving across the floor, and then it was gone."

"I felt someone on the battlements. He stood next to me, first making me feel warm and then cold as he walked away. Isn't this just the greatest place?" Virginia exuded happily. She had always wanted to see the Dover cliffs and Dover Castle, and now she had done both. Most importantly, she had shared them with Rob. Rob and William looked at each other and nodded, like doting husbands with their women.

They stopped to see Mrs. Parker, the landlady at the bed-and-breakfast who had befriended them on their first stay in Dover. She greeted Rita and Virginia warmly, and introduced the couples to her son, who had just returned from a protracted business trip. She proudly showed them changes she had made in the little house during their absence. A newly acquired antique phonograph and tea service made lovely additions to the living room.

Later, as they strolled to the hotel, Virginia and Rita saw the fog once again covering the view of the castle, reminding them of their first trip to Dover. Taking Rob's hand, Virginia pulled him closer. She did not want to lose him in the shadows that filled the valley.

Making arrangements to leave for London on the nine o'clock train, which promised to be in operation the next day, Virginia and Rob said goodnight to Rita and William at their bedroom door. They all doubted that they would sleep much in their excitement to return to London and then to the States.

Quickly entering their massive room and closing the door behind him, Rob hungrily took Virginia into his arms. "You didn't think I'd let you sleep tonight, did you?" he asked with his nose buried in her hair. His fingers were already loosening the buttons on her blouse.

Chuckling huskily, Virginia responded as a shiver of desire ran up her body, "I'd hoped you wouldn't. I've had enough nights of simply sleeping."

Hungrily consuming her mouth, Rob groaned as his hands pushed the blouse from her shoulders. "There won't be any more as far as I'm concerned. I'm home now where I belong. I've slept alone too much myself."

Rob's hands moved wildly from her shoulders to her breasts and then to her hips. At each place, he lingered long enough to leave a burning print on Virginia's cool flesh. His imprisoned desire for her was still too great for him to control his passions.

Virginia could not resist the urgency that dictated their actions. She alternated between clinging to him and pressing him onward as her lips and tongue tasted his hot flesh. She gasped and groaned as his fingers eased between her thighs and hotly stroked the moist flesh. She cried out as he quickly carried her to the bed and buried his face between her breasts, teasing each nipple with his teeth. Hungrily, he pulled each one into his mouth and sucked until she dug her fingers into his back and writhed with the passion burning between her legs. His fingers again danced in her wetness, and she moved her thighs in a circular motion in response.

"Oh, Virginia! I want you so much!" Rob groaned as her hurrying hands slipped on the condom and eased him into her wet recesses. Lifting her hips to meet his and placing her feet around his waist, he thrust into her, driving his full length as she opened to receive him.

Arching her back, Virginia allowed the undulating waves to devour her body. Her face and chest burned from Rob's kisses and her own passion. Her hips kept up a constant battle with his as she fought to control her desire and his.

Finally, she surrendered to the pulsating pleasure that spread through her as he drove deeper and harder into her. Her every muscle and nerve tightened in response to the quickening pace. Her breath came in puffs as she clung to his shoulders, barely able to tell if she moved with him or if his energy carried her along. As the moment of release racked her body and his, she cried out his name, realizing that it did not matter who controlled the passion.

With only their choked breathing disturbing the silence of the night, Virginia and Rob lay wound in each other's arms and legs. Their bodies were so tightly entangled that it was impossible to tell them apart in the moonlight that shone on the rumpled bed. No dreams of a train speeding through tunnels would disturb Virginia's sleep.

Sixteen

London was alive with excitement and noise. Construction was going full swing in sections of the city that had long needed repair. Young men had traded their computer joysticks for shovels. Flowers grew in great profusion everywhere. Children played in the streets and parks. Everyone smiled gaily as summer lingered in England.

Quickly unpacking in Virginia's apartment for their last stay in London, they joined the throngs of people scurrying along the streets. Once again, Virginia took Rob to all of her favorite places. At times he seemed to be genuinely happy to be back in London and with her, though she occasionally saw concern playing across his smooth brow.

Sitting in Hyde Park feeding the birds, Rob seemed especially distant. Virginia rested her hand on his, and he brightened. She decided that all he needed was reassurance and love, both of which she would freely give. After all, they had taken a big step in putting their lives ahead of the desires of their corporation. Both hoped that their careers would not falter.

That night they ate dinner in a small oak-paneled carvery that smelled of roast beef and Yorkshire pudding. They sat at a table in the corner, away from the laughing families.

"What's troubling you, Rob? Are you sorry we came to London? You seemed happier in Paris. Would you like to return? I don't care where we live, as long as we're together. There are plenty of expatriate black people in France. We could have a good life there." Virginia gazed into his eyes.

"No, that's not it at all. I guess I'm just adjusting to the sudden freedom. This is the first time in my adult life that I've taken any real time from work. I've always wedged my life into the crevices of business life. I'll get used to it. It must be a change for you, too. Don't worry about me. I'm just trying to figure out my next step, that's all." Rob tried to sound nonchalant as he wondered about his future. He had taken a big risk in asking to be removed from the Rome assignment to return to the States. His boss had said all the right words, but Rob was still concerned about the thoughts that he had not expressed. Those were often the ones that could return to haunt him.

"You're right. Both of us have taken a risk. It'll work out. You can always start your own business. With your credentials and expertise, you'd have clients beating down the door. I've given thought to teaching on the college level, or consulting. It's time for a change for both of us." Virginia smiled confidently. This new beginning had given her a sense of liberation of which she had dreamed for a long time.

"You've been reading my mind. Consulting would open all kinds of doors for us. I'll definitely think about it," Rob responded as he gave Virginia's lips a lingering kiss that promised more to come.

Seeing him put on a brave smile almost broke Virginia's heart. He was trying so hard for her sake to make everything perfect. In many ways, she wished he would stop and let things take their own course. She wanted him to realize that she was happy with him the way he was, and did not need anything more than his love.

The days passed quickly as the two couples again enjoyed the sights of England together. They journeyed out into the countryside for picnics, visited castles in York and Westminster, and wandered the streets of Stratford-upon-Avon, Canterbury, and Bath. They traveled by train into Scotland, where they walked the Royal Mile, stopping to shop along the way. They were delighted to see that the farther away from London and the south of England they traveled, the less damage there was from IRA attacks. Everything was peaceful and untouched. This was the England of textbooks and fairy tales.

Each day Rob grew more confident about their plans. He even began to talk about leaving the company and opening his own firm. As they enjoyed new sights together, the feeling of exploration replaced the worry of taking time away from work and striking out on his own. At Stonehenge they marveled at the ancient rocks. In Bath they admired the Roman ingenuity that had harnessed the underground waters and turned them into community bathing pools. On a trip to Wales, in Cardiff, they laughed together at the antics of strutting peacocks as the males displayed their colorful tail feathers for the entertainment of the dull brown females.

At night they lay in each other's arms and listened to the singing of the nightingale in the tree outside the apartment. Virginia and Rob explored each other's bodies by the light of the setting sun. They giggled like little children as they unashamedly enjoyed their nakedness. They reveled at the pleasure they could quickly invite by a well-placed kiss or touch. They groaned and sighed as the tide of passion washed over them and left them spent and weak. And finally they slept soundly, each cradled in the assurance that the other would still be there in the morning.

Like many tourists, they soon felt to an uncontrollable desire to return home. Choosing the slow route, they booked passage on a cruise ship leaving from Liverpool and arriving in New York a week later. They had spent a leisurely two months in London, and it was time to go home. Autumn had begun to touch London, and bring with it the first chill of September nights.

Virginia had found life on a ship quite pleasurable when she had once vacationed with her family, but she was not prepared for the grandeur that awaited them when they boarded the ocean liner. Instead of the middle deck inside cabin that her parents preferred, Rob had booked the best the ship had to offer on the world's premier cruise line. They found themselves surrounded by shining brass and polished crystal. Huge chandeliers sparkled from the ceilings of the dining room, foyer, and lounges. Water in the pool beckoned to them as they strolled the decks or lounged in deck chairs. Waiters in spotless white jackets with vivid red cummerbunds and black trousers stood by to do their every bidding. Stewards turned down their bed and left chocolates on the pillows every night. The tables were set with creamy bone china, glistening silver, and sparkling crystal, all displayed on spotless white damask clothes. So many glasses and forks greeted them that Virginia often did not know where to begin. Fresh flowers bedecked every table, and every stateroom displayed a basket of fruit, teas, cheeses, crackers, and jams for snacks.

They dressed for dinner in clothes Rob and William had purchased for them in fashionable Knightsbridge before leaving London. The men wore dark business suits, or the tuxedos they had also picked up on that last shopping spree. They dined on caviar and paté, sipped champagne and brandy, munched truffles and escargot, and savored the flavor of thick tender steaks, buttery lobster, and succulent shrimp. The transatlantic crossing created memories that they would share for the rest of their lives.

Virginia and Rita treated themselves to facials and manicures the second day at sea. They laughed at the irony of blacks being able to enjoy luxury previously reserved for the wealthiest of whites. Much had changed since the end of segregation.

While the women were being pampered, Rob and William practiced skeet shooting off the bow, and played cards into the night. They became quite proficient at poker and blackjack. Each won enough at the gaming tables to pay for gold and diamond bracelets that sparkled on Virginia and Rita's wrists.

At night they danced until the wee hours, and were always the last to leave the floor. Rob excelled at the fox trot and tango. William enjoyed swaying to the big band sound and New Orleans jazz with Rita in his arms, while using one crutch for balance. They all enjoyed getting down with the mellow tunes from the heyday of Smokey Robinson, and the Motown sound.

William and Virginia always engaged in lively conversation as he slowly guided her in small circles on
the dance floor. "That'll have to do until my leg
heals, Virginia. Then we'll dance at your wedding,
if you'll include an old married man on your card,"
he said, beaming. They planned to settle down in
New Jersey as soon as the ship docked. He already
had a position in another communications firm waiting for him. While they had played in London, William had made phone calls home that resulted in a
job that would start in a few weeks and pay twice
his former salary.

"Of course, I'll save one for you," she said. "I
couldn't possibly consider myself married without a
dance with my old friend. I couldn't be happier for
you and Rita. You're both such wonderful people,
so loving and giving, you deserve each other. I don't
know what I would have done without her compan-
ionship while Rob was away. I would have been so
lonely." Virginia smiled as they returned to the table
where Rita and Rob waited.

Rita and William and Virginia and Rob found that
they were most comfortable with each other despite
the number of other people on board. They knew
each other's paces and comfort zones. They did not
have to worry about making small talk. Sometimes,
they socialized with another couple from Washington, DC, when it was time to play cards or sip night-
caps in the bar. Mostly, however, they were content
to be alone.

Their love for each other deepened with each
passing day. Virginia and Rob became almost inseparable, always holding ends, kissing, and gazing into
each other's faces. Once they closed their cabin
door they left all the problems of world outside.

Rob's hands possessed Virginia's body as if tomorrow would never come. Her fingers clung to him as if to keep him with her forever. They had been separated too much to believe that these good times would really last.

Once they were alone, Rob pulled Virginia tightly into his arms and crushed her to him while his lips burned tracks from her eyelids to her lips. He lingered, gently teasing her tongue with him until she gasped as desire rose within her. His fingers unfastened the straps of her evening gown and carelessly dropped it to the floor in his need to caress her smooth skin.

Virginia groaned with anticipated pleasure as he lowered her to the bed and removed her lacy bra and panties. She raised her hips to reach his exploring fingers and lips as he placed kisses on her flat belly and between her shapely thighs. Her hands pressed him to her as the hunger mounted. Her fingers teased his shoulders, back, thighs, buttocks, and manhood until he groaned with an undeniable demand for release. She only paused long enough to put on a condom. Then she guided him into the moist recesses of her womanhood. Their bodies joined and struggled for the pace that would satisfy their need for each other.

Their bodies met and lingered, only to pull away tantalizingly. Thrusting, panting they came together again in a primal dance that left them breathless and tired, yet feeling a unique oneness that came from sharing soul and body. Then they rested in each other's arms as the gentle rocking of the ship lulled them to sleep with her head on his shoulders and their arms and legs intertwined.

As the days passed and they drew closer to New

York, Rob's anxiety deepened. He had never felt as if a sword hung over his head, but now he felt it swinging closer every day. He partially wished that he had resigned, rather than simply asking for an exception. At any rate, he was preparing himself to make the next step and to break free from his former corporate life.

Virginia, on the other hand, had already decided not to continue in corporate work. She was ready for a change. Marriage and a new job looked very appealing to her.

At eight o'clock on Sunday morning, Virginia and Rob joined Rita and William on the deck as they sailed into New York Harbor. The sun shone brightly as the Statue of Liberty raised her torch high to welcome them. The level of excitement was high as everyone on board cheered and spun noisemakers to celebrate their return to the States. Rob pulled Virginia against him and kissed her soundly. After being away for so long and experiencing so much, they were finally home.

Standing on the pier beside waiting taxis, Rob and William embraced. Virginia could see the pain of parting on their faces. Although they had promised to remain in touch, their lives would be changed by the paths that they had decided to take. She and Rita held each other and whispered their good-byes. They promised to attend each other's weddings, to write, visit, and to send photographs of their houses and children. They promised never to become so busy that they could not find the time to share their thoughts and dreams, no matter how many miles lay between them.

Collecting their things, Virginia and Rob took a cab to the airport for the flight to DC. They had planned to stay with his parents first while looking for a place to live in town. After a few days there, they would drive to Towson to see her family. As the taxi wove in and out of traffic, they marveled at the hectic pace of Manhattan after living in England, where everyone moved more slowly and stopped to exchange pleasantries or smiles. Passing the Empire State Building, Times Square, and Central Park, Virginia was relieved to see that change had not touched the vibrant city. So far, home looked just as she remembered it.

Arriving in DC, Virginia discovered that her former city still sparkled. The months away from home had not changed the city in which business leaders and politicians conducted the affairs of state of the nation and the world. The houses looked the same, too.

Rob's parents' house looked charming and welcoming. Pots of geraniums and begonias bloomed along the steps and under the white-and-yellow striped awning. The family's cat, Toby, lounged on the welcome mat, waiting for someone to let him into the house. He rose from his resting place, meowed, and happily rubbed himself against Rob's legs when they walked up the steps.

"I sure am glad to see you, old boy," Rob said, picking up the fat cat and lovingly scratching him behind the ears. Toby purred loudly and nuzzled his head against Rob's chest.

Virginia saw a frown fleetingly play across Rob's forehead. Gently, she placed her hand on his and asked, "Are you okay? We've had a busy day."

"No, I'm all right. Don't worry, it'll pass. Just my old conservative nature setting in again. I should be at work, remember? Old habits are hard to break."

Rob set Toby on his feet and led Virginia by the hand to the front door.

Virginia and Rob had not told his parents when they would arrive, wanting to surprise them. As they rang the doorbell, Rob surveyed the front yard and the porch of the stately Victorian structure. He had spent many happy years there. Now, instead of bringing home a lame bird or an adopted kitten, he brought the woman who would soon be his wife.

Rob's dad opened the door, and at first he did not recognize the man who stood on his porch. As the shock of seeing his son vanished, he threw open the door and pulled Rob into his arms. Tears of joy welled in his eyes and rolled down his handsome brown face. Looking into Rob's eyes he said, "So you decided that you'd had enough of Europe and decided to come home. It's about time!" Smiling a hello and pulling Virginia to him with his free arm as if he'd known her for ages, he embraced them, calling to his wife. They moved into the cool foyer and left the world outside on the sidewalk.

As they waited for his mother to join them, Rob looked around the old familiar house. His mother had kept everything exactly as it had been when he left. She had not changed the deep burgundy-and-mauve striped slipcovers on the sofa and chairs, or the matching drapes. Gold-fringed mauve throw pillows were still piled on every seat, completing the look. Dishes of chocolate overflowed crystal and china plates on every table. Magazines highlighting the accomplishments of American athletes, business professionals, and theatrical celebrities lay casually on the coffee table and tumbled out of the magazine racks. Vases of flowers added color to every corner.

The familiar fragrance of her perfume lingered in the room, as if she had just left.

"Rob! You're home, my son," his mother exclaimed tearfully. "I've missed you so much. Nothing has been the same without you. And you've brought this wonderful young woman with you." She hugged her only child tightly and gazed tearfully into his face. Then she stepped back and examined him for signs of not eating. Finding him in good condition, she hugged him once more and then turned her attention to Virginia, hugging her.

"Now that you're here, we can begin planning your wedding! Rob wrote us all about you. I can hardly wait to be a grandmother!" she added gleefully.

Everyone laughed at her exuberance. Virginia's cheeks glowed pink at the mention of children. She had been so busy with work and the constant problems of maintaining a long-distance romance that she had not taken time to think beyond the moment. Rob's mother had made the future sound so imminent.

Word of Rob's return quickly flooded the neighborhood. Soon the house overflowed with friends, family, food, and laughter. The dining room table was quickly set buffet style as mouthwatering treats tempted everyone to partake of the impromptu welcome home celebration. Roast beef, baked chicken, potato salad, string beans cooked with ham and honey, and candied sweet potatoes were piled high on every plate. Everyone remembered to save room for chocolate cake, strawberry shortcake, and homemade ice cream. People hugged and kissed both of them as they freely discussed Virginia and Rob's wedding plans or swapped stories of Rob's childhood adventures. Everyone was extremely proud of the neighbor boy who had done so well for himself. In no time at all, Virginia felt as if she had known all of them for her whole life. Rob's family and friends had opened their arms to her, and she felt at home among them.

Long after the streetlights came on, the last person wished them a happy life and went home. Finally, they were alone with his parents, and could catch up on the time they had missed.

Rob and Virginia had just settled into the sofa when the front door opened. A tall leggy woman dressed all in red walked in unannounced. It was obvious from the smile on her fabulously beautiful bronze face that she was used to turning heads. Virginia could see that the woman was no stranger. From the way she greeted Rob's parents and the frost in the air, Virginia saw that an old relationship had existed between them.

Rob shifted uneasily as the lady in red made her way to where he sat with his arm around Virginia's shoulders. He looked as if he had been slapped across the face . . . hard. Virginia observed that he was clearly uncomfortable with the woman's visit, and wondered about the cause of his reaction. It was clear from the tightness of his mouth that he remembered every detail of their shared past. She immediately felt that this woman's presence was a threat to their relationship.

Rob rose slowly and extended his hand to greet the outstretched hand offered to him. Looking from the visitor's carefully made up face to Virginia, he said, "I'd like you to meet Ronny Saunders, an old friend. Ronny, this is my fiancée, Virginia Summers."

Without taking her eyes from Rob's pinched face Ronny purred in a whispery soft, sugary voice, "An old friend? Is that what I've become to you? Why didn't you tell Virginia about us? Let *me*, Rob dear. I can tell that this needs a woman's touch. Virginia, I'm Rob's wife."

No one moved as the words hung in the air. The room suddenly seemed cold and threatening to Virginia as she listened to Ronny's words repeat in her head . . . *Rob's wife!* Virginia could not believe that the vibrant, undeniably beautiful woman was married to the man she loved. What else had he forgotten to tell her? What other secrets had he kept that would come forward to jeopardize their future?

Virginia looked at Rob's parents for confirmation. One glance at their rigid postures and tightly composed faces told her that this woman had spoken the truth. Gazing up at Rob from her seat on the sofa, she saw that he looked frozen in space. A look of disgust distorted his features. His outstretched hand was now clenched in a fist at his side. His breath came in short puffs, and his face looked dark and frightening.

Turning her attention from Rob to Virginia, Ronny looked her over critically. She was aware of her own beauty, and evaluated everyone against herself. She assessed Virginia's stunned, wide, hazel eyes, full lips, shapely figure, and freely flowing thick hair as beautiful in their own way, but definitely not in a league with hers. There was something in Virginia's manner that spoke of an upbringing away from the sophistication of the big city. No, Ronny decided, Virginia was no match for her in beauty or bearing. Being a woman who had everything and everyone she wanted, Ronny had no reason to lie to herself. She decided that the gentleness of nature that radiated from Virginia must have been the attraction for Rob. He must have found Virginia's quiet reserve a relief from her own vitality. Raising her eyebrows in private amusement, she wondered if he were ready for a little excitement once again.

"Rob, dear, you should have spared the poor girl the embarrassment of not knowing what to say by telling her about us. That really wasn't very kind of you to spring our marriage on her like that," Ronny cooed, perching on an ottoman across the room from where Virginia sat, stiff and straight, on the sofa. She wanted to have a clear view of the enemy.

"If my new assignment hadn't distracted me, it would have been our *former* marriage," Rob corrected, resuming his seat next to Virginia and taking her ice-cold hand in his. "We were separated six months before I transferred, if you remember correctly."

"So we were. I guess that explains why you didn't tell her about us. The separation must have erased me from your memory," Ronny replied, dripping sugar and venom with every word.

"No, it wasn't the separation that made me forget, although it certainly helped to erase you from my mind. Anyway, I remember every minute now . . . including the two years spent with you, Ronny. I *could* say that it's nice to see you again, but I'd be lying," Rob said with a crispness in his voice that Virginia had never heard.

Virginia did not know how to react to this new discovery, and the impact it could have on her life with Rob. She wanted this evening to end, for Ronny to disappear, and for everything to return to the way it was. Deep inside, she knew it never would.

Holding her hand more tightly, Rob cleared his throat and continued. "I should have told you about her sooner, but there just wasn't the right time. The marriage was doomed almost from the start, and should have ended when we found out that we weren't compatible. I'm sorry for not telling you about her, but I couldn't find the words. In London and on the ship, I tried to tell you, but I just couldn't. We were so happy. The marriage would have ended long before now if the transfer hadn't interfered."

Before Virginia could respond, Ronny burst into the conversation. She had been silent, observing the tenderness between Rob and Virginia for as long as she could stand it. She was not accustomed to sharing the attention with anyone.

"Rob, why don't you tell Virginia about our wedding? She might find the details enjoyable, since she's sitting in the room where it took place." Ronny smiled with malicious joy at seeing Virginia flinch with pain and betrayal.

Rob shot her a look that said he would have thrashed her if she had been a man. Controlling his temper, he spoke in a flat voice, as if reading from the newspaper. He hoped that his bland recounting of the story would defuse the impact of Ronny's appearance.

"It was a small ceremony with only about fifty guests. The furniture had been moved out to make room for the chairs. My best friend was the best man. Her father gave her away. We traveled to Paris for our honeymoon. We stayed in a hotel across the street from the Louvre, and visited Notre-Dame and Sacre Coeur. That's how I knew the way to them without benefit of a map, and why I didn't want to

see them again. We ate on the Champs Élysée, saw
a show at the Moulin Rouge, and rode in a carriage
through the Bois de Boulogne. When we returned,
we settled here in a house round the corner. I sold
it before going to Europe. During our brief marriage, Ronny played around with a jazz piano player,
a drummer, and an actor, to name a few. I didn't
leave out anything, did I, Ronny?"

"No, I don't think you forgot anything. My only
question of you, my dear husband, is where do we
go from here?" Ronny asked. She was cool and
calm, almost like a spider studying its prey.

Virginia found that she could not move. The
shock of this terrible discovery had frozen her to
the sofa. All she could do was think about Rob and
this woman in love, in each other's arms, and in
Paris. She felt numb, helpless, and fearful of the
future that had seemed so promising until Ronny's
arrival.

Rob's father spoke for the first time since Ronny's
dramatic entrance. Virginia could tell that the effort
at civility toward the intruder put a great strain on
his nerves. He was controlled and dignified, but furious with the intrusion into his home and his son's
happiness.

"You have shown remarkably poor taste, even for
you, in coming here, Ronny. I would appreciate it
if you'd leave now. Anything else you have to say to
Rob can wait until morning. You've done enough
already to spoil his homecoming. We're all very
tired, the hour is late, and we're ready to call it a
night." Rob's father's lips trembled with his struggle
for composure.

Rising from her seat, Ronny smoothed the skirt
of her impeccably tailored dress and glanced from

Mrs. Robinson to Rob and Virginia on the sofa. Gliding toward the front door, she paused and turned for one last look at the devastation she left in her wake. Satisfied with the results of her visit, Ronny could make her grand exit.

"I suppose it is getting late. Virginia, you will want to retire to that charming upstairs bedroom, the first one at the top of the steps, if I remember correctly. Rob and I spent our first married night there. The walls probably still echo the sounds of our lovemaking. Goodnight, all. I'll be in touch, Rob. There's much that we still need to work out." Ronny glided from the living room into the foyer.

"How dare you!" Rob's mother sputtered, rising from her chair. Ronny's intrusion into their family time had violated every code of etiquette. She had sat quiet long enough. She had to silence this dreadful woman.

Before his mother could reach her, Rob burst from the sofa and grabbed Ronny by the shoulder. He would not let his mother finish with Ronny for him. He wanted the satisfaction himself.

"There's nothing to discuss. You'll hear from my lawyer in the morning. Stay away from me, Ronny. It's over between us," Rob hissed, spinning her around to face him.

"My relationships are never over until I say they are. Ask your friend Tommy, he'll tell you. I played him every which way before I cut him loose. You don't have to see me to the door. I can let myself out. Sleep well, everyone," Ronny oozed, shaking herself free from his grasp with a smile of pure wickedness. The clicking of her heels echoed in the still night air as she walked down the sidewalk.

Rob looked from Virginia's stricken face to that

of his parents. He did not know what to say. His future was shattered by a woman he had pushed from his mind, and a relationship he had not taken the time to end. He should have tied up all loose ends before going to Europe. Ronny would have been out of his life if he had. Now it was too late. The damage had been done.

The slamming of the screen door at Ronny's departure broke the spell that had held Virginia prisoner. Rising to her feet, she walked slowly to Rob's parents. She could not stay another minute in that house.

"Thank you both for welcoming me into your home," Virginia said, tears brimming in her eyes. "I really must be going now. Please don't try to detain me. I need time and distance to work things out."

Picking up her purse and straightening her shoulders, Virginia walked past Rob on the way to the door. He reached out for her, but she shook his hand off. Not even his touch could comfort her now.

"Don't worry about me. I'll spend the night with my old roommate Edwina. She'll be happy to take me in. Tomorrow, I'm going home to the farm. Please don't try to contact me. Too much has happened tonight. You should have told me about her at the corporate New Year's Eve party, when you first met me. At the very least, you should have used any number of other opportunities to tell me. You blew it, Rob, big time. Anyway, I need some breathing room. Goodnight." She slipped her engagement ring from her finger and eased it into the pocket of his jacket.

"Virginia, wait," Rob managed to say as his heart pounded painfully in his chest. "I love you. We can work this out together. I meant it when I said that

I'm filing for divorce tomorrow morning. I'll be free in no time. I know I should have told you about Ronny from the beginning, but she just didn't seem important. I wasn't thinking straight. I know I was being selfish. All I knew was that I'd finally found a woman who cared for me without interest in my money or social status or position in the company. I was wrong, I know that now. Don't leave me, Virginia. I'll make it all work out, you'll see."

"I know you love me, but I can't handle any more of this right now. I've never loved anyone except my family until I met you. Now, I find out that you're married. I feel betrayed, bruised, abused. I have to get away and think. Good-bye." Virginia whispered all this without turning to face him. She would not take the chance that the sight of his tormented face would stop her.

Virginia did not look back as she walked into the night, away from the man she loved. She did not see happy lovers as they passed on the street and stared into her tear-streaked face. She could not hear their whispers as they questioned the cause of her distress. She could not think of anything other than putting distance between herself and the terrible truth of Rob's past association with that woman.

Seventeen

Standing in front of the only door that would open to security and comfort, Virginia did not stop to wonder about the lateness of the hour. She took hold of the knocker and let it drop. The sound shattered the silence in the hall as it echoed through the building and drowned out the pounding of her heart in her ears. Virginia only knew that she would be safe as soon as she was inside.

"Virginia!" Edwina exclaimed, flinging the door open and pulling her friend into the apartment they had shared less than a year ago. "I'm so happy to see you. When did you get back? How was the trip? Where's Rob? Let me look at you. What's wrong? You look terrible. I thought everything was going well."

Virginia looked around the little apartment at all the familiar sights as Edwina's questions circled madly around in her head. She knew she must look exhausted. Her whole world lay shattered around her shoulders like a tattered shawl.

"I don't know where to begin, Edwina." Virginia said with a sigh as she dropped her bags and sank into the comfortable sofa. "So much has happened since we arrived this morning. Let me sit for a while.

I'll tell you everything as soon as I've collected my thoughts."

"Oh, that was so thoughtless of me. I should have insisted that you rest. You must be tired from your trip. I'm just so excited to see you that I forgot to ask you in. Let me make you some tea. I'll be right back." Edwina scurried off, only to return in no time at all with a cup of steaming strong tea.

Although the evening was warm for September, Virginia relished the feel of the hot cup in her hands as she sipped the soothing elixir. She could feel her friend's eyes on her, and sense her impatience to know all the latest news. Virginia did not blame her; she would have been just as curious if Edwina had arrived on her doorstep late at night with her face streaked with tears.

"Let's see. Where should I begin?" Virginia mused, staring into the dregs at the bottom of the cup. "I guess I'll get right to the point. I just found out that Rob's married."

Edwina's jaw dropped, and she stared, uncomprehending at Virginia. At first she thought her friend was suffering from some kind of trauma related to travel. The idea that the man she loved could possibly be married was ridiculous, too far-fetched to be believable. It was impossible. But, as she stared into Virginia's tormented face, Edwina began to accept the truth of her statement.

"What gave you that idea? You've been with him since the New Year's party, when you first met. Surely he would have said something, or shown some signs before now." Edwina sank onto the sofa beside Virginia.

"I met her. I met his wife. Rob says that after

he filed for separation from her, he transferred
and forgot all about her. He never said a word
while we were in London, practically living together every weekend. Even after I joined him in
France, he didn't mention a wife. On the ship returning home, he mentioned a faceless woman
who tormented his dreams, but I never guessed
that he had been married to her. I thought she
might have been a beautiful Frenchwoman with
whom he had fallen in love and just couldn't tell
me . . . sort of a flirtation. I never dreamed . . ."
Virginia's voice trailed off as fresh tears streamed
down her cheeks.

"Don't cry, Virginia." Edwina said, trying to
soothe her friend's battered feelings. "It'll all work
out. I've sure that he was telling the truth, and
would have told you everything if he hadn't guarded
the little time you had together so carefully. You'll
see. After all, you haven't been wrong about Rob
yet." She hated to see her usually cheerful buddy
so dejected.

"Maybe, but I'm not going to sit around here waiting for him. I've decided to go home to Towson
tomorrow. I'll rent a car and head out early. I need
to put as much distance between Rob and me as I
can. I need time to think. The last thing I want to
do is to stay here and run the risk of seeing him
with her." Virginia wiped her tears with her soggy
fistful of tissues.

"I'll go with you. Everyone in the office will be
happy to have me out of their hair. All I've done
for the past week is talk endlessly about your return," Edwina said, concern filling her voice. Edwina had missed her so much while Virginia was in
Europe. She hated the look of despair that pulled

at the corners of Virginia's mouth. This was not the reunion Edwina had envisioned.

"I'd love to have your company." said Virginia. "Let's turn in and get an early start tomorrow. My parents will be so happy to have both of us stay for a while. You'll love the farm . . . and my brothers. I'll feel better as soon as I have some of my mother's home cooking." Virginia smiled through her tears at the thought of home and her family.

Snuggled deeply into her pillow, Virginia slept fitfully that night. Dreams of women in red dresses and speeding trains plagued her. When she awoke, she was more tired than when she had gone to bed. Knowing that she would soon be home and in her old room made it possible for her to shower, dress, and eat a surprisingly hearty breakfast. Having Edwina with her brought to mind all of their happy times in Washington.

In their hurry to leave for the train station, Virginia almost stepped on an envelope that someone had slid under the door. Inside was a note in Rob's familiar handwriting.

Dearest Virginia,

"I know the shock of finding out that I'm married was great, but I beg you to find it in your heart to love me again, and to forgive me. I did not deliberately set out to hurt you, and despise myself for what I've done. You're the source of my life and happiness. Without you, I am nothing.

As I promised, I'm on the way to see my attorney. By the afternoon, he will have filed the necessary divorce papers. I will come to you in Towson when they are final, and I am free. Until then, I will not trouble you. I only ask that you remember all that we've

shared and not let this unsettled business come be-
tween us.

Forever,
Rob

Grabbing her bags, Virginia stuffed the envelope
into her pocket. She would read it again later, when
her heart did not hurt so much. For now, she
needed to catch the train that would take her home
to safety.

Home, the farm, her parents, and her brothers . . . Virginia felt better already. As soon as she
pulled her little rental car into the driveway, she felt
revitalized. The cares and worries of Washington,
with all of its noise and cars and people dashing
madly from place to place, slipped away from her
as the fresh country air filled her nostrils. Along the
route to her parents' house deep in the countryside,
she pointed out her grammar school and high
school, the family's church, and the local grocery
store. She wanted Edwina to love the little antique
shops, the playgrounds, and the farmland as much
as she did.

Once beyond the town limits, green fields of corn
and alfalfa, peach and apple orchards, and patches
of peas and strawberries stretched as far as the eye
could see in all directions. Cows, horses, and the
occasional sheep grazed peacefully in the pastures.
Whitewashed fences dotted the horizon, separating
pastures from yards. Silos and haystacks, red barns,
and chicken houses added color to the never-ending
expanse of green.

However, Towson was not only horse and farm
country. Malls sprawled over the former fields. Hous-

ing developments had replaced haystacks. Towson was a thriving cosmopolitan town.

Breathing deeply, Virginia inhaled the sweetness and let her soul run free through the fields as she ran barefoot through the thick grass. Edwina laughed, kicked off her shoes, and joined her, hurrying to catch up. Stopping only long enough to pick some daisies from a patch beside the pond, they swung their suitcases as they laughed and talked on the way to the large white house with green shutters and roof standing guard on the hill.

Pushing the front door open, Virginia called into the cool silent house, "Mama, I'm here. Anyone home?"

From the back of the house, the gentle sound of splashing water and the soft sweet melody of her mother's voice reached her ears. Suddenly realizing how much she had missed her home and family, Virginia rushed into the kitchen and threw her arms around her unsuspecting mother.

"Virginia!" her mother shrieked in surprise, "How you startled me! Why didn't you call to tell us you were coming home? I could have planned a special dinner to welcome you back."

Not waiting for an answer, Virginia's mother pulled her daughter into her arms and hugged her close. It had been a long time since they had embraced, and she had missed Virginia's happy laugher. The farm had not been the same without Virginia and the boys. Now they were all home again, and she was happy once more, yet she wondered what had brought her daughter home alone, without a phone call. It was not like Virginia to act impulsively. She wondered what had driven her out of Washington, but she did not ask, knowing that Virginia would tell her in her own time.

Not waiting for introductions, she included Edwina in her motherly embrace and said, "You must be Edwina. I'm so glad to meet you finally. I'm sure you girls are hungry. It'll only take me a few minutes to get the food on the table. Tell me everything about the trip from Washington."

As she bustled around the kitchen, Virginia and Edwina filled her in on the uneventful trip and about the activity in Washington that they had gladly left behind. Neither of them mentioned Rob. Mrs. Summers did not ask about him, knowing that Virginia would explain his absence in her own time.

Putting their lunch of cold fried chicken, hot, buttered, freshly baked biscuits, garden fresh salads, and ice tea on the table before them, Mrs. Summers excused herself and ran to the field to find her husband and sons. They would be as excited as she was to see Virginia and Edwina.

"Your mom sure is a good cook," Edwina said, adding some homemade peach jam to her biscuit. "My mom never took the time to bake anything. Growing up in the city, we always bought our bread from the bakery around the corner. It was good, but nothing like this."

"Her biscuits have won prizes at the county fair," Virginia answered with pride. She had not realized how hungry she was until her mother placed the mouthwatering food on the table before her. Now she had to restrain herself from gobbling the delicious meal.

She almost did not hear the slam of the back porch door as her father and brothers entered. "Virginia!" the three of them shouted in unison. They were all dressed in denim overalls, plaid shirts rolled up at the sleeves, and thick, muddy, brown boots. Their faces were dusty and smudged with sweat from hard work in the barn and fields. Regardless of the layers of grime, Virginia thought them the most handsome men she had ever seen. Her brother had come home for a vacation, and the clean living of farm life.

"Don't you dare come into my kitchen looking like that!" Mrs. Summers shouted in mock despair. "Wash up outside and knock off some of that dirt before you come in here."

"Yes, Mama," the three men answered as they scurried off. They might tower over the diminutive woman, but she ruled the house.

"You look even prettier than you did the last time I saw you—for a sister, that is," Cliff said when he finally returned, giving her a squeeze that caused her to gasp. He looked considerably better for having scrubbed his face and hands at the well.

David added, "I'm sure glad you've finally come home. It's not the same without all of us being together. It's like when we were kids again having you here, too."

"You must be Edwina," Mr. Summers said, seeing the visitor standing off to the side watching the greetings. "Welcome to our home. We've heard so much about you from Virginia. Please forgive our dustiness. If we'd known you two were coming, we would have dressed up a bit. I hope your enjoy your stay."

"I'm sure I will," Edwina replied, "This looks like a fun place to spend some time."

"I'd be happy to show you around, if Dad can spare me for a while," David offered. He was two

years older than Virginia, tall, handsome, and showing interest in Edwina.

"You won't be much use to your daddy if he
doesn't let you go anyway," Mrs. Summers inter-
jected. She had not missed the sparks that flew between her youngest son and Virginia's friend. "Why
don't you hitch up the wagon and drive Edwina
around the property? I'm sure she'd rather ride
than walk. The paths are rather overgrown."

As soon as the kitchen emptied out, Mrs. Summers began tidying up as a way of giving Virginia
the opportunity to strike up a conversation. By the
time she had washed the second plate, Virginia began lightening her heart as she dried the dishes.
There was so much she needed to tell her mother.
The older woman was ready to listen and advise, if
asked.

"It's over between Rob and me, Mama. I found
out that he was married. He says that he got too
busy with the job to follow through on his divorce.
I believe him, I guess. I don't think he meant to
deceive me. But it's over just the same." Virginia
spoke softly.

"Don't be too hasty, dear. I know your feelings
are wounded, but, from what you tell me Rob's a
good man from a good family. You could do much
worse. Don't decide anything until you've given
yourself a chance to step back and take a look within
your heart. You might find that what you've shared
with him has given you a strong enough foundation
to withstand this. There were some things I needed
to overlook with your father, and I'm glad I did. Just
give yourself some time. You'll feel better after you
sleep in your old room for a few nights," Mrs. Sum-

mers counseled, rinsing the last pan and placing it on the counter.

With a sigh, Virginia responded, "I hope you're right, Mama. It's just . . . well, I'll try."

"That's my girl," Mrs. Summers said, planting a kiss on Virginia's forehead. "Why don't you go for a walk? The exercise will do you good . . . give you a chance to work things out, too. I can finish these few things myself."

"Okay, Mama. Thanks for listening," Virginia said as she planted a kiss on her mother's forehead.

As Virginia strolled across the yard, the family's black Labrador retriever Shadow joined her. The playful dog bounded around, inviting her to play tag with him. When she would not join in, he settled down for a leisurely walk to the woods that led past the fish pond, the barn, and the chicken house. He left her side only once—to chase a rooster that quickly flew atop a fence post with a great deal of angry flapping of wings.

As usual, Virginia enjoyed walking around the family's farm. It was one of the last holdouts against the encroachment of citified ways into the country. They owned three hundred-fifty acres of prime land that builders had tried repeatedly to purchase. As long as her parents refused to sell, the farm would survive to give her a comfortable retreat when life became too heavy.

Virginia did some of her best thinking while taking in the sights and sounds of the countryside. Today was no exception as she allowed her mind to return to Rob, London, Paris, and promises kept and broken. She only hoped that the beauty of the landscape and the tranquillity of her surroundings would ease the heaviness in her heart. Maybe then she would be able to forgive him.

Following the wagon tracks into the woods, Virginia walked the path that wandered past a stream that swelled into a small lake and served as their swimming hole. Finally she stopped and sat on the bank. A fallen tree made a perfect perch for watching the lazy stream bubble and flow, dappled silver, green, and yellow by the sun shining through the trees. Shadow splashed through the shallow water, putting his head underwater as if looking for something in its depths. Finding nothing, he returned to Virginia's side and shook water from his dripping coat all over her.

"I might as well go for a swim. You've gotten me all wet," Virginia exclaimed, laughing, as she rose and stripped down to her bra and panties.

Walking slowly into the cool clear water, Virginia at first shivered at the change in temperature. Then she abandoned herself to it as she soaked away the heat of the day. Easing into its gentle caress, she swam to the center and pulled herself onto the platform. Lying back on the warm boards, she allowed the tension to ease from her body as the sun's rays penetrated her frame, warming her to the bone. With Shadow at her side, she fell asleep as the water lapped around her.

When she awoke, the sun was low in the sky. In the distance she heard the sound of the wagon as it made its way home. Swimming quickly to shore, she pulled on her clothes and rushed to the road. Waving her arms, she stepped out into its path as David and Edwina approached. It was obvious from their smiles that a new friendship had bloomed between them.

"Climb on," David shouted as he slowed the wagon to a crawl. Just as she had when she was a kid, Virginia clambered aboard the wagon, and Shadow jumped on beside her. As Virginia nestled among the pails of wild blackberries, the wagon picked up speed on its way home. The smell of the berries made her hungry. Feeding some to herself and some to Shadow, she munched contentedly until her fingers were stained blue-black. She could imagine the delicious pies and jam her mother would make with them, if she did not eat all of them.

Her memories of evenings at home were validated as the family settled around the dinner table. Mrs. Summers placed before them steaming bowls of shimmering greens and rice, heaping plates of steak, and biscuits dripping with butter. When they all thought they would pop if they ate another mouthful, she placed before them slices of thick blackberry pie and homemade ice cream. No one thought about cholesterol or calories.

After the delicious meal, the family gathered to play card games and Scrabble. They were not television fans, and preferred conversation to mindless network programming. Sensing the contentment of the people, Shadow settled under the table between their feet for a nap. The women challenged the men at bid whist for nearly three hours before calling it quits without a clear victory. As everyone retired for the night, Virginia turned out the lights and put Toby, the cat, out for his nighttime mouse patrol in the barn. Looking into the quiet night sky, Virginia saw stars she had not seen in the months she had lived in Washington, London, and Paris. She felt at peace. The only thing that would have made her

feel better would have been Rob standing by her
side.

With a sigh, she turned out the light and slipped
between cool white sheets. The moonlight streamed
through her window and played on the dolls and
stuffed toys that lined her dresser. Turning to face
the window, she watched the twinkling of the evening stars through the leaves and listened to the
song of the lark in the trees. She fell into a deep
sleep in her own room and her own bed. The troubles of Washington and the unfulfilled dreams of
her life with Rob were far away. Not even the train
dreams disturbed her slumber.

The weeks passed quickly as Virginia and Edwina
lolled around the farm. Edwina had turned a few
days leave from the office into a sorely needed vacation. They picked berries and vegetables, swam,
cooked, and relaxed away two glorious weeks until
it was time for her to leave and return to work. Before too long, Virginia should return, too, but she
was not sure she wanted to live in Washington again.
After her experiences in the city, the quiet life of
the country made her feel warm and content; she
did not want to lose that feeling. She could open
her consulting firm anywhere.

Rob wrote to her daily, begging her to forgive him
and telling her about the progress he had made in
obtaining a divorce. He reminded her of the good
times they had experienced together and pleaded
with her to remember them, not the harsh reality
of his wife's existence. She read each letter with interest, but she never answered any of them. Every
day that passed made the separation between them
hurt a little less. She had not stopped loving him,

but she had forced herself to imagine a life without him.

During the day, she kept busy with farm chores so that he would not invade her thoughts. Yet, her memory of his hands on her body, his fingers in her hair, the sound of his voice, and the smell of his aftershave mingled in her thoughts, and often made her weak and light-headed. At night after the farm was asleep and dreaming, her resolve abandoned her and left her open and vulnerable. She awakened wet with perspiration from her imagined couplings with him. She could feel his hands on her breasts, his lips on her mouth, and his body melding with hers. She longed for him to be with her, to put out the fire that he had awakened in her, and to take her into his arms. She ached to press herself against him, to surrender to his warmth, and to feel him give himself to her. She had learned to enjoy the release, the closeness, and the whispered words of love. She missed their moments together.

The last time she'd had the train dream, Rob had stood on the platform beside her. Their luggage had sat in piles around their feet, and they had both been smiling and happy. In her sleep, Virginia had known that they had reached the end of their travels. When she awoke, she was alone, but not lonely.

Against her will, Virginia often found herself laughing at the antics of her brothers—especially David, who wrote to Edwina every day and eagerly ran to the mailbox to see if she had responded. He gloomily peered over Virginia's shoulder when she received one of the pale pink envelopes and he did not. She could see that he had fallen hopelessly in love.

Often she lay out on the platform for hours, just

napping or gazing at the sun-speckled leaves. Sometimes Cliff joined her when he had finished his chores. He climbed up without disturbing her, and listened to the sounds of nature around him. She would wake to find him sleeping peacefully beside her. Sometimes she would spend the time alone with her thoughts. Occasionally David swam out to pester her until she abandoned the platform, leaving him to read one of Edwina's letters in solitude. Unable to stand the separation, he had rushed to Washington and proposed to Edwina. Now they were busily planning their Christmas wedding.

As October approached, Virginia decided that she would not return to Washington, at all. Not wanting to chance running into Rob, she decided that she would strike out on her own. When she healed, she would open a consulting business and become her own boss.

Still, Virginia felt unfulfilled. She phoned the principal of her high school, who had invited her to teach business and economics at her alma matter when she had first graduated from college. Then, the pull of the big city had been too strong. The allure of the corporate world and its financial rewards had been too great. Instead of earning a master's of education, she had followed the business route. Maybe he might still need her. Although the school year had already begun, he might be willing to add her as a guest speaker.

Luckily, the principal offered her a job teaching advanced placement courses for the rest of the semester. The man who had originally held the position had left for greener pastures. Virginia could start immediately.

Rob's letters stopped around the same time, but

she hardly noticed. Virginia was too busy preparing for school. There was so much she wanted to do to make the classroom comfortable, and her lessons stimulating and exciting. She knew that she would have to catch her students' attention early in order to have a successful semester. Students felt little respect for substitutes. Virginia wanted to make them change their minds.

Her first day was filled with apprehension and excitement as she stepped from the warm sunshine into the cool darkness of the classroom. The talking teenagers immediately stopped to stare at the newcomer. They had heard that their substitute teacher had grown up in the neighborhood, moved to the big city of Washington, worked for a major corporation, and had traveled to Europe. Now, the paragon stood before them as an authority figure, as well as an honored alumna, to guide them through their studies. They knew more about Virginia than she did about them, but in time she would learn.

"People, Virginia began, placing her purse, briefcase, and vase filled with flowers on the desk, "I'm Miss Summers, and I'll be your teacher this year. I'm sure we'll get along fabulously, learn wonderful things, and have a great time. Let's get started. I have many stories to share with you about life in America's big corporations, but not until you know the basics. Take out your textbook and turn to chapter one. Who would like to begin?"

She looked around at the sea of quizzical cynical young faces. Some of them looked as if they wanted to raise their hands, while others appeared not to trust her. It seemed like centuries ago that she had sat at one of those uncomfortable desks waiting for the teacher to call on her. Now she was the teacher.

Time had passed so quickly, and so much had happened. She did not have time to dwell on that now. There was much to be done. She had to assess the knowledge of her students and assign group business cases. The business of learning was at hand.

She pushed thoughts of Washington and Rob far back in her mind as she unbuttoned her sleeves and scanned her attendance sheet. "Evelyn Andrews, would you please read the first page—under The History of Economic Development in the United States?" Her first day as teacher had begun.

Every night Virginia returned to her parents' house tired, but happy. She loved teaching the reluctant scholars the most. She enjoyed seeing the lightbulb of recognition and appreciation shine in their eyes. She also enjoyed sharing stories of the wonderful places she had visited in books and in her travels. They sat with their eyes wide as they listened to her fill their heads with pictures of faraway places and exciting people. She worked hard to decorate the room with photographs of distant places, current events, and famous people pulled from magazines. She anxiously awaited their return every day as they learned to trust and respect her.

Eighteen

One Saturday long after the warmth of the late October Indian summer had all but faded from memory, Virginia decided to put her work aside and lounge by the roaring fire in the living room. She had almost finished grading her latest stack of papers, and had nothing pressing to do until dinnertime, when she would help her mother in the kitchen. Winter break started the next day, and she was feeling relaxed and ready for the holiday. Right now, she was alone, with time on her hands. Her mother was busy making apple butter for Christmas gifts, and her father was working in the field tying up the last of the haystacks. Her brothers had come for the weekend to help. They were herding the cows from the distant pastures in anticipation of the first snow that would eventually blanket the farm.

Virginia loved this time of year as everyone prepared for the holidays. The smell of freshly baked Christmas presents in the pantry, the aroma of the tree by the window, and the garland trailing down the banister always filled her with contentment. The entire farm lay ready for something wonderful to happen. The lake lay quiet, too, with hardly a ripple disturbing the surface. All of the fish seemed to know that cold weather had arrived. They stayed close to the bottom, exploring muck and decaying water grasses. Only once in a while did they hop into the air to glisten in the fading sun.

Virginia could feel the joy of the holiday infiltrate her bones. While at school, she had to appear focused on her work, for the good of the children. They were already excited about the final bell that would signal the week away from homework and tests. She had to pretend that the holiday did not make her heart sing with anticipation and cause her to wish daily for snow and a white Christmas. Now, however, in the privacy of her living room, she could relax and let the season wash over her.

Lying on the thick rug in front of the fireplace, Virginia stretched lazily and gazed into the fire. Her hair fanned out around her in a radiant halo as her lean body relaxed under the spell of the lapping flames and warming heat. Her eyelids grew heavy as the sweet smells of the holiday surrounded her. A cup of eggnog sat untouched, within easy reach of her long tapered fingers.

Too subdued to move, Virginia did not stir as a warm body eased itself onto the carpet and pressed its warmth against her. She did not open her eyes as the intruder gently dropped holly berries onto her stomach.

"David, stop that! You're being a pest. Go away! I won't have you ruining my serenity," Virginia cried, brushing away the berries. She refused to give her brother the pleasure of interrupting her moments of leisure and contentment.

Again the annoying little berries tumbled onto her body and rolled onto the floor. Squinting into the semidarkness, she said in mock anger, "All right, you asked for it, David. Just for that I'm going to . . ."

Turning, looking into laughing deep brown eyes, Virginia gasped as Rob's mouth covered hers in hungry kisses that she found herself returning with enthusiasm. Pushing him away slightly, she marveled at the depth of her feelings for him despite the betrayal.

"What brings you here? This is a surprise." Virginia spoke breathlessly, struggling to regain her composure. She was glad for the rosy glow from the fireplace that masked the blush on her cheeks.

"Unexpected, but hopefully not unwelcome," Rob replied, brushing his fingertips softly over her cheeks and down her neck. He allowed them to linger on the swell of her soft breasts under her thick sweater.

"Not unwelcome. You just caught me by surprise, that's all," Virginia responded with difficulty. It had been so long since she had seen him, had felt his touch, and had tasted his kisses that she was quite startled by her unbidden response. She had hoped that her emotions would not betray her the next time she saw him, but she had been wrong.

"I drove down here to show you this. Since you never answered any of my letters, I thought I should bring it in person." Rob pulled an envelope from the inside pocket of his green-and-brown wool plaid jacket. Sitting up, he opened it, smoothed the pages, and handed the document to her.

Virginia read silently as the firelight played on the thickly stacked sheets of paper. She could hardly believe her eyes. In her trembling fingers, Virginia held Rob's divorce papers freeing him from Ronny. The pain of betrayal had been so great that she had not wanted to believe that he would do it, but he had kept his word.

Watching her intently as the emotions played across her face while she read, Rob spoke quietly. "I know how I've hurt you, and I'm sorry. I tried to explain in my letters that my life has been empty without direction since you left me. I can't imagine spending any more lonely days and nights without you. Do you think you could love me again, Virginia? I want us to be together for always. I can't imagine spending my life without you. I'm blessed with wonderful memories of our time together, but they mean nothing without you in my arms."

"I never stopped loving you, Rob. I was just crushed emotionally. I felt betrayed when I found out about your marriage. I just couldn't get past the feelings without getting away from you completely. I couldn't even stand the idea of writing to you. Some days I didn't open your letters, at all. I let them pile up on my dresser until I could face the pain of reading your words while knowing that you belonged to someone else. When they stopped, I thought the worst, but was relieved, too. Fortunately, I had a teaching job to give me satisfaction, but I still missed you." Virginia rested her hand lightly on his. The love she felt for him struggled to push away the lingering memories and the residual pain.

"I love you, Virginia. Will you marry me?" Rob asked, heartened by her response. He took her tentatively into his arms. So much had happened that he still had his doubts about their future, even as he hoped for happiness together.

"Yes, darling, I'll marry you, but on one condition. I can't bear the thought of giving up my teaching, or moving back to the city. Can't we make a life here where the air is clean, people make time to care about each other, and life is slower and more quiet?" Virginia waited, hoping that in his vulnerable state Rob would agree.

"I don't see why not. I can open my consulting business anywhere. If you're agreeable, after this school year you might want to join forces with me. We'd make a dynamic duo. This looks like a good place to raise children, too. It's much better than the busy city. As a matter-of-fact, I already checked on the possibility of opening an office here. The realtor said it should be ready by the end of next month. Do you think that gives us enough time to get married and find a house?" Rob smiled playfully. The glow from the fire highlighted his handsome features.

"That's more than enough time. I've never wanted a lengthy engagement or a big wedding. I know a perfect house for us. It's just down the road from here. It has plenty of bedrooms, a barn for horses, a chicken house, and a great pond out back." Virginia clung to his arm. She had long envisioned owning one of the other remaining farms, and looked forward to living near her parents in their old age.

Rob chuckled at her enthusiasm as he slipped a ring from his pocket and onto her finger. He had come prepared with hopes for a reconciliation and a ring to prove his devotion. He was relieved that Virginia had forgiven him, and agreed to start again.

"What happened to my other ring?" Virginia asked, staring at the shimmering larger diamond that had replaced the original one.

"I hope you don't mind, but I traded it for this new one. I thought our new beginning deserved a new ring," Rob responded, trailing kisses from her ears to her lips.

"Are you sure you won't miss the big city? Life is awfully quiet around here sometimes. For the most part, there's really not much to do. Antiquing, boating on the lake, horse racing in season, and visiting Baltimore and DC are the highlights of activity here. We spend a lot of time reading and fishing. We're a close community, but there's plenty of local gossip." Virginia breathed deeply of the combined fragrance of Rob's aftershave and Christmas fragrances.

"I'll have all the excitement any one man can handle loving you, raising our children, and advising my clients. What more could I want?" Rob took Virginia's hands in his and placed burning kisses on the palms of each. Slowly his lips trailed tingling tracks along her cheeks and ears.

"It's almost been a year since I met you." Virginia chuckled softly as she pushed Rob away gently.

"I know. What'll we do this New Year's?" Rob asked, refusing to be distracted from her soft neck.

"What we're doing right now suits me just fine," Virginia replied as she tightened her arms around his warm body.

Snuggling together, Virginia and Rob held each other close as the flickering flames played on the shiny oak floors in brilliant ribbons of red, amber, and gold. For the first time they had no place to go, no corporate problems to solve, and no long-distances to keep them apart.

Perfectly happy, they lay on the carpet before the fire.

Coming in November from Arabesque Books . . .

__SECRET DESIRE by Gwynne Forster
1-58314-124-3 $5.99US/$7.99CAN

Victims of a harrowing robbery, widow Kate Middleton and her young son are rescued by police captain Luke Hickson. Neither of them expect, much less welcome, an instant spark of attraction. But when trouble strikes again Kate realizes the only place she feels safe is in Luke's embrace. . . .

__SHATTERED ILLUSIONS by Candice Poarch
1-58314-122-7 $5.99US/$7.99CAN

When a hurricane damages fiercely independent Delcia Adams's island campground, she must hire Carter Matthews to help her rebuild. The more she lets him help, the more she discovers that the handsome stranger is a man of dangerous secrets . . . and irrestible fire.

__BETRAYED BY LOVE by Francine Craft
1-58314-163-4 $5.99US/$7.99CAN

All Maura Blackwell wants is money to save her grandfather's life and all her former flame Joshua Pyne wants is a child of his own. When the two strike a bargain to wed, neither of them expect an undeniable love—or the inexplicable urge to turn their make-believe marriage into the real thing.

__A FORGOTTEN LOVE by Courtni Wright
1-58314-123-5 $5.99US/$7.99CAN

As the administrator of a major ER, Dr. Joni Forest faced down personal and professional turmoil to make the unit respected. Now, the ER's former head, Dr. Don Rivers, is back, challenging her leadership—and reigniting the simmering desire between them. Now, the couple must come to terms with unresolved pain and career pressures in order to claim true love. . . .

Call toll free **1-888-345-BOOK** to order by phone or use this coupon to order by mail. *ALL BOOKS AVAILABLE NOVEMBER 1, 2000.*

Name_____

Address _____

City _____ State _____ Zip _____

Please send me the books I have checked above.

I am enclosing $_____
Plus postage and handling* $_____
Sales tax (in NY, TN, and DC) $_____
Total amount enclosed $_____

*Add $2.50 for the first book and $.50 for each additional book.

Send check or money order (no cash or CODs) to: **Arabesque Books, Dept. C.O., 850 Third Avenue, 16th Floor, New York, NY 10022**

Prices and numbers subject to change without notice. All orders subject to availability.

Visit our website at **www.arabesquebooks.com.**

SIZZLING ROMANCE FROM
FELICIA MASON

For the Love of You   0-7860-0071-6 $4.99US/$6.50CAN
Years of hard work had finally provided a secure life for Kendra Edwards but when she meets high-powered attorney Malcolm Hightower, he arouses desires that she swore she would never let herself feel again . . .

Body and Soul   0-7860-0160-7 $4.99US/$6.50CAN
Toinette Blue's world is her children and her successful career as the director of a woman's counseling group . . . until devastatingly handsome, much younger attorney Robinson Mayview rekindles the flames of a passion that both excites and frightens her . . .

Seduction   0-7860-0297-2 $4.99US/$6.50CAN
C.J. Mayview goes to North Carolina for peace of mind and to start anew. But secrets unravel when U.S. Marshal Wes Donovan makes it his business to discover all there is to know about the beautiful journalist . . .

Foolish Heart   0-7860-0593-9 $4.99US/$6.50CAN
Intent on saving his business, Coleman Heart III turns to beautiful consultant Sonja Pride. But Sonja has a debt to pay the Heart family, and she is determined to seek revenge until she finds out that Coleman is a caring, honorable man to whom she just might be able to give her heart.

USE COUPON ON NEXT PAGE TO ORDER THESE BOOKS

Own These Books
By *Felicia Mason*

__**For the Love of You** $4.99US/$6.50CAN
0-7860-0071-6

__**Body and Soul** $4.99US/$6.50CAN
0-7860-0160-7

__**Seduction** $4.99US/$6.50CAN
0-7860-0297-2

__**Foolish Heart** $4.99US/$6.50CAN
0-7860-0593-9

Call toll free **1-888-345-BOOK** to order by phone or use this coupon to order by mail.

Name _____

Address _____

City _____ State _____ Zip_____

Please send me the books I have checked above.

I am enclosing $_____

Plus postage and handling* $_____

Sales tax (in NY, TN, and DC) $_____

Total amount enclosed $_____

*Add $2.50 for the first book and $.50 for each additional book.

Send check or money order (no cash or CODs) to: **Arabesque Books, Dept. C.O., 850 Third Avenue, 16th Floor, New York, NY 10022**

Prices and numbers subject to change without notice.

All orders subject to availability.

Check out our website at **www.arabesquebooks.com**

MORE ROMANCE FROM
ANGELA WINTERS

__A FOREVER PASSION
1-58314-077-8 $5.99US/$7.99CAN
When congressman Marcus Hart hires Sydney Tanner for a genealogy research project on his family, he is instantly intrigued with her cool attitude. But they must confront unbelievable family resistance and simmering, long-kept secrets together if they are to gain a world of love.

__ISLAND PROMISE
0-7860-0574-2 $4.99US/$6.50CAN
Morgan Breck's reckless spirit leads her to make an impulsive purchase at an estate that, in turn, plunges her into the arms of sexy investor Jake Turner. Although Jake is only interested in finding his missing sister, their intense passion just may force Jake to surrender to love.

__SUDDEN LOVE
1-58314-023-9 $4.99US/$6.50CAN
Author Renee Shepherd decides to visit her sister in Chicago and is drawn into an investigation surrounding the suspicious death of her sister's colleague. The executive director of the company, Evan Brooks, is somehow involved in all of this and it's going to take much trust and faith for Renee to risk everything for sudden love . . .

Call toll free **1-888-345-BOOK** to order by phone or use this coupon to order by mail.

Name_____

Address _____

City _____ State _____ Zip _____

Please send me the books I have checked above.

I am enclosing	$_____
Plus postage and handling*	$_____
Sales tax (in NY, TN, and DC)	$_____
Total amount enclosed	$_____

*Add $2.50 for the first book and $.50 for each additional book.
Send check or money order (no cash or CODs) to: **Arabesque Books, Dept. C.O., 850 Third Avenue, 16th Floor, New York, NY 10022**
Prices and numbers subject to change without notice.
All orders subject to availability.

Visit our web site at **www.arabesquebooks.com**